LOLLIPOP

LOLLIPOP

Marc Pye

SCEPTRE

Grateful acknowledgement is made for permission to reprint excerpts from the fllowing copyrighted material:

The lines from *The Real Frank Zappa* by Frank Zappa © 1989 are reproduced by permission of Macmillan

First published in Great Britain in 2000 by Hodder and Stoughton
A Sceptre Book
Hodder and Stoughton
A division of Hodder Headline

10 9 8 7 6 5 4 3 2 1

British Library Cataloguing in Publication Data

Pye, Marc
Lollipop
I.Title
823.9'2[F]
ISBN 0 340 76608 5

Typeset by Hewer Text Ltd, Edinburgh
Printed and bound in Great Britain by
Mackays of Chatham plc, Chatham, Kent

Hodder and Stoughton
A division of Hodder Headline
338 Euston Road
London NW1 3BH

Acknowledgements

Thanks to my family and friends for being so supportive and having faith in me to become a writer. (You know who you are.) Thanks to the people who had *no* faith in me – you just made me more determined. (I feed off your negative energy.) A special big thanks to Shefali Malhoutra, Mark Grindle, Des Dillon, Jimmy McGovern and Giles Gordon for being there in 'the wilderness years' and helping to make a dream come true. Thanks to the Rangers and Celtic fans for all your help with the songs (and the stories), the guys from The Blue Bears web site and Celtic plc.

'Some scientists claim that *hydrogen*, because it is so plentiful, is the *basic building block of the universe*. I dispute that. I say there is more *stupidity* than *hydrogen*, and **that** is the *basic building block of the universe*.

Stupidity is *replicating* itself at an astonishing rate. It breeds easily and is self-financing.

The person who stands up and says '*This is stupid*,' either is asked to 'behave' or, worse, is greeted with a cheerful '*Yes, we know! Isn't it terrific!*'

When Hitler was doing his shit, a whole bunch of people thought **he** was terrific, too. How could they be wrong? There were so *many* of them; they thought they looked good together – their arms all went up at the *same time*.'

Frank Zappa: *The Real Frank Zappa*

'*We are all Jock Tamson's bairns*.'

Robert Burns

Day One

It was the week before Christmas. The pubs were dead. It seemed everyone in Glasgow was skint this time of the year – saving their money for Hogmanay. Except for the boys in Finlays – it was a cause for a celebration: Celtic had just beaten Motherwell 3–0. The boys were wearing their colours and looking forward to a repeat performance in two weeks at Ibrox. The fact it was approaching Christmas was irrelevant as the decorations were obscured by pictures and pendants around the place, emphasising to the untrained eye that this was very much a Celtic supporters pub. The faces of Jock Stein, Bobby Murdoch, Kenny Dalgleish and the Celtic squads from over the years loomed down on the drinkers from various dusty framed pictures. Green and white scarves draped over the gantry, tarnished brown by years of cigarette smoke. A Celtic shirt autographed by the European Cup Winners squad of '67 and a signed fiver by Pele were proudly on display behind the bar, offering a conversation piece for the lonely afternoon drinker or visitor from out of town.

The owner, Francie Gallacher, was lending a hand behind the bar. Francie, now in his fifties, was an ex-boxer who'd spent his money wisely, having the foresight to plough his winnings into a dilapidated old pub in the Gallowgate. Market research meant nothing to Francie. He relied on gut instinct for the décor of the place and the clientèle it would attract. Giving the place an Irish-sounding name and cashing in on the two most important aspects of Glasgow culture, as he saw it – religion and football – he used his contacts in the sporting world to ensure that a few big-name ex-Celtic players were among the celebrity faces present for the opening night. Invites were like gold dust; just as rare were Protestants. Francie had made it clear: this pub was for Celtic supporters – **CATHOLICS ONLY**. If Rangers supporters wanted somewhere to drink, they could go to a fucking Rangers pub.

The great Rangers/Celtic divide in the city had been the cause of many an argument – death, even. To the majority it was more than a game, it was a way of life. The bigotry and hatred went hand in hand and nobody expected it to change. Francie, for one, hoped it didn't. He had a gold mine here at Finlays and he knew it. Besides, the crack was good. Everybody was friendly and there was no shortage of conversation, particularly when Celtic were battling for top of the league.

The place had worn well, even though the emerald-green carpet was now permanently sticky with beer and stained with Buckfast. The chrome and mirror interior, a theme Francie had pinched from a London nightclub after a memorable Wembley weekend on the pish, had also long since become fashionable in pubs, but he liked the idea it made the place look bigger; plus, if the mirrored walls in Finlays were running with condensation, as sure as night followed day, he knew the takings would be up: those mirrored walls acted like Francie's weathercock, and tonight they were flowing like a river.

Malkie drove through the city centre, wondering how he'd managed to get talked into this one: 'It'll be a laugh,' they said. He looked in the rear-view mirror at the boys: Shug, Chic and Scobie sat in the back. He'd often considered if it was just a Glasgow thing – changing someone's name at school so it bore no resemblance to their original. He didn't know of any other city where you were likely to meet a seventy-year-old with the unlikely name of Jo-Jo or Chalky. He glanced at Shug: Hughey McNab. Same name as his old man – how imaginative. Malkie had known him since primary school. Hugh had become Shug in secondary, round about the same time that Charles Mathieson had become Chic, like thousands of Hughs and Charleses before them. Malkie's own name was miraculously conjured from his surname Malcolm, and the same applied to Scobie.

Malkie remembered their first day at school and how innocent they'd been. A million years away from the jaded lunatics who now sat in the car. Who'd have thought that Shug and Chic would have ended up doing borstal for nicking cars, Scobie would be a total waster and he, himself, would have lost all ambition to be a footballer after the promise he'd shown to talent scouts from Rangers and Motherwell. He'd fucked it up big-style, and there was no turning back the clock. He looked at his own reflection: crow's feet already, or was it just the effect the streetlights had on his face? He'd be twenty-five in a week. Fucking ancient. He spent most of his time lately checking if the bald patch on the back of his head was getting any bigger. The guys all took the piss out of him – called him slaphead, so he now had it shaved into the wood, he'd grown a goatee and kept it trimmed short. An ex bird told him that's what guys did when they were losing their hair – it made you look less bald. But it only made Malkie more aware of how sparse his dome was getting. He was constantly reminded every time he went to a nightclub toilet: his whole scalp would shine back at him in the mirror. It made him depressed when he realised how he must look to women. Like an old cunt. He was aware of getting older and he didn't like it one bit. Only now was he beginning to get his life in some sort of order. Last month, after burying his mother, the realisation finally hit him: you only get one shot at life. He'd been fucking about for far too long, so he finally decided to take his brother up on the offer of a job in his Liverpool pub. It was a change of scenery and a chance maybe to have his own place one day. If big bro' could do it, then so could he. Fuck it. It was better than hanging round here with these losers.

Malkie glanced at Scobie in the mirror, skinning up another joint. That's all he did lately, smoke blaw. If he had to run for his life he'd probably keel over in a fit of the giggles. Malkie watched Scobie as he looked out of the window and screwed up his face. He hadn't a clue were he was. You could take Scobie out to a pub in Easterhouse and he'd think he was in Wishaw. He was a harmless cunt really. Young girls liked mothering him because of his chubby baby features and the fact that he laughed all the time. Not like Shug. Malkie couldn't remember the last time he'd heard him laugh. Malkie glanced at him again in the mirror. The cunt was away with the mixer. This had to be his stupidest idea of all time – going to Finlays: the fucking lion's den.

He watched Shug's eyes dart about as he got his bearing. Pale-blue pupils staring ahead like a man possessed, occasionally scanning from side to side, observing passers-by. There was no telling what was going on behind those eyes. You could be talking to him and they'd be flicking about, his brain elsewhere – always scamming; looking for an angle. If you were talking about someone he didn't like, you could see a sneer come across his face as he plotted against them. He was unstable, no doubt about it. Then again, having an old man like Big Shuggie McNab was enough to make anyone mental.

Shug's head turned as though on a swivel and he looked out of all the windows simultaneously. Speedin again, thought Malkie, whizzed oot his nut. The middle of winter and the sweat was running down his forehead, sticking the overgrown strands of his mousey-brown hair to his head. Malkie remembered years ago the pictures in the paper of Paul Gascoigne when he turned up for practice with that haircut – fringe brushed down across his forehead. The next day there was a picture of George Michael with the same style. That afternoon Malkie went to the Paki's for a pint of milk and passed at least a dozen boys with the same cut. That night he met Shug. Same haircut, what a surprise. Malkie decided against it, choosing to have some individuality.

Shug rubbed his thin, unshaven chin, wiped the sweat from his eyes and opened the window to get some air.

'Fuck sakes, man,' said Chic, 'it's fuckin freezin . . . Malkie, turn the heatin up, will ye?' Malkie hit the heater – it was already full up. He glanced in the mirror at Chic and shrugged his shoulders. Malkie's car was a heap of shit, there was no denying it. Chic glanced back at him, shook his head in disgust and looked out of the window. Malkie watched him pull up the collar of his jacket and fold his arms. Poor cunt, thought Malkie, having to slum it with the rest of them. Chic was becoming a pain in the arse lately. Pretentious. All designer clothes, sunbed tan and highlighted hair. The vain bastard.

Malkie watched the headlights from a passing car glint off Chic's polished teeth as they chattered away. Some nights if they were in a dark club, that's all you could see – a pair of teeth talking to you. Chic had them polished every couple of months. Not bad for a 'doleite'. All paid for by punting whatever he could get his hands on – perfume, watches, and ringing the occasional car with Shug, a little pastime that had earned them their spell in borstal when they were kids. It hadn't put them off though. Chic's main source of income lately was from blocking phone boxes.

Last Sunday Chic had called Malkie, arranging to meet him in a pub at the bottom of Sauchiehall Street. When Malkie got there Chic told him to put his money away – the beers were on him tonight. Chic motioned for Malkie to follow him outside. He walked a few yards to a phone box and looked back at Malkie. 'Keep an eye oot, eh?'

Malkie nodded, puzzled by what was going on. Chic went inside the phone box, picked up the receiver and pretended to make a call. Malkie watched him fiddle about and pull something from the coin return. A pile of silver coins came clattering into the tray and Chic scooped them out, opened the door and flashed his designer smile at him. 'Whit was that?' asked Malkie.

Chic came out of the call-box. 'Aboot five an a hof quid,' he said, before moving on to the next one. Malkie watched him stick his fingers up the coin return and pull on a piece of string.

Later on, in the pub, Chic explained his scam: on Friday night he'd gone the length of Sauchiehall Street, blocking all the coin returns on the phone boxes with rolled-up gaffer tape tied with string. He'd stuffed the ball of gaffer tape up the coin return with a plastic ruler and left the string hanging out of sight but where he could still get his fingers to it. Punters used the phones all weekend and chose to give up on their change rather than report the fault to BT. And now here they were on Sunday night, cashing in. By the end of the night they'd made over fifty quid. They'd been for a curry, drank in every pub in Sauchiehall Street, and both got taxis home, courtesy of Joe Public. Ingenious. Chic said he'd seen it on a crime programme on TV – a bunch of boys in London had been doing it for ages. These programmes were great. If you ever needed a scam the cunts handed it to you on a plate.

Chic saw nothing wrong with what he was doing – he had to make a living. It was simply this: the dole was his basic, everything else was commission.

Chic huddled up in the back seat, turning away from Shug and Scobie. The front seat was fucked – some sort of pin had gone, making the seat slide backwards and forwards whenever Malkie braked or accelerated. Alton Towers didn't have a look-in.

He pulled his collar up again and shivered, then stared in amazement as Scobie nudged him and offered him a joint.

'Is that gonnae warm me up, is it?' he asked, looking at Scobie's saucers for eyes.

Scobie looked at the joint and considered if it was possible. Could THC raise your body temperature as well as lowering your sugar level? He'd have to give it some thought. He opened his mouth to give an educated guess, but all that came out was a slurred, 'Aye . . . *ah'm* awright.'

'Yir cunted,' said Chic. He hated it when Scobie was like this: he'd laugh at anything. You could punch fuck out of his arm and he'd howl with laughter – he was beyond help.

Earlier tonight, before Malkie picked them up, Scobie had insisted they go up and see Agro Dave. He was called Agro Dave because he was agoraphobic. He never left the house. Scobie heard that Dave had some good skunk and he didn't want to miss out on it. He'd finished the last of his rocky and didn't fancy going the weekend without a blaw. He'd had enough of that rocky shite. It was too mild for him – he had to pack a joint full of it before he could even taste the stuff. He thought about what Chic had said to him on the way to Agro Dave's. 'Ye must be buildin up a resistance tae it then.'

Scobie had looked at him and laughed. 'Bollocks – a resistance tae hash?'

As they turned the corner into Agro Dave's street Scobie saw that the lights were off. 'D'ye think he'll be in?' he asked Chic.

'Course he'll be in . . . he's a fuckin agoraphobic, ya daft cunt!'

Scobie thought about it as they approached Dave's and burst into laughter as it hit him. 'Oh, right . . . ah forgoat!' He laughed hysterically.

Chic watched as the door slowly opened on a chain

and the hairy bearded figure of Dave peered at them through the opening.

'Awright, Dave man' – Chic smirked at Scobie – 'ye comin oot fir a pint?'

Scobie held his sides and fell over the hedge.

Dave opened the door wider and looked at them both as he pulled up the collar of his padded lumberjack shirt. He wondered if they were taking the piss, although he could see Scobie was totally off his cake. 'Naw, man,' he said. 'Yir awright . . . ah'v goat a video ah want tae watch.'

Scobie pulled himself out of the hedge and calmed down. 'Any blaw, Dave?'

Dave unhooked the chain and opened the door. 'Aye, moan in.' Dave turned around on his shiny worn moccasins and shuffled up the hallway.

Scobie and Chic stepped into the dark council house, smelling the incense in the air. Scobie liked it here. It was peaceful. Some nights if there were nothing on the TV he would take a wander down to see Dave and watch a video. Dave had a great collection – mostly horror, slash and gore. He could quote the entire script from *The Texas Chainsaw Massacre*. Dave was a member of a mail-order video club and would buy three or four videos a week. Scobie was always asking to borrow some of his films but Dave wouldn't let them out of his sight. What would happen if Scobie forgot to bring them back? He'd have to leave the house to chase him up and there was no way he fancied that.

So Scobie accepted the rules. If he wanted to see a film he'd just have to go to Dave's and watch it. It was better than the pictures anyway. He'd arrive with a bit of blaw and they would sit and talk for hours, watch a horror and have a few pipes. If Scobie was a bit short Dave would always let him have some on account. He was a good cunt Dave, even if he did have some strange ways.

Chic and Scobie followed Dave into the living-room. On the TV, a young blonde girl with a ripped dress, covered in blood, was pinned up against the wall screaming her head off. Scobie looked about the room, lit by a couple of flickering candles and the glow from the TV. 'Sit yirsels doon,' said Dave, gesturing at a director's chair from MFI that some wit had written 'Dave' on in felt pen. Chic sat in an old velvet armchair that had candle wax dripping down the armrests. He glanced at the TV as a guy in a ski mask held a meat hook aloft and plunged it into the girl's forehead.

'It's awright, Dave man, we're no stayin long,' said Chic.

'Whit can I dae ye fir?' asked Dave.

Scobie rubbed his hands together in anticipation. 'Ah hear ye've goat yir hons oan a nice bit ay skunk?'

'Certainly huv.' Dave reached for a tennis ball off a shelf laden with videos. 'How much d'ye want?'

'Quarter awright?' asked Scobie, reaching for his money.

Chic picked nonchalantly at the wax, watching as

Dave give a quick shake and a squeeze of the tennis ball and out popped a quarter.

'Nice wan.' Scobie handed over the cash. 'Oh, an, er, mah pal's after some ay that whizz ye gied us laist week. Any left?'

Dave nodded and headed out the door. 'Ah'll be back in a minute.'

Chic watched Dave go into the bathroom and shut the door behind him. Scobie breathed in the sweet smell of his newly acquired skunk.

'Haw you!' said Chic.

Scobie looked up. 'Whit?'

'Where dis he keep hus speed?'

'Fuck knows,' said Scobie. 'Bathroom cabinet? How?'

'Fuckin better hud be,' said Chic. 'Ah've seen where he keeps hus blaw . . . ah'd hate tae think where he keeps his whizz.'

Scobie sniggered and set about skinning up. The door opened and Dave came back in, carrying a handful of wraps.

'Tenner awright?' asked Dave.

'Er, ah wis thinkin mair ay twenty?' said Chic, digging in his jeans and pulling out the money.

'Nae bother.' Dave took the twenty off him and handed over the wraps.

Chic stood up, ready to leave and saw Scobie rummaging in his pockets for his lighter. He was glued to the TV and starting to get comfy. 'Moan you.' Chic kicked his foot.

Scobie ignored him. He licked a cigarette along the join and peeled the paper away. 'Let's jist huv wan fir the road,' he said, sprinkling tobacco along the skins. 'We've loads ay time yet.'

Chic looked at his watch and sat back down again. Scobie did have a point. Malkie wouldn't be picking them up for at least an hour.

'Ah'll git some beers, eh?' said Dave, walking off to the kitchen.

Chic waited till he was gone and sniffed one of the wraps. Deciding it hadn't been up Agro Dave's ring-piece, he opened it, licked his finger and dipped it in. Scobie heated up a corner of the hash with his lighter, watching Chic for the verdict. Chic tasted his speed and grinned as the sour-sweet taste hit his tongue. 'Look out, ladies,' he said.

Chic peered out of the window of Malkie's car. He could see the lights of The Barrowlands in the distance. Almost there, thank fuck. The sooner this was over and they could get to the warmth of a club the better. He was looking forward to ditching the others and taking off with that Yvonne bird from last week. Now that was a session and a half. Chances were she'd be in Archaos later and up for another shagfest. Just as well he'd scored that whizz.

He'd met her last week when he was out with a couple of boys from the gym he'd recently joined. She kept walking past him, giving him the eye. The boys were nudging him but he was too pished to do anything about it. In the end they pushed him up in front of her, saying, 'Speak tae the lassie fir fuck sakes.' He said hullo. She said he looked like David Beckham, so he said she looked like Xena. Within an hour the Warrior Princess had abducted him and taken him back to her flat. She was all over him like a bad suit, but he'd run out of whizz and was having trouble getting it up after the amount of drink he'd poured down his neck.

He asked her if she had anything that would wake him up a bit. She said she had some Pro Plus. She took them out of a drawer, tossed him the packet and went into the kitchen. Chic quickly got to work, taking ten pills out of the packet, crushing them on the table with a glass and snorting the lot through a rolled-up fiver. The sour caffeine taste ran down the back of his throat, but it did the trick. Within half an hour he had a hard-on that a cat couldn't scratch. On the job all night – didn't sleep a wink.

Thinking he was on to something, he tried the same thing the following night when he got lucky with big Louise, a leggy blonde he'd had his eye on for some time. He swallowed another ten pills in the pub bogs, necked a couple of Beck's and jumped in a taxi with her. When they got back to his place and he got her kit off he found he couldn't get it up – total opposite of last night. He went to the bog to see if he could instil some life in the old chap but when he got back Louise had gone. He knew what she was thinking: he was pathetic, with a wee dick to boot. He'd seen her since in a couple of pubs, sniggering to her mates. One of her pals had passed him on the way to the bogs and wiggled her little finger at him. Bitch. He'd a good mind to go over and explain to Louise that it wasn't him – it was the tablets. Pro Plus, for fuck's sakes. 'Poor man's speed.' He didn't know what was worse: being labelled a needle dick or a tight bastard.

He was itching for another shot – just to show her what she'd been missing. But how the fuck do you ask a bird like that for a second chance? She'd laugh in his face. He decided to leave caffeine pills alone and stick to the proper stuff in future.

Chic knew what his problem was: he was led by his dick. It made all major decisions in life for him. He never wore a rubber either. His angle on AIDS was: 'If y've goat it, y've goat it an there's fuck aw ye can dae aboot it.'

Chances were he already had a couple of kids littered about, especially from when he worked at Butlins down south a few years ago. There was one he knew about – to Susan in Easterhouse. A four-month-old boy she'd named Declan. He said it sounded like a Fenian name. She said unless he was prepared to commit to her and the baby he had no right to say what she called it. So, was he ready to commit? Was he fuck. Sure, the kid looked a wee bit like him but they all looked the same at that age, didn't they? It could be anybody's.

Chic had been to see her and the wean a couple of

times recently, mainly to get a ride out of her – she was always up for it. That's how she ended up in the state she was in now. Daft bitch. The last time he came to visit she said she was skint and was having trouble managing. She'd had to give up her job as a temp to watch the wean. He told her not to worry: if other birds can do it then so could she. She told him she needed a hand – *financially*.

Money?

He clocked the way she was looking at him. There was no way he could help – he was on the dole, remember? She said that he'd better come up with something fast. She wasn't having her baby – *their* baby – suffering because its da was a lazy basta. She said that if he didn't come up with some cash soon then there were channels she could go through to make sure that he did pay. He told her to get to fuck – money-grabbing wee cow that she was.

The Barrowlands sign loomed above them and lit up the inside of the car as Malkie drove along the Gallowgate, approaching the bar. He had a bad feeling about this; the wind-ups, jokes, whatever you wanted to call them, they were getting out of hand. This was the maddest thing they'd done since Scobie climbed up on the chapel roof and played 'The Sash' on a portable CD player while mass was coming out. So much for God-fearing folk: what a fucking uproar. They went bananas. A big guy in a Sunday shirt ran to his car, opened the boot, came back with a jack and hurled it up at Scobie. Scobie, the poor bastard, was an easy target. Stoned out of his nut, hanging over the edge of the roof and holding on to his sides in a fit of the giggles. The bloke soon knocked the smile off Scobie's face: the jack opened in midair, wrapped round Scobie's head and knocked him off the side of the roof: **coconut!** Scobie never did get those front teeth replaced. He looked like an extra from *Deliverance* – all he needed was a piece of straw hanging from his gub and a banjo in his hand.

Malkie pulled the car up. Shug got out, zipped up his parka and looked towards Finlays. Malkie wound down the window and Shug leaned in. 'Ten minutes, right?' he said.

'Right.'

'An keep the engine runnin.' He walked up the icy pavement and opened the door. Steam belched out into the street, along with the sound of singing and cheering that came from inside. Shug glanced back at the car, grinned like a maddie and walked into the pub.

He looked about the smoke-filled room as though he was in here to meet someone. He tried to hide his look of disgust as a fat bloke in front of him led a crowd in a rendition of 'Go home, British soldiers', turning round to sing the words in Shug's face, expecting him to join in and be as fired up as he was. Shug gave a knowing grin and squeezed past him to join the queue at the bar.

* * *

Evelyn looked about for familiar faces in the crowd. She was starting to lose interest. It had been Mick's idea to come here. She'd wanted to go into town – the dancin. She was getting in the Christmas mood, but Mick was being his usual sensible self: he had work in the morning, so she'd to settle for a quiet drink in Finlays.

She knew one or two of the girls who came here with their men, but it was really just a place for the guys to meet up and quickly ditch the women at a table. She'd pre-warned Mick that if he left her on her own she was getting a taxi home, so he'd been trying his best to entertain her. She looked up at him. He was thinking of something to talk about, God love him. It wasn't as if this was a first date. After six years of marriage there wasn't that much he could tell her. She knew it all. She looked at his hair – it needed cut. Her pal, Angela, fancied him with his hair long. The wee bitch made no attempt to hide it, although it was always done in fun. She said he looked like Daniel Day Lewis. Angela always flirted with him and winked at Evelyn; said with a name like Donnelly he must have a bit of the Irish in him, and come to think of it, *she* wouldn't mind a bit of the Irish in *her* too. Mick, the stupid bugger, never caught on. The closest he'd ever been to Ireland was taking Evelyn to see the Corrs at the SECC. She loved him to bits, though. He was a good husband and a great dad to wee Jamie.

She thought about the wee feller – just turned five – and remembered when the other mothers in her street laughed as they warned her about 'the terrible twos'. When Jamie was a toddler he'd had more tantrums in shopping malls than Evelyn cared to remember. He could still have his moments now if he didn't get his own way. Mick was good with him, though. He had a way of calming him down just by speaking to him. She tried it but it never worked as well for her and she always lost the place with him and skelped his arse. He was a good kid really. She liked to watch people's faces when he smiled at them. Those dimples could melt your heart.

She pulled a long strand of hair from her cheek. It was hot in here; didn't they have any fans? She was sure they turned up the heating just to get you to buy more drink. She pulled her long hair away from her neck and into a ponytail, wrapping the hairband round it, thinking what a waste of time it had been trying to do anything with her hair tonight – the minute you walked in this place it always went as flat as a pancake. She looked up at Mick again. He looked nice in that grey top she'd got him from Asda. He always whinged about wanting to pick his own clothes but, if the truth be known, he couldn't pick his nose. He was clueless when it came to fashion. When he got in from work tonight she told him she wasn't going anywhere with him dressed like a tramp. She pulled out a carrier bag and held the top up. He started pulling the usual faces, saying it wasn't really his style. He appreciated the thought and all that, but . . . She told him to shut up and try it on. She sat and watched as he pulled it over his head, saying it was too baggy, complaining that the sleeves were too tight and the neck was too low. Was she sure it wasn't a woman's? When she said she'd take it back he said, 'Naw, Naw, it's awright, it'll dae fir a night oot.' An hour later in the pub he was telling her how much he suits grey and that he should let her buy more of his clothes. It was always the same carry-on, thought Evelyn.

She smiled to herself and looked up at him, not realising he'd been talking away to her.

'So the doctor pulls oot a suppository fae behind hus ear an goes tae write a prescription wi it, right? He looks at it an goes, "Suppository? Aw, some bum's goat mah pen!"' He cracked up laughing.

Evelyn shrugged her shoulders. She'd missed half the joke. 'Ah don't git it,' she said.

'Ye niver git any ay mah jokes.'

'That's cos they're stupid!'

'They're no stupid; listen . . . the doctor, right, he should huv a pen behind hus ear, right?'

'Right?' She looked about the bar and saw Angela in with her new boyfriend. That was a lovely dress she had on. A black diamanté slip dress Evelyn had told her she'd seen in the window of Frasers. Must have cost her a few bob anyway. Or her boyfriend, more like – Angela said that he was loaded. Evelyn thought about asking them over but remembered Mick said he wanted it to be just the two of them tonight. They hardly saw enough of each other as it was.

'Y' know whit a suppository is?'

'Eh? Oh, aye.' She turned to face him and look interested again. She knew what her problem was: gasping for a fag – it was all she could think of. Deciding to put herself out of her misery, she reached into her bag and pulled out a pack.

'Ah thought ye wis tryin tae pack them in?' said Mick.

'Ach, it's Christmas, ah'll dae it in the New Year.'

'Aye, right, same day the Pope signs fir Rangers.'

'Ah will – ah promise.'

He took a mouthful of lager and watched her rummaging in her bag. She pulled out a lighter. 'Look, d'ye want tae hear this joke or no?' he asked.

'Aye.' She lit up a cigarette and took a long satisfying draw.

Shug moved up the queue and glanced up at a picture of the Pope behind the bar. He felt a sneer coming on, but remembered where he was and quickly hid it. Francie gave the bloke in front of Shug his change then looked Shug up and down. Shug knew the look: who's this cunt?

'Yes, young feller?' said Francie, managing a festive smile. No need for the third degree, it was almost Christmas after all.

'Beck's,' said Shug.

Mick was still fighting a losing battle. 'So there's a patient away wi the doctor's pen up their erse. Dae ye git it?'

Evelyn looked at him, puzzled; what the hell was he

on about? That wasn't the least bit funny. 'Na, that's stupid,' she said.

Give up, thought Mick. He shook his head in defeat, picked up his pint and looked about the bar. Big Ronnie and the boys were in tonight. Ronnie threw his head back and laughed at one of his pal's jokes. Mick's focus was drawn to the scar that ran from Ronnie's right eye, all the way down to his jaw. He never did ask him how he got it. He'd rather wait till Ronnie divulged that info. What he did know was that whatever happened to Ronnie that night was fuck-all compared to what happened to the cunt who gave him the scar.

'We don't really huv anyhun tae talk aboot any mair, dae we?' asked Mick.

'Ye want a divorce?' Evelyn smiled.

'Ach, ye know whit ah mean. Ah'm tryin mah best here.'

Evelyn took his hand and gave it a squeeze. 'Ye don't huv tae amuse me – ah'm quite happy jist bein oot, thanks.'

Mick smiled at her for a moment then got up. 'Budge up a bit,' he said. She moved up the bench she was sitting on. He sat next to her and put his arm round her. 'Ye want tae sit oan Santa's knee an tell us whit ye want fae yir Christmas?' he said, nuzzling her ear.

She looked down at the empty bottle in front of her. 'Well, ye could stert by gittin me another Hooch . . . *Santa*.'

Mick cast his eyes across to the busy bar. 'Aye, gies a

minute till the queue goes doon a bit.' He watched Francie serving a bloke in a parka who had his back to the crowd. There was something about this guy . . . something familiar. Mick watched him turn round and look about the bar before he realised. 'Aw shit.'

'Whit?' said Evelyn.

'It's yir Shug – hide!' He jumped up and slid on to the chair facing her so he had his back to the bar.

Evelyn looked about; he must be mistaken. 'It cannae be. He widnae come in here? He'd huv tae be mental.'

She watched as Francie placed the bottle on the counter in front of Shug. 'Wan eighty, son.'

Shug unzipped his parka and reached into his inside pocket. He pulled out a fiver and offered it to Francie.

Francie could hardly believe his eyes. He stared disbelievingly at the Rangers scarf that hung round Shug's neck. Francie half laughed in exasperation, took back the bottle of beer and gestured with his thumb. '*Oot!*'

'Whit?'

'Yir no gittin served . . . Moan, oot!'

'How no?' said Shug.

'How no? Are ye daft, son? Get oot afore ah huv ye dragged oot. Ye don't come in here wi they colours oan.'

'Whit? This?' Shug looked at the scarf innocently. 'It's Sampdoria!'

'Is it fuck, it's Rangers!'

'It's Sampdoria! Hoanest. Moan, mate, gies a beer, eh? Look, ah'll tek it aff, right?' He took the scarf off. 'It is Sampdoria though.'

Mebbe it is, thought Francie. Ah'v no bin tae a match in ages. Besides, these cunts change their strips twice a season these days. 'Aye, well, it looks like a Rangers skerf tae me,' he said. 'Put it in yir poakit, right!'

'Aye, awright.' Shug put the scarf in his side pocket. It hung loosely at his side.

'Wan eighty.' Francie handed over the Becks. 'An keep it in yir poakit – ah don't want any trouble.'

'Aye, aye.'

'Ah mean it.' He turned and put the money in the till. 'Soaft shite.'

Mick had his head bowed. 'Whit's he dein noo?' he asked, not daring to look up.

'Ah don't believe it,' said Evelyn. 'He's jist goat served . . . wearin a Rangers skerf!'

'Yir jokin.'

She watched as Shug walked away from the bar. 'Ah wish ah wis,' she said. 'Shit, he's comin ower!'

Suddenly Shug changed direction, walked over to the window and pulled out the scarf.

Chic wound down the window again. It was a toss-up between freezing your balls off in Malkie's shitey cold motor, or having the windows closed to keep in the heat and ending up as stoned as Skobie, breathing in that shite he was smoking. Scobie offered him the joint again. Now he knew why they called it skunk – it was minging. He shook his head; paranoid enough, thank you. He hated it when Scobie did that – it must have been the tenth time he shoved that smelly bastard of a thing under his nose and he'd turned him down. He did the same with crisps. You could be out for a pint with Scobie; he'd have a pint of heavy in one hand and a packet of cheese and onion in the other. After every mouthful of beer he'd offer you a crisp. How many bastarding times did you have to say no? 'Shove yir fucking crisps up yir erse, ya daft cunt!'

Chic wiped the window and looked across to the bar. Shug suddenly appeared at the window of Finlays, waving the scarf like he was at the match, and raised his bottle of beer as if to say cheers to Chic. Chic nudged Scobie, who turned to look out of the window and focus his gaze. He took a deep draw on the joint and sniggered as the smoke billowed from his nostrils.

Malkie couldn't help but smirk at Shug's audacity. 'That cunt's mental, man! Ah didnae think he'd dae it!'

'Ha! Ah know,' said Chic. 'Look at um, crazy basta!'

Shug danced a jig, still waving the scarf, then quickly disappeared from view as an arm dragged him away from the window. Scobie started coughing on the smoke and almost collapsed in an uncontrollable heap.

'Shit! They've goat um.' Malkie turned round. 'He'll no be long noo . . . Chic man, shut hum up will ye!'

Ronnie's hand was wrapped firmly round Shug's throat, pinning him up against the wall. He rubbed the scarf in Shug's face. 'Whit's this, eh? Eh?'

'Whit took ye so long?' choked Shug.

'Cheeky basta! Whit ye dein in here wi this? Ya blue-nosed cunt!'

Evelyn knew she had to move fast. She grabbed Mick's arm. 'Mick, he's gonnae kill um.'

'Good, he deserves it.' He slid further down in his seat.

Shug grinned at Ronnie. 'Er, Fenian basta,' he said. 'Yir turn.'

Ronnie couldn't believe the audacity: had he heard this cunt right? He looked at his mates: they shook their heads in disbelief. A voice piped up: 'Ronnie, man, ye don't want banned. Tek the cunt ootside an brek hus legs.'

Just one of the many options on offer tonight, thought Ronnie. He moved his face closer to Shug's. 'Ah'm lookin at a deid man. Yir comin wi me – ootside.'

Evelyn grabbed Mick's arm again, digging her nails in. 'Mick, stoap um.'

'Whit? No way, he'll kill me an aw!'

Shug pulled a sour expression and drew his face back from Ronnie's. 'Yir breath smells ay pish – whit huv you bin dein?'

That was it. So whit if ah git banned, thought Ronnie. There's plenty mair pubs in Glasgow. He dropped Shug back down on his feet and punched him square in the face. Shug flew across the pub with Ronnie wading over to finish the job.

'Mick!' screamed Evelyn.

Mick's arse was up off the seat like lightning. He

knew if he didn't do something now he'd get it in the neck off Evelyn for days. 'Shit! Awright. Haw! Ronnie, whoah! Wait a minute. The boay's no right in the heid, man, leave um!'

Shug lay on his back, nursing a bloody nose, thinking twice about getting up. Ronnie stood over him, daring him.

Mick intervened. 'Ronnie!'

'Stay oot ay it!' warned Ronnie.

'Ah know the boay, he's no right, he cannae help it!'

'How *d'you* know um?'

Shug sat up, grimacing in pain and managing a smarmy smile. 'Ah'm hus brar-in-law,' he said. 'Awright, Mick.'

Ronnie looked at Mick disbelievingly. 'Yir fuckin jokin.'

'Ah'm no,' said Mick, ashamed.

Ronnie looked down at Shug, then back at Mick in disgust. 'Get um oot ay here!'

'Cheers, Ronnie.'

Ronnie walked back to his table, shaking his head at his confused mates.

Shug wiped his nose and looked at the blood on his hand. 'Aye, cheers, Ronnie, ya dick!'

'Shut it, you!' said Mick, helping Shug back on to his feet. 'Moan, git oot.'

Evelyn came marching over. 'Yir lucky he didnae kill ye – ya stupid basta ye. Whit ye dein comin in here wi Rangers colours oan?'

'Well, somebody hud tae.' Shug pinched his nose to stem the flow.

'Ah'v hud it wi you, ah'm sick ay ye!' She stormed off to the toilet.

'Moan.' Mick helped the limping Shug to the door.

'Ye couldnae lend us a fiver could ye, Mick – fir a Joe Baxi? Ah'm a bit skint. Ah'll gie ye it back.'

Mick pulled out his money. 'Er, ah'v only goat a tenner oan us, ah'll huv tae git ch—'

Shug snatched the money off him as quick as a flash: a miraculous recovery. 'Aye, that'll dae, cheers . . . see ye.' He left the pub, walking normally again.

Mick turned and walked back to his seat. He passed by Ronnie and the crew and gave a sheepish smile. Ronnie picked up his pint and swigged it, ignoring Mick like a bad relative at a wedding.

Shug reappeared in the doorway, took a glass of whisky off a table and threw it over a Celtic flag hanging on the wall by the door.

'HAW! RONNIE! RONNIE!' he shouted.

Ronnie took another mouthful of his pint. 'What now?' He looked over to the door and saw Shug set fire to the whisky-soaked flag.

'RANGERS YA BASTA! GIT IT UP YE!' He gave Ronnie the finger.

Ronnie nearly choked on his pint. 'That was fucking it!' Tables went flying as Celtic supporters dived out of their seats and made for Shug. Evelyn came out of the toilet and looked about. 'Here we go again.' She'd seen this scene before – her engagement, her wedding. Shug, doing what he did best: winding up Catholics.

Shug overturned a table near the door to slow them down and ran from the pub, laughing.

Malkie watched Shug come running out of the pub, a crowd of people following him throwing bottles and glasses. One smashed off the car door.

'Jesus Christ!'

'Ha ha, ooh fuck,' laughed Scobie.

'Hurry up, git in!' Chic opened the door.

Malkie frantically revved the car and Shug dived in. Pint glasses and bottles rained down as Malkie let the clutch out and the car tore off down the street.

'You are wan lucky basta' said Chic.

A glass smashed off the rear window: Chic instinctively ducked. Shug calmly took the joint off Scobie and took a long draw.

'Here.' Malkie looked in the rear-view mirror and passed back a handkerchief. 'Yir nose is bleedin.'

Shug took it and wiped his nose. 'Money!' he said.

'Eh?' Scobie stared blankly. He'd forgotten what they'd come here for. Wasn't it a pint? What happened?

'A bet's a bet', said Shug. 'Tenner each, moan.'

'Oh, aye, right.' Chic handed over a tenner. 'Here ye go. Nice wan, Shug.'

'Aye, it wis worth it; here.' Malkie passed back a tenner.

Scobie rummaged in his jeans for money, remembering what the bet was about now. 'Thirty quid fir ten minutes work, eh?' He laughed, digging deep in his jeans. 'No bad, Shug, mah man, no bad at aw.'

'Forty,' Shug sneered. 'Ah tapped mah stupid brar-in-law fir a tenner an aw.' He looked out of the window. 'Droap us near the toon, Malkie.'

'Right.' This'll do, thought Malkie. No need for long goodbyes. He'd be well gone in the morning. No reason to deal with these mad cunts again. Best not to remind Shug he was going, he thought – act normal. If he says, 'See ye th' morra', best just to say, 'Aye.'

Malkie pulled up at the back of the St Enoch's Centre. Shug got out, still smoking the joint, slammed the car door and banged his goodbyes on the roof. Malkie tore off down the road. Shug took off the scarf, its purpose now served, dumped it in a bin and walked off towards Argyle Street: the night was still very, very young.

Evelyn hated all the Rangers/Celtic crap, and all the bullshit that went along with it, just as much as Mick. Her Auntie Jean hadn't spoke to her since Evelyn announced her engagement. 'Merryin a Tim?'

Evelyn stood in the kitchen with her ma, Irene. 'Aye! Tim or no, I'm gonnae merry hum . . . ah luv hum, so it's nuthin tae dae wi you!'

Jean looked at Irene and pished herself laughing. Evelyn thought there must have been some secret code going on that she wouldn't get till she was in her forties. Her ma had long ago explained about periods, babies, all that stuff . . . so what was the big joke she'd missed out about Catholics?

'Hus he goat red hair?' Jean laughed.

Evelyn wasn't in on this, whatever it was. She looked at Jean like she was mad.

'They're sleekit bastards,' explained Jean. 'If he's goat red hair he's *double* sleekit! There's nuthin mair sleekit than a ginger Tim!'

That was the night Evelyn stood up for herself. No one was going to take the piss out of her – or Mick.

'At least he's no a fanny!' she said.

Jean looked puzzled. 'Whit's that supposed to mean?'

'Yir Boabby,' said Evelyn, 'he's a fanny. A wee diddy who's scared tae mek a move withoot askin you furst! At least ah'v goat a man, a *real* man, Tim or no, ya auld bag, ye!'

Jean looked to her sister-in-law for back-up, but Irene was too gobsmacked to do a thing.

'Ah think ah'd better leave,' said Jean, grabbing her coat.

'Aye, ah think ye better hud,' said Evelyn. She looked at her mum, expecting a roasting but Irene never said a word – probably thought better of it after Evelyn's display.

Irene was glad Hugh wasn't in to have heard Evelyn speak to his sister like that; he would have killed her, but something needed to be said. That night Irene went to bed feeling proud of her little girl. If she could handle Jean she could handle anything the other bigots threw at her.

* * *

Evelyn sat on the edge of the bed and looked about the room. Those curtains needed changing; they'd been up since the summer. Maybe she'd get her mum's pal, Audrey, to make her a new pair when Christmas was by with. In fact the whole room could do with decorating. She wasn't going to mention it to Mick. He'd go nuts: 'It wis only done laist year!' The bedside units annoyed her: plain white. They'd had them since they moved in. She'd seen lovely units in MFI just the other week, wardrobes to match. She'd break the decorating to him first then eventually bring the conversation round to the units. Now definitely wasn't the right time though.

They'd been sitting there far too long without saying a word. She turned round and looked at him, hoping he'd calmed down. Mick sat holding a bloodied towel against his head; his new Asda top and his hands were also covered with blood. Looking back, it would have been safer to jump in the car with Shug. The minute Shug left Finlays, some of the crowd turned their unwelcome attentions on Mick for being related. He was halfway out of the door, still arguing his point with Ronnie, when he felt a whack on the back of his head and heard Evelyn scream. Bottled in his favourite pub. What a red neck – you couldn't get more embarrassing.

'Ah'm soarry,' she said. 'I know ah sais that ah widnae git ye involved again . . . bit he's mah wee brar. Someone hus tae look oot fir um, noo an again. He aywis looked oot fir me when ah wis wee.' She lit up a cigarette. 'I know whit yir thinkin; bit he's no mental.

He disnae need loackin up. No again. Every time they loacked um up he came oot worse then when he went in. The furst time wis the worst, he wis only ten. When he came oot he widnae speak tae mah ma or da fir months; an then when he did, aw's he wid say tae them wis "bastards". He's jist goat a destructive personality; he cannae help hissel.'

'Shite,' said Mick.

'It's no shite,' retorted Evelyn.

'Aye it is. Total-utter-wan-hunnert-per-cent-no-question-aboot-it shite!'

She shrugged, drew heavily on her cigarette, looked about the room for a diversion: she didn't want to get into it.

'Ah'v heard it aw before, Ev, every excuse unner the sun – *the boay's a loner, dis hus aen thing, wants tae be left alaen, ye cannae depend oan um, hus mind wanners, it's no hus fault* – bollocks! That's aw it is. There's wan word that sums aw that bollocks up: dae ye want tae know whit it is?'

No answer.

'Eh? Ah'll tell ye: *selfish*, that's aw. Ye cut through aw that crap an that's whit yir left wi, a selfish basta. Dae ye know whit ye git if ye look up *selfish basta* in a dictionary? A picture ay yir Shug lookin up at ye.'

'Aw shut it!' she snapped.

'Naw, *you* shut it! Ah'm sick ay this pish. Every time *he* sterts, *you* stert. It's like bein oan a fuckin merry-go-roon. Ye huv tae let go ay um, Ev; he's a grown man.'

In the next room moonlight streamed in through the half-drawn curtains. Five-year-old Jamie was sitting up in bed trying to play with a Power Rangers toy to take his mind off the argument. They were at it again. A single *thump* came from the next room: he flinched on cue.

The front door slowly opened and Shug came in quietly, carrying a sausage supper and an opened can of beer. Straight away he heard the noise coming from the bedroom. Uh-ho. **Soapy bubble**, he thought. The can of beer dropped to the floor with a thud and squirted everywhere. 'Aw, shit!' He picked it up, trying to stop it from going everywhere, and dropped his sausage supper in the process, scattering chips all over the carpet. 'Basta!'

Mick was in mid-rant when he heard the noise in the hall. 'Whit's that?'

'Great. Noo yiv woke the wean up, ah'll niver git um back tae sleep.' She went to get up.

Mick held his hand out to stop her, opened the bedroom door and turned on the hall light.

Shug stood in front of him on a squashed sausage, the supper in one hand, and trying to pick beer-soaked chips out of the carpet with the other.

'Ah don't believe this!' Mick shook his head.

'Awright, Mick, man,' said Shug, looking up. 'Soarry aboot the noise. Did ah wek ye up? Whit happened tae yir heid?'

'Whit is it?' Evelyn came out and saw Shug. 'Oh, shit. Mick, don't stert.'

'Oh ah'm no gonnae stert,' said Mick, trying to be calm. 'Ah'm no the wan who sterts things, remember.' He pointed to Shug. 'That's *hus* joab. Ah'm the wan who cleans up the mess afterwards. *You* deal wi it this time. An ye kin stert by tekin that key aff um an tellin um tae git tae fuck! Ah'm away tae mah bed, some of us huv tae be up fir work in a couple ay oors.' He went back into the room, slamming the door behind him.

Jamie jumped at the noise.

'Whit are ye dein here?' Evelyn hissed. 'Ye cannae stay – he'll kill ye!'

'Mah da's pished again.'

'So whit? He's aywis pished!'

'Aye, bit he's really bad th' night. Kept kickin fuck oot mah door, gien it, "C'moan then! Haw, big man, think yir too big fir a smack, ya cunt!" Aw that pish. Ah hud tae git oot afore ah decked the basta.' He offered the chips to Evelyn, who waved them away irritably.

'Look, Shug, yir gonnae huv tae move oot ay mah ma's – git yir aen place or somehun. Ye cannae keep oan stayin here. Is there naebody ye kin stay wi th' night?' She cast a worried glance towards her bedroom.

'Kin ah no stay here, like?'

'Mick's goin mental aboot the trouble ye caused in the pub. He'll no let ye stay. No after that.'

'It wis jist a laugh – goat a wee bit oot ay hand, that's aw. Anyway, tell um tae git tae fuck. It's yir hoose an aw, ye know.' That was the thing with Shug, he always had a way of justifying things, even if he was way off the mark.

Piggy in the middle, thought Evelyn.

'Moan, Ev?' He held his hands out, palms up. 'Y'll no know ah'm here, ah'll go straight tae bed – ah'm knackered. Look, ah'll be oot ay here in the mornin, right. Ah'll away ower tae Malkie's th' morra . . . ah promise.'

'Ah'm sick ay this, Shug,' she sighed. 'This is the laist time, ah mean it. It's causin arguments wi me an hum aw the time.'

'Don't worry aboot it. Away tae yir bed; ah'll git these cheps up.'

'Forget the cheps, ah'll git them th' morra. Jist git in there.' She pointed to the spare room. 'An don't mek a sound.'

'Cheers, Ev.' He went into the room and closed the door. 'Your usual room, sir?' He smiled to himself as he placed the sausage supper on the bedside unit. He took off his shirt and lay on the bed. This was the life. Peace and quiet. No mad alkies running about, keeping you awake all night.

Mick was sitting up in bed as Evelyn came in. 'Well?'

'Well whit?'

'Is he away?'

She sat on the edge of the bed and nonchalantly set the alarm clock. 'Aye.'

'No he's no. Ah didnae hear the front door go.' He pulled the towel away from his head, got up and looked in the mirror. It had stopped bleeding. About time. It was the first time he'd been hit by a bottle; he hoped it would be the last.

'Look, Mick, ah'm tired.' She got into bed. 'Ah don't want tae argue. Kin we talk aboot it th' morra?' She lay down and turned her back to him.

'This is th' morra. It's hof past three! Ah want tae know whit yir gonnae dae aboot um!'

'It's jist fir th' night, he's goin tae Malkie's th' morra.'

'Is he fuck!' He made for the door. 'He's goin tae Malkie's the noo!'

She dived out of bed and got between him and the door to stop him leaving the room. 'Mick! Stoap it!'

'Ah telt ye he's no stayin!'

'It's jist fir th' night. He's goat naewhere else tae stay, he'll be oot in the mornin, hoanest. Mick! Leave it, will ye!'

Shug came out of his room, squinting and scratching his head. 'Fuck sakes, man. This's worse than oor hoose.'

He could hear Jamie sobbing. He looked towards Jamie's room, then to Evelyn and Mick's. He tutted in disgust, opened the door and peered inside. 'Wee Man,' he whispered.

The light from the hall lit up the room. He could see Jamie sitting upright on his pillow, with his back against the wall and his knees curled up against his chest. Buzz Lightyear grinned manically at Shug from Jamie's *Toy Story* pyjamas. Shug slowly crept into the room. 'Haw,

Wee Man. It's me. Ye awright? Eh?' He picked Jamie up and hugged him. 'Moan, yir awright, pal, it's jist yir ma an da huvin a carry oan; it'll be awright in the mornin. D'ye want a story?'

Jamie shook his head sadly. He wasn't in the mood. Poor wee basta, thought Shug. Imagine huvin they two hof-wits fir yir ma an da.

'Ah know whit ye kin huv,' said Shug. 'Wait there the noo.' He put Jamie back on the bed and went into the kitchen. He took a loaf from the breadbin and butter from the fridge. 'If that's whit bein merried is, man, ye kin keep it,' he muttered to himself. It was all that fuckin Donnelly's fault. Fuckin Boghopper that he was. Evelyn was all right when she used to see that Andy Clarkston – good Orangeman. Banged up now but – for assaulting his wife if he remembered rightly.

Shug buttered two slices, took a bag of sugar out of the cupboard and poured some on to the bread, then went back into Jamie's room and sat on the bed.

Jamie had stopped crying. The arguing had also stopped. He handed Jamie the sandwich. 'Here ye go, Wee Man. Wan ay yir Uncle Shug's famous magic sugar pieces. An why dae we caw thum magic?' he prompted him.

Jamie took a bite. 'Cos they taste magic.'

'Aye, that's right, pal. Pure magic.'

The bedroom door slowly opened and Evelyn came in. She sat on the bed, kissed Jamie on the head and stroked his hair. 'Sorry, son. Ye awright?'

'Aye. Uncle Shug made me a magic piece.'

'Oh, that's nice,' she said to Shug, half joking, through gritted teeth. 'So's ye kin git sugar all ower yir bed. Whit huv ah telt ye aboot gien um them? Hus teeth'll fall oot.'

'Ah made you enough ay thum when you were wee. They niver did you any herm.'

'Aye, suppose so.' She smiled.

A brief moment of nostalgia had passed between them. Evelyn thought how things had changed since they were kids. Things were different now. A lot different. She took the remainder of the sandwich and the plate from Jamie and brushed the sugar off his duvet.

Jamie lay down in his bed and Evelyn tucked him in. She kissed him goodnight and motioned for Shug to leave.

'Listen,' he said, offering a half-hearted apology, 'Ah'm sorry fir causin ye grief wi Mick.'

'Don't worry aboot it. He's like a bear wi a sore heid. In fact he *is* a bear wi a sore heid.' She managed a smile.

'Is it bad?'

'Nah, it looks worse than it is. He could huv done wi a couple ay stitches though, bit he'll no listen tae me.' She picked the plate up and walked to the door. Shug followed.

'Is he gonnae phone in sick?' he asked.

'Him? Nae chance. Ye know whit he's like when it gets near Christmas: ye niver see um fir workin. Ye could cut both hus legs aff an he'd still manage tae drag hissel in.'

They stood at the bedroom door, looking at Jamie.

'He jist wants tae gie me an the wean a good Christmas, that's aw,' she said.

'Aye, he's no a bad cunt, Mick . . . fir a Catholic.'

She smirked, bit her bottom lip and punched him in the bicep.

'Aya!' He grabbed his arm.

He went back to Evelyn's spare room and lay on the bed. He lit up a cigarette and stared at the curtains: illuminated bright orange by the glow from the streetlight.

The dull orange light shone through Evelyn and Shug's bedroom window.

Shug was fast asleep in his bed. Evelyn sat on her bed crying and playing with a doll to take her mind off her parents' argument. Her father roared again. She jumped off the bed and dived in beside Shug. He woke up, unaffected by the noise. 'Whit ye dein?'

'Ah'm scared.'

'It's awright, he'll no come in here.'

'He might dae.'

He turned over and closed his eyes. 'Away intae yir aen bed; if he catches ye in here he'll kill ye.'

There was a loud thump. The mother screamed.

Evelyn almost jumped out of her skin. She clung to Shug, petrified, crying. 'He's gonnae dae hur in.'

'No he'll no. If he hits hur then *ah'll* hit *hum.*' He sat up in bed and put his arm around her to comfort her. Her shoulders were shaking up and down. 'Hoad on the noo,' he said.

He got out of bed, went out of the room and along the hall. He opened the door of the living-room and the smell of drink hit him. A trail of spaghetti ran down the wall; a broken plate lay at the foot of it. He looked about the sparsely furnished room for more signs of damage. The white woodchip paper that had been trying to free itself from the walls for years was permanently stained brown above where his father always sat. The thin red curtains moved as though someone was hiding behind them. They always took on a life of their own when it was windy outside. If you didn't know that window had a cracked pane of glass you'd swear there was a ghost in the house.

His father sat on the couch with his back to the door. Shug looked at the back of his head, wobbling unsteadily – always a good sign he was away with the budgies. He didn't hear Shug come in. His mother sat in an armchair, smoking nervously. She saw Shug and cast a worried glance between him and his father. She motioned with her eyes for him to get out before he was seen. Shug ignored her and went into the kitchen.

'No so lippy noo, eh?' growled Shug's father. 'Eh? Ya fuckin cow! Don't you *ever* question *me* aboot money . . . it's goat *fuck all* tae dae wi you how much ah spend . . . fuck all . . .'

Shug buttered two slices of bread and poured sugar on them. He listened as his father went on and on like a broken record. He knew they'd have to listen to this long after everyone had gone to bed, then in the early hours they'd be woken up by him smashing up the house, shouting to himself as though he was being attacked. Shug looked at the knife in his hand and gripped it tight. Enough was enough. Somebody had to do something about him.

Shug put the knife in the sink and took the sandwich into the living-room. He stood behind the couch for a moment, looking at his father in disgust. 'Haw you, shut it! Don't talk tae mah ma like that!'

His father turned round and focused on him. His head jerked back then fell forward again as though it were too heavy. Shug looked at the state of him, sitting there in his jeans and denim shirt – his mad hair, slicked back and piled up on his head like a Teddy boy. Everybody else's da had normal long hair. Shug was always getting slagged at school because of his da. The kids all called him Elvis. Shug couldn't stick him any more. He wasn't a da, he was someone who lived in their house and terrorised them.

'Whit? Whit are *you* dein up? Away tae yir bed, ya wee basta, afore ah tan yir erse,' said **THE KING.**

'No! *You* away tae *yir* bed, ya drunken . . .' He decided against swearing: not a good idea. 'Yiv woken Evelyn up an she cannae stoap greetin!'

'Well tell hur if she disnae stoap hur greetin ah'll come

in there an gie hur somehun tae greet aboot, eh? Tell hur that!' Then he saw the sandwich. 'Haw, whit's this?' He focused on the mother. 'There ye go, that's where aw yir hoosekeepin money's goin. That wee basta's eatin ye oot ay hoose an hame . . . that's the mystery solved.'

Shug's mother got up and walked over to him. 'C'moan, son, away tae yir bed, eh; ah'll tuck ye in.'

Shug looked up at the clock. It was half past ten, yet she still had her overalls on from work. She looked thin and tired, like she worked all the time at that factory and never got any thanks for it. She never smiled any more and her mouth was permanently turned downwards, as though she'd been unhappy for so long she'd stuck like that. She always used to say that to him when he pulled faces: 'If ye don't stoap it y'll stay like that.' Maybe that's what happened to her? She never said that to him any more. She never said *anything* any more. Shug looked up at her thin tired face and saw she had the beginnings of a black eye. He turned to his father, raging. 'Did you hit mah ma?'

'Aye, ah hit yir ma, an if ye don't get oot ay mah sight ah'll gie you some an aw.'

'Ya big basta!' Shug punched him hard in the face, then stood with his fist raised as if to say, '*Do you want some more*?'

His father, taken by surprise, sat dazed for a moment. Blood trickled from his nose. He wiped it away and looked at it on his hand.

Irene was frantic. 'Hugh! Don't hit um, he wis only protectin me. Hugh!'

She awaited the inevitable reaction from Big Hugh. Instead his face broke into a proud smile. He looked up at her. 'Did ye see that? Did ye see it? Eh? Ha! Wee basta nearly broke mah nose.' He reached out for Shug. 'Ha ha! Ya wee cracker, c'mere.'

Shug pulled away, defiant. 'Na! An if ye ever hit hur again . . . ah'll kill ye!'

'Aye, ah bet ye will, ah bet ye will,' laughed Hugh. 'Fair play tae ye, wee feller, fair play . . .'

Shug went back to the bedroom with the sandwich.

Evelyn sat on Shug's bed; wide-eyed, straining to hear what was going on. Big mad Hugh was laughing his head off in the other room.

'Here ye go.' Shug got into bed and handed her the sandwich.

'Ta. Why's he laughin?' she asked.

'Cos he's mental.' He wiped her eyes with the sleeve of his pyjamas and put his arm around her. 'Ye awright noo?'

She nodded and took a bite of her magic piece.

Shug looked away from the streetlight and leaned across to the ashtray. 'Huh, happy days.' He stubbed out his cigarette.

The bedroom door slowly opened. Jamie's face peered from behind it: a cheeky grin.

'Ha, kin ye no sleep either?' Shug smiled.

'Na. Ah could sleep in yir bed though.' Jamie climbed up on the bed.

'Aye, awright. In ye get.'

Jamie climbed under the covers and cuddled up to Shug. Shug put his arm around him and looked down at him lying in the crook of his arm.

'Wee Man.' He smiled.

He was the reason Shug liked staying here. After all the shite that went on in his life, one wee smile from the little guy made him forget all his troubles.

Jamie closed his eyes and sighed deeply. Shug vowed things would be different for this wee guy. He wouldn't have the upbringing that he and Evelyn had – not if Shug had anything to do with it.

He remembered when Evelyn went into labour. It seemed like yesterday. She'd been trying to get hold of Mick at work but the phone was constantly engaged, so she phoned her ma's house, hoping to catch one of them in. Shug was in the bath at the time. He wrapped a towel round himself and answered the phone. Evelyn told him the baby was coming. Without drying himself he quickly pulled on a T-shirt, jeans and trainers and jumped in the Fiesta he'd *acquired* only that morning. If she'd phoned two hours later the car would have been away – sold to Harry at the Gorbals and Shug would have had all the hassle of having to nick something else.

Fate, that's the way he saw it.

He drove through every red light in Drumchapel on the way to Evelyn's. He bounded up the stairs and saw the door was already open. He walked into the living-room to find her sitting there, quite calm, with her bag packed and a bath towel between her legs, soaking up the water.

He helped her down the stairs and into the car, carrying her bag while she tried to hold the towel in place like a big nappy, laughing through the contractions about what the neighbours must think of her.

He drove to the hospital and a nurse bunged Evelyn in a wheelchair. He told Evelyn if she needed him he'd stay in the waiting area.

They whisked her up to a ward. A nurse on the desk took his details and told him to go home, saying she'd call him. Shite, he thought. Aye, so you will. No way was he having that.

Shug was the last person you could call religious, but he did nothing but pray that Evelyn and the baby would be fine. He sat in the waiting room with his head in his hands, refusing to catch anyone's eye. He didn't want happy bastards talking shite to him. This was serious – his sister could die in there, the baby could die – anything could happen. An hour later the nurse came and led him to the delivery room. Evelyn had been calling for him and wouldn't calm down until they brought him in. The midwife stood at the bottom of the bed. Evelyn was lying with her legs open and holding a mask over her face. Shug diverted his eyes from her, choosing to fix his focus on the midwife's enormous arse instead. She turned round and eyed him up and down like he shouldn't be here, as though men were bastards for putting women in this position. She said now he was here he might as well make himself useful. She led him to the side of the bed and showed him how to hold the gas and air mask over Evelyn's nose and mouth. He looked down on her, lying sweating, wincing in pain. She tried to smile at him through the mask. He smiled back, not knowing what to say. He hoped his smile said it all: she would be all right. Her contractions got slowly worse until forty minutes later it actually happened and Shug watched dumbstruck as this perfect little boy was carefully extracted from his sister.

Jamie was handed to Evelyn and Shug stared in amazement at this new life. An addition to the family. A wee person with big hands and feet. Shug reached his hand out to touch Jamie's toes. 'Look at the size ay they feet, Ev . . . he could play fir Rangers,' was all he could think of to say.

She smiled at his awkwardness. 'Sit doon,' she said.

He sat on the side of the bed and she sat up and handed Jamie to him. He gently took him from her as though he might break. She lay back, exhausted and watched him as he stared down at Jamie's tiny little face, then shook his head in amazement and burst into tears. She sat up again and rubbed his back. He wiped his eyes and said he was sorry. He felt so stupid, greeting in front of his sister. Maybe it was the relief that her and the baby were okay. Whatever it was she understood. She never mentioned it again.

Later he drove to Govan and got Mick from his work. Mick was raging that no one had called him, but soon cheered up when he saw Evelyn and his new son. Shug made his excuses and left them to it.

When he arrived home Shug opened the door of the Fiesta and picked up the soaking wet bath towel off the back seat. It was covered in the fluid that kept the wee guy alive for nine months. Amniotic fluid he'd heard the nurse call it. He could smell it – the whole car smelled of it, like a sea breeze. Salty, fresh. He picked up the towel, put it to his face and breathed deep: life. That's what it smelled of – Jamie, a brand-new life.

Day Two

Mick walked past Jamie's room and saw Jamie standing in front of his mirrored wardrobe, dressed in his school blazer, scuffed shoes and trying to tie his school tie. He reminded Mick of one of the old boys from the bowling club in that uniform. 'The midget bowler' Mick sometimes called him.

'Whit *you* dein up?' asked Mick.

'Gittin ready fir school,' said Jamie.

'But it's only hof six.'

Jamie looked at him, not realising the relevance. He continued to wrap his tie in knots. Mick walked off to the bathroom and had a piss. The door opened and Jamie breezed in and stood behind him. Mick was used to it by now. Every time he went to the bathroom someone would want in. If he was having a shite there would be at least three of them in there, Mick on the bog, Evelyn brushing her teeth and Jamie telling the pair of them all about school. There wasn't one space in the house where he could get five minutes to himself. It was all part of being a family he supposed – he wouldn't change it for the world.

'Da, kin ye fix mah tie fir us please.'

'Aye, gies a minute, eh?' He washed his hands, splashed some water on his face and looked in the mirror at his cut head. How was he going to explain this one to the boys in work? There'd be no need to – most of them would already have heard what happened in Finlays. Whit a reddie, he thought. He dried his face and turned round to Jamie. 'Come in here an ah'll show ye.' He walked out of the bathroom, indicating for Jamie to follow, and went into Jamie's room. Mick stood him in front of the mirror, unfastened his tie and stood behind him, reaching his arms over Jamie's shoulders as though he were putting the tie on himself. Jamie laughed at the way Mick went about it.

'Ah cannae dae it the way yir ma dis it,' explained Mick. 'Anyway, ye should be able tae tie yir aen tie by noo – yir auld enough.'

'Ah kin *nearly* dae it.'

Mick fastened the tie, straightened the knot and folded Jamie's collar over it.

'There ye go.'

'Ta.'

He went into the kitchen with Jamie following closely behind, and put the kettle on while Jamie sat down at the table.

'Kin ah huv Coco Pops please,' asked Jamie, looking up at Mick who was leaning against the fridge reading the paper.

'Hmm?' Mick glanced at the telly page.

'Coco Pops. Mah mammie aywis dis it fir me.'

Mick lowered the paper and put it down on the worktop. 'Whit *doesn't* she dae fir ye? Yir auld enough tae git yir aen breakfast ye know,' he said, taking the cereal out of the cupboard and placing it down on the table in front of Jamie.

'Ah telt hur that but she sais ah aywis mek a mess.'

'Aye, well try no to, eh?' He put a cereal bowl down in front of him, then opened the fridge, took a pint of milk out and placed that down in front of him also. Jamie looked at him as if to say, 'Aren't you going to do it for me?' Mick picked the paper up again and gave him a look back that said, 'Get on with it.'

Evelyn came in, wearing her dressing-gown, bleary-eyed and yawning.

'Ye want a cup ay tea?' asked Mick.

'Aye, please.'

'Ah wis gonnae let ye sleep in.'

'How can anyone sleep wi the racket you two mek?' She glanced at the cut on his head, remembering the noise the bottle made when it hit him last night. 'So how are ye?' she asked warily.

'Wonderful. Never better,' He snorted, folding the paper again and putting it on top of the fridge.

'Ah wis only askin.'

'Ah've goat a splittin headache – didnae git much sleep.'

She went over to the drawer, took out a bottle of paracetamol and handed it to him!

'Thanks.' He filled a glass with water and clicked open the lid on the tablets.

'Ye want tae try an git yirsel an early night, th' night,' she said, sitting down at the table.

Jamie lifted up the box of Coco Pops and tilted it above his bowl. An avalanche of brown cereal poured out, filling the plate in seconds and spilling on to the table and floor.

'*Jay-mee!*' Evelyn grabbed the box from him and stood it upright on the table.

'Soarry.' Jamie got off the seat and started picking Coco Pops off the floor one by one, crunching them underfoot in the process.

Mick stood at the sink with his head tilted backwards, swallowing the paracetamol, while glancing at the mess with a wry grimace.

'Here, sit back up on the chair an git yir breakfast,' said Evelyn. She poured the excess cereal back into the box then added milk to Jamie's bowl.

'So, whit aboot laughin boay?' said Mick, putting the teabags in the cups and pouring in boiling water. 'Still in his pit is he?'

'Aye,' she said.

He handed her a cup of tea and sat down at the table. 'Jist as long as he's still no in it when ah git back fae work. Ah like a bit ay peace an quiet when ah git hame at night, no?'

'Aye, ah know. Don't worry, he'll be away,' she said, sipping her tea.

Mick turned to Jamie, aware he was being stared at.

'Da, y've goat a cut oan yir heid,' said Jamie, scrutinising the scab on Mick's forehead.

'Aye, ah know,' said Mick. 'A man did it in the pub laist night.'

'Did ye hit um back?'

'Er . . . aye – no, no, ah didnae. Ye shouldnae fight, son.'

'But you sais if someone hits ye, y've tae hit them back.'

'Aye, ah know, but er . . .' He looked to Evelyn for help. She sipped her tea and smiled at him as if to say, 'Get yourself out of that one.'

'Oh, ah forgoat tae tell ye,' said Mick, eager to change the subject, 'see the ship ah wis tellin ye about the other day?'

'The big helicopter carrier?' said Jamie, remembering.

'Aye, that's the wan – *HMS Ocean*,' said Mick excitedly. 'Well it's comin intae Govan oan Seturday. Ah'll tek ye tae see it if ye like. It's massive.'

'Aye.' Jamie munched at his cereal as if the offer sounded reasonable.

'Ah'll show ye the bits ah welded, eh?' He raised his eyebrows at Jamie and drank his tea.

Jamie nodded. Evelyn looked at them both and shook her head, amused, trying to work out who was the bigger kid.

Archie looked up at the clouds forming above his head and fastened the top button on his waterproof coat. He lifted up the peak of his hat and scratched his hot head, thinking that as long as he was a lollipop man he'd still never get used to the clothing. When it was raining he had to wear the oilskins the council had supplied him to keep him dry, but all they did was make him sweat and stop his clothes from letting the heat out. He ended up soaking. He was looking forward to a couple of weeks off work. The rain and snow was starting to get to him. No good for old bones. This would be his tenth year in the job. He'd been a plasterer by trade, working for the council. But then the cutbacks came, followed by the voluntary redundancies. He'd discussed it with his wife Jean, and they both decided, as he wasn't getting any younger, he should take the redundancy. He still did a few homers but the jobs started getting few and far between and he needed something to occupy his mind. At the time he was only fifty-five and hated to think he was already on the scrap heap. He didn't feel fifty-five. He still had his hair, although it was now grey and thinning on the top. He'd kept himself fit by going for walks every day and always tried to eat the right foods. There was life in the old dog yet.

Jean had heard through a friend that they were looking for lollipop men so Archie applied and got the job. It was a bit strange at first, but he soon got used to it. Some of the kids were right wee characters. He'd come home every day with another story about them that would tickle Jean. Things they'd said, stories and jokes they told him.

It was different now. He still had the kids but Jean was gone. It was almost two years. When she died he'd decided to give up his job – didn't see the point – but it was the kids and the parents that kept him going, persuaded him to carry on. They told him he was doing something worth while, making a difference. It was good they cared. He always said the people of Drumchapel had heart. Archie had been born and bred here and had no desire to leave, no matter how hard the memories were. He would probably die here too: not for a while though, he hoped.

He took a firm grip on the little girl's hand, held his lollipop aloft and stepped out into the road. He saw her safely across, then turned to cross back over.

A stampede approached: shouting, screaming kids. Archie hurried back over the road, almost getting run over in the process. 'HEY! WAIT! WAIT THERE . . . STOAP!'

A group of eight-year-old schoolboys were running around, hitting each other with their bags. He tried to get some order and lined them up at the kerb. 'Right, you lot, stoap that, c'moan noo.'

'Piss aff!' came a boy's voice.

Archie turned: wee Frankie, he might have guessed. This kid's attitude was becoming a problem. His parents needed to smack his arse. Best to ignore it he thought . . . then again, he wasn't putting up with this wee swine speaking to him like that when none of the other kids did. 'You whit?' said Archie.

'You heard me, ya auld basta, or are ye deif as well as daft?'

'What's yir problem, son?'

'You! Ah'm auld enough tae cross the road masel. I don't need you tae help me; an ah'm no yir son, right?'

'Fair enough. Huv it yir own way.'

He wasn't going to win this one. Not today, anyway. The wee bugger just wanted an argument. Well he wasn't getting one. Archie took two of the boys by the hand and surveyed the traffic. The boys showed no embarrassment, only for their friend's behaviour. This was becoming a regular thing, Frankie giving them a showing up.

Frankie skulked behind them. One of the kids turned round to him. 'Fuck sakes, Frankie, gie um a brek, eh? The auld boay's only dein hus joab!'

'Shut it. He's no holdin mah hon, right? Big poof.'

Archie led the kids across the road and Frankie walked off on his own. He stood and watched Archie on the other side of the road, pretending to box with his pals: silly old bastard.

The kids were clearly enjoying the attention. One of them decided to show off his kick-boxing skills. Archie played along by launching into a mock Bruce Lee impression, nearly putting his back out in the process. They laughed at him. He was all right, old Archie – good for a laugh. They gave him a wave and walked off to school.

SCREECH.

Archie looked round.

Frankie was dodging in and out of cars to catch up

with his pals on the other side of the road. A middle-aged man in a blue Volvo sounded his horn at him. Frankie gave him the wanker sign.

'Silly wee bugger,' said Archie, shaking his head. He crossed back over again. A second group of children were waiting to cross. Standing on the kerb was a small fair-haired boy in an outsized Adidas jacket with the sleeves turned up. He was engrossed in a Game Boy. He glanced up at the road for a second then automatically went to cross, but Archie had eyes in the back of his head and grabbed him by the back of the coat with one hand and lifted him on to the pavement.

'Haw you! Whit are ye up tae?'

'Level eight,' said the kid, staring at the Game Boy without blinking.

Nearby, a car went through a puddle, sending a spray of muddy water on to the pavement. Fifteen-year-old Jaqui grabbed her friend Siobhan away from the road so they wouldn't get soaked. Siobhan didn't care if a bus hit her; she was too upset to care about anything any more. Her long blonde hair was stuck to her cheeks with tears. Jaqui sat her down on a small brick wall that surrounded the garden of a house across the road from the school and tried her best to console her. 'Ah telt ye no tae go oot wi um, dint ah?' She drew on her cigarette, chewing gum at the same time. She flicked the ash on to the pavement and sneered, making her stony-faced expression even more frightening than usual. Jaqui had a look about her that said she wasn't right in the head, but she was all there and a bit more. 'He's a basta,' she said. 'He chucked me an aw, jist cos ah widnae gie um it.' She cracked her gum to emphasise her point.

Siobhan let out a gut-wrenching sob. Jaqui wasn't known for her patience.

'Aw fir fuck sakes, Siobhan, stop yir greetin, yir stertin tae git oan mah tits.' Jaqui had seen this a million times before. She knew what Siobhan's trouble was: she'd been blessed with looks that made heads turn, a figure that belonged on a Milan catwalk, not on a fifteen-year-old schoolgirl from Drumchapel, and a nature that made her an easy target for guys to use her.

Jaqui was forever telling her she should toughen up: use them and dump them before they did it to her. The longest Jaqui had been out with anyone was three weeks. Her cut-off period was always two – maximum, whether she liked the guy or not.

One time she went on a fortnight's holiday to Spain with her mum and dad and forgot to finish with Mark Drysdale. She dumped him the minute she got back, outside the chippy, then swanned off displaying her new tan, planning how to get her hooks into Mark's pal Barry. She saw the way he looked at her. It would only be a matter of days.

Jaqui was an old hand at the 'Game'. Siobhan, on the other hand, had a lot to learn. Jaqui watched her friend standing there, breaking her heart in the middle of the street, thinking there's no way she'd ever give herself a showing-up like that. She looked over at the crossing as Archie came walking over to them.

'Will we be huvin the pleasure of yir company crossin the road, ladies?'

Jaqui shook her head and dug her hands in the pockets of her three-quarter-length leather coat to try and keep them warm.

Archie looked down at the boy, playing with the game. 'Girls, eh?'

'Aye,' said the kid, still engrossed.

'C'moan, you, switch that thing aff, y'll gie yirsel brain damage; look, ah'll show ye how tae dae the green cross code. Ah'm no aywis gonnae be here, ye know.'

Siobhan, by now, was an emotional wreck. In a desperate search for comfort she threw her arms around Jaqui and sobbed louder. Jaqui was startled by the public display of emotion, but she mellowed and hugged her back. 'C'moan, babe, he's no worth it – he's a wanker.'

Siobhan forced out a single burst of a laugh amongst the tears. 'Ah know he is . . . but Jaqui ah luv um!'

Archie came back across the road.

'Archie man,' said Jaqui, 'dae us a favour: skelp her roon the jaw fir us, she's dein mah boax in.'

'Aw, Siobhan,' said Archie, 'c'moan, pal . . . whit's up, eh? It's no like you tae greet.'

Siobhan turned to Archie, the big surrogate father, and put her arms around him.

Jaqui was having trouble dealing with all this emotion. 'Ah cannae honnel this pish,' she said, lighting another cigarette off the one she was still smoking.

'It's Bobby Turner,' sobbed Siobhan. 'Ah luv um, bit he sais he disnae luv me any mair . . . he's chucked me.'

'Why?' asked Archie.

'Ah don't know . . .'

'Aye ye dae.' Jaqui flicked away the old cigarette and drew heavily on the new one. 'It's cos ye would'nae gie um it – same reason he chucked me. Basta!'

Archie gently put his forefinger under Siobhan's chin and raised her head up. The face of an angel with streaming eyeliner and smudged lipstick looked up at him. 'Siobhan, yir a beautiful girl . . .'

'No ah'm no.'

'Aye ye are; yir a beautiful lassie wi yir whole life ahead ay ye. But this boy . . . Bobby. Ah hate tae tell ye, hen, but he only wants ye fir wan thing.' It was the same old story: love 'em and leave 'em. He remembered when he was her age, thought he'd found the right girl, only to have his feelings thrown back in his face, leaving him with that sick, empty feeling in the pit of his stomach that didn't go away for days.

'I know it hurts, hen,' he said. 'Ye feel like someone ye love has died, don't ye?'

She nodded, sniffed and wiped her eyes. 'Aye . . . worse.'

'Well, the gid news is the pain goes away. Before ye know it y'll be in love an it'll be the real thing. Ah'm tellin ye the right boy fir you is oot there an yir gonnae meet him wan day.'

'Aye,' said Jaqui. 'Keith fae Boyzone.'

Siobhan sniggered.

Jaqui saw she was on to a winner and started singing 'Picture of You', doing the routine from the video at the same time.

Siobhan laughed out loud and wiped the tears from her face, realising she should be used to this by now. Guys were in no short supply, but they all had one thing in common: they all fed her a load of shite and, like a sucker, she fell for it every time. They told her what she wanted to hear, until they realised she wasn't going to 'drop 'em', then it was a different story. Jaqui was always telling her to get tough. Maybe it was time to take her advice – she was fed up feeling like this.

She looked at the make-up on the back of her hand. 'God, whit a state tae git intae.'

Archie handed her a freshly ironed handkerchief.

'Thanks, Archie.' She wiped her face. 'If only you wis fourteen again, eh? You could huv bin mah mister right.'

Whit? . . . Fourteen? Ah widnae be fourteen again if ye paid me a million quid – too much hassle. Come on,' he said, checking the traffic before stepping out into the road and holding up the lollipop. Siobhan and Jaqui followed him.

'Ta, pal,' said Siobhan, kissing him on the cheek as she passed. She stopped, remembering the handkerchief and went to hand him it back.

'Keep it,' he said.

'It smells of Old Spice.' She laughed.

'Hey, there's nothing wrong with Old Spice, hen.'

'Haw,' said Jaqui, 'y've goat Scary Spice, Posh Spice . . . noo we've goat *Auld* Spice there.' She pointed to Archie and laughed.

'Go oan . . . Git!' he said, threatening to bat them with the lollipop.

Siobhan smiled at him and tucked the handkerchief in her pocket. Jaqui gave him the thumbs-up as they walked off to school. She was glad Archie had sorted it. She knew what *her* game plan would have been: tell all the girls who fancied Bobby, 'He's a basta!' Followed by a public humiliation of him in front of the whole school, including his mates: probably tell everyone what a wee dick he had, even though she'd never seen it. It would have made her and Siobhan fall out for a while, but would have been worth it just to see the look on Bobby's face. Archie's technique was better but. She could always get Bobby alone and ridicule him senseless some other time without Siobhan ever finding out.

Archie smiled to himself as he watched them walking off to school. 'Claire Rayner, eat yir hert oot?'

Shug looked over at the swing-park. It hadn't changed a bit since he was a kid: littered with the glass of a thousand Buckie bottles, trampled into the asphalt over the years. It was like a Tom Jones song: 'The Green Green Glass of Home.' When Shug was a kid, and this was all grass, he used to play cricket on it with Scobie. It used to be dead flat – like a cricket ground.

He remembered the day it was built. Scobie had hit the ball a cracker. Shug turned and ran after it. He nearly shat himself when a JCB came thundering through the gates towards him with a gang of workmen marching behind it. One of the workies picked up the ball and bowled it back. It whizzed past Shug at the speed of light. He was impressed: this workie knew how to bowl properly. Shug couldn't bowl like that; he'd seen it on the telly, but every time he tried he'd always end up holding on to the ball too long and it just battered into the grass at his feet.

He hated playing cricket at school games when Billy Sharkey was on the other team. Sharkey was a great bowler – made it look dead easy. He'd take his time walking back up the field, polishing the ball on his leg. He'd eye the batsman for a minute like he was saying, 'I'm gonnae git you . . . yir oot, mate.' Then he'd jog, gradually building up speed towards the line, with his eye fixed on the batsman all the time. Then came the swing, like a propeller. Sometimes you'd never see the ball – just heard the stumps clatter when the ball made contact with them.

Shug always tried to watch Sharkey's feet, because he'd stop dead before the line – every time – never once crossed it. How the fuck did he do that? Shug figured Sharkey counted his paces as he walked away from the line. Shug tried it, but could never get it to work out.

Paces weren't the same as running – they were always shorter; everyone knew that. No matter how many times Shug tried he always ended up over the line with the ball still in his hand, and Sharkey pishing himself laughing at him.

Could have been a professional, that lanky cunt. Where was he now, eh? Selling mobile phones for a pish wage, that's where. Cricket was for fannies anyway. Only the English were into that: English fannies. The Pakis were good – always tanned the English. Aye, he liked watching the Pakis play the English. The Pakis cheated like fuck, but nobody cared . . . just as long as they kept beating those English bastards.

'Y ready?'

'Eh?' Shug turned back round as Jamie returned with the football. 'Aye, on ye go.'

Jamie dug his heel into the grass, placed the ball in it and walked backwards. Shug settled into the goalmouth, between his jacket and an Asda bag with a stone on it.

'An steppin up to the ball noo is Jamie Donnelly, the youngest ever player tae play fir Scotland.'

Jamie smirked as he walked away from the ball, trying to hide his smile. He coughed and tried to look serious, but he loved it really when Shug did the commentary.

'Scotland two, England two. One minute remainin ay extra time an Scotland huv been awarded a penalty. It's aw doon tae this young man. The crowd go silent . . .'

Jamie ran at the ball and gave a kick, managing to

scuff the top of it. It rolled towards the goal. Shug saw it coming a mile off but dived the opposite way. Jamie smiled as he watched it trickle into the goal. Shug got back up on his feet with a look of bewilderment on his face: how on earth had the young chap done that, sent him diving the wrong way with just a look? Amazing! He ran over to Jamie with his arms outstretched.

'It's there! This young Scottish international has surely saved the day. The final whistle goes – it's all over! Scotland three, England two!' He picked Jamie up and danced about with him. 'Jamie Donnelly's hat trick will surely go doon in history as one ay the finest moments in Scottish football . . . and the crowd are goin wild!' He spun Jamie round. Jamie laughed out loud, enjoying the attention. He looked for the ball and saw it rolling towards the duck pond. He pointed to it and did a Teletubby voice.

'Uh – oh.'

Shug looked at the ball, then at Jamie. They ran after it, laughing their heads off. Shug managed to reach it just as it went in the water.

Max pelted across the grass, ears pinned back for less wind resistance. Somewhere, miles behind him, he thought he could hear his owner shouting his name, but he couldn't be sure. He knew he was on to a beating for running away. It wasn't the first time; it definitely wouldn't be the last. But it was too late now – he was too far gone – caught up in the excitement: there was a ball over there.

He ran at the boy and tried to grab his arm. The boy screamed and pulled his arm back. Max stood in front of him, barking. He'd had an idea: the boy could wrestle with him until the big guy fished the ball out of the water, then they could all play together. He jumped at the boy again, so the boy would hit him on the head, push him away – anything to start the game. But the big guy had to spoil it all by going too far. He came tearing over and booted Max in the ribs – three times. Max yelped in pain: there was no need for that – what was the problem? Max stood back, winded, taking stock of the situation.

'Get tae fuck, ya basta! Go oan!' Shug ran at him. Max backed off and saw his owner was already halfway across the field. The lead was going back on any minute – that was a certainty.

'Haw!' shouted the owner. 'HAW! Fuckin leave it alean!'

Shug stood between the dog and Jamie. 'Whit? Talkin tae me, ya stupit basta? If that thing comes near hum again ah'll brek its fuckin neck; then ah'll stert oan you, ya cunt! Git it oan a lead – there's weans playin aboot here!'

Max's owner wasn't accustomed to being spoken to like a dick, but the guy did have a point. Fuck it. He'd take it out on the dog. 'MAX! Git here – noo!'

Max skulked over to get his lead back on. He knew what was coming next: he tried to crawl up his own arse, knowing his back legs were due a kicking the minute he was out of sight of any witnesses. He dug his paws in and was promptly choked as the chain tightened round his throat: resistance is useless, he thought, as he was dragged, whimpering, back across the park.

Shug looked down at Jamie, 'Ye awright, Wee Man?'

'Aye. It tried tae bite mah sleeve.'

'Moan.' Shug picked up his jacket and they walked over to the duck pond.

Old Mrs McFarland, a regular in the park, stood at the duck pond, watching Jamie and Shug. She emptied the last of the breadcrumbs in the bag over the railings, then screwed up the bag and put it in a bin. She reached in her heavily quilted blue coat, pulled out a pair of men's thermal gloves and started to put them on. Her daft-looking mongrel, a cross between a Jack Russell and a Cairn Terrier, was tied up by his lead to the railings.

'Ah seen that,' she said. 'It's a damn disgrace, lettin a dog run roon like that where there's weans.'

Shug put his jacket on. 'Aye, ah know – the idiot.'

She looked down at Jamie. 'Is yir laddie awright?'

Shug rubbed Jamie's hair. 'Aye, he's awright, int ye, son?'

'Aye,' said Jamie.

She gently nudged Jamie's arm. 'Mah doggie'll no bite ye, son. He'll gie ye a nasty lick though – he's nae teeth.'

Jamie bent down and stroked the dog's head. The dog wagged his short brown tail and licked Jamie's face, glad he wasn't being tarred with the same brush as mad Max. Jamie laughed. 'Whit's hus name?' he asked.

'Coco.' She smiled at Jamie, then Shug. 'Ach, he's a lovely wee feller – looks jist like his da. He's goat yir eyes.'

Shug was secretly chuffed: stupid old bag thought Jamie was his. He wished he was: he'd make a fucking better job of bringing him up than that pape, Mick. 'D'ye think so?' he asked, looking at Jamie's eyes smiling back up at him. 'Aye, ah suppose he hus.'

Archie walked down the street, carrying his shopping bags. He stopped outside his local pub and counted his change.

Skint.

Two young guys came round the corner and almost knocked him flying.

'Whooah! Soarry, mate,' said one of the guys. 'Ye awright?'

'Aye! Nae problem, son.'

'Archie?'

'Aye!' replied Archie warily.

'Archie man, ah thought it wis you – how ye dein, mate?'

Archie hadn't a scooby. 'Er . . . no bad.' He looked at the guy's face, searching his dark features, trying to place him. This bloke knew him from somewhere but Archie was damned if he knew where. He hoped this wasn't the start of dementia.

The guy laughed. 'Ye don't remember me, dae ye?'

'I'm soarry, son, mah memory's no—'

'Paul McCardle. Ah used tae go tae St Francis' . . . it must be aboot ten years ago noo.'

'Bloody hell, so it is.' They shook hands like long-lost friends. 'The laist time ah saw ye, ye must huv been aboot three foot tall; now look at the size ay ye!'

'Aye, long time, eh? Oh, this is mah pal Davie. He's English, but he's no bad, no.'

'All right, mate.' Davie shook Archie's hand. 'Ow d' y' know this reprobate then?'

'Oh, I used tae tek um across the road when he wis a nipper. Ah'm a lollipop man. Is that a Scouse accent?'

'Yeah.'

'Ah served in Korea wi a bunch ay Scousers – Kings Regiment, d'ye know it?' asked Archie.

'Sorry, mate, can't say I do.'

'Scousers, eh?' said Paul. 'Irishmen wi their brains kicked in! Ha!'

'Oh aye?' said Davie calmly. 'The only thing gettin kicked in'll be your balls if y' don't shut it.'

Paul laughed to Archie. 'Y'd huv tae get them aff the missus furst. She keeps them in hur purse when ah'm oot wi hum.'

'Ye married?' asked Archie.

'Aye, two years noo, wi a lassie.' He felt about in his inside pocket, 'How's Jean keepin? Mah ma's aywis sayin, "Ah wonder how wee Jean's gettin on. It's bin years since ah seen hur." Ah, here it's.' He pulled out the photo. He looked up – Archie looked serious: It was *that* look, Paul realised. 'Oh, fuck . . .'

'Tell yir ma she's in a better place, eh?'

'Soarry, Archie man, ah didnae know. How did, er . . . ?'

Archie took a deep breath. He thought he was over it, but when someone asks you out of the blue like that it was always guaranteed to hit you like a ton of bricks. 'Cancer. It'll be three years come April . . .'

'Ah'm soarry, mate.' Paul nodded at the pub. 'Come in fir a pint, eh? Ah'll show ye ma lassie's photie.'

'Oh, no, ah cannae, son . . . er, ah'd love tae bit ah huv tae get these messages hame.'

'Niver mind them, moan hae a dram wi us, it's fuckin freezin oot here. Ah'm buyin, moan!'

Davie was all for talking to the old feller, but in the warmth of the pub with a pint in front of him. He held the door open, hoping they'd get the hint. The warm air wafted out, along with it the smell of decent ale, cigar smoke and microwaved pies. Laughter rang out from the corner of the bar. It was tempting. Paul made a grab for Archie's arm to drag him in. Archie was embarrassed. Time to come clean.

'Ah cannae, son, ah'v nae money left – ah'v jist bought all mah messages. Another time, eh? It wis nice seein ye again.' He went to leave.

Paul grabbed his sleeve and dragged him back towards the door. 'Archie, wait, listen. Ah don't want yir money, ah jist want yir company, right? C'moan, huv a drink wi me an mah pal. Fir fuck sakes ah huvnae seen ye fir years; it's no charity, ye know – ah jist wannae buy ye a bevvy! Come on, gies yir patter.'

'Aye, awright. But jist the wan, eh?' said Archie, giving in as they walked into the pub.

'Aye, aye.' Paul smiled. 'Jist wan.'

Mick's boots scuffed on the stone steps as he wearily walked up the close stairs, picking shards of metal from his hair. His Mizuno rucksack slipped off his shoulders and he was sure he heard his flask smash inside. He slipped the rucksack back over his shoulder, too tired to check. A good bath and a cold can while he watched the film. That's all he asked for after a long day at the shipyards. That, and a bit of peace and quiet. He'd been listening to his workmates all day going on about how the place would shut down. He was sick to the back teeth of hearing it. It hadn't happened yet, he told them. What was the point in worrying about it till they knew for sure?

He'd worked at the shipyard since he left school. He wanted to go into the army but his old man told him he should follow in the family footsteps in shipbuilding – it was a decent living. So Mick became a welder.

He coughed and leaned over the close stairs, spitting the gritty black catarrh over the edge. He'd have asked to get put on another job instead of sitting in the arse-end of a ship, welding all day, breathing in that black shit, but the gaffer was a bit of a cunt and he'd make him suffer. Besides, he needed the overtime. Another few days and he'd have it finished.

He watched as the black bogey descended to the bottom of the close, hoping that no one would come out of their door and get it on the napper. It could have done them a serious injury: there was more iron in that bogey than in a packet of cornflakes.

He felt the scab on his head. It had been bleeding at work with all the *experts* in the canteen probing it for signs of glass. The decision they'd reached was unanimous – a clean cut made by the hard base of a Budweiser bottle. No need to worry about it. Fucking forensic officers, the lot of them.

He opened the door, came in and put down his bag, then hung his jacket up in the hall. He looked into the living-room and saw Jamie sitting on the floor, playing with his toys. Jamie raised his head and smiled at him. 'Hi ya!'

'Hi, pal. How ye dein?'

'Fine.'

Mick could smell the dinner. His stomach twitched, reminding him he was starving. 'Mince, ya dancer.' He'd go into the kitchen and kid on he was having a riveting conversation with Evelyn while he stood and dipped bread in the pot till she got the dinner ready.

He walked into the living-room and noticed Shug sitting among a pile of beer cans, watching an Ally McCoist video. This room was Mick's sanctuary, the place he relaxed in after a long day's work. He could watch what he liked on the telly. Sometimes, after a few cans, he would look up at the large family picture on the wall and wonder how he ever got to be so lucky. The minute he saw Shug sitting on the floor, *his* floor, all that was taken away from him. The telly wouldn't be his own tonight, neither would his flat or his family – they'd be taken over by that idiot who Mick was duty-bound to be hospitable to. Well, it wasn't going to happen tonight. He was going to put a stop to it this time. Shug looked up at him as Mick came into the room.

'Awright, Mick? Super Ally – some boay, eh?'

Mick wasn't amused. 'Whit are *you* still dein here?'

Shug continued to stare at the TV. 'Aw, that's nice, innit? Cheers, brar-in-law.'

'Ah thought ye wis goin tae Malkie's.'

'Ah wis – ah did. Only ah forgoat, dint ah: Malkie's away.'

'Away where?'

'Liverpool, workin – GO OAN! Ya dansa!' he shouted at the TV.

Evelyn stood over the cooker, stirring a pot of mince with a wooden spoon. She took a potato masher out of the drawer, picked up a spoon and scooped a lump of margarine on to the potatoes. She turned round as Mick came in.

'Oh, hi.' She looked at his expression. 'Bad day at work?' She smiled warmly.

The smile was returned with a frown. 'Whit's goin oan?' he asked.

'Don't go blowin yir stack, Mick.' She stirred the

mince. 'It's jist until mah da sobers up. He's still oan a bender. Ye know whit he's like ower Christmas.'

'Ah'm no huvin hum stayin here ower Christmas. Ah telt ye laist night, get um tae fuck!'

'He cannae stay at Malkie's, he sterts a new joab the morra in L—'

'Aye, ah'v heard, Liverpool. So whit aboot whit's-hus-name? Scobie, an the other dickheid. Can he no stay wi them?'

'Ah don't know, why don't ye ask um?' She started getting the plates out.

He'd had enough of this. He sighed and stared at the floor. 'No. Why don't *you*?' He turned round and walked out.

'JAMIE!' she shouted.

No answer.

'*JAMIE!*'

'WHIT?' Jamie shouted back from the other room.

'Dae us a favour, pal, an set the table!' She started mashing the potatoes.

'Aw!'

'C'moan son, an bring they empty cans in wi ye.'

Mick slammed the front door and went down the stairs, putting on his jacket. He'd made his position clear last night. The pair of them were taking the piss now. He put his arm in the sleeve of his jacket and felt the cheap lining rip again. Why was it every leather he bought always had that shite gold lining that ripped the minute you put your hands in the pockets or sleeves? He forced his arm up the sleeve and tucked the protruding lining back into the cuff.

Evelyn came out into the close and looked down the stairs, drying her hands on a tea towel and pulling her arms into her sides. She shivered as the cold air that howled through the close blew against her thin blue cotton top.

'Mick! Where ye goin?' she asked, wondering what was going on.

Mick stopped and struggled with the zip. 'Oot mah mind!'

'Bit yir dinner's ready. When will ye be back?'

He looked up at her. 'Well, that's up tae you, isn't it?'

'Whit dae ye mean?'

'Y've hud yir laist chance, Ev. Ah'll be back fir mah stuff th' morra. Ah telt ye, ah cannae stay in the same hoose as that dick wan mair night.' He pulled his collar up and plunged his hands deep into his lining-free pockets.

'Bit it's jist th' night – he'll be away th' morra.'

'Well if that's the case y've nuthin tae worry aboot, huv ye, ah'll be back. Bit if ah git back an he's still here . . . then ah'm away fir good. It's up tae you . . . see ye.' He carried on down the stairs.

She looked over the banister at him. 'Mick? Mick!'

He walked out. The front door battered against the frame with the wind. He meant business. Her lip was trembling almost as much as her body. The icy blast from the street blew up the close stairs as the front door banged open with the wind then slammed shut again. She shuddered and walked back into the flat.

In the living-room Jamie had his arms full of empty beer cans and was taking them to the kitchen. Shug saw her coming back in, turned back to the TV and, without taking his eyes off the screen, held up an empty.

'Gonnae git us another can, Ev.'

That did it. She couldn't control her rage. She knocked the can out of his hand and started slapping him.

Shug pushed her away. 'Whit? Whit is it? Git aff us will ye, ya mad bitch, ah'll git wan masel. Fuck sakes, eh! Ah only wanted a can.'

'Mick's away because of you! That's it, yir oot ay here th' night!' She burst into tears. Jamie looked up at her, then at Shug, not knowing what was going on.

'Don't blame me fir the state ay yir marriage.' Shug got up and grabbed his parka. 'Ah'm no stayin roon here tae watch you greet, ah'm away fir a beer.'

'Aye, well don't come back!' she cried, grabbing a drying tea towel off the radiator and wringing it in her hands.

Shug stopped and stood at the door. 'Look, don't worry aboot Mick . . . gie um a couple ay days tae calm doon an he'll be back. Then ah'll git oot yir way, right?' He walked out of the room.

She continued to cry, and wiped her eyes with the tea towel that had 'The Lake District' written all over it. A reminder of happier times. Jamie put down the beer cans and wrapped his arms around her legs to comfort her. She drew him close and stroked his hair.

'Aw come on, boays. Let me git a roon in, eh?'

Paul put his hand on Archie's shoulder and pushed him gently back down in his seat.

'Naw, ah sais. We're earnin, so we're treatin ye. Now shut it an gies another wan ay they Scouser jokes.'

Archie wasn't one to argue. After rooting through all his pockets he'd found he'd just enough money to get the boys a pint. But every time he tried they sat him back down again – wouldn't hear of it. The last time he managed to make it to the bar after he'd been to the toilet, only to find himself being physically lifted off his feet by Paul and manoeuvred back to the table to the bemused looks of the crowd in the pub. 'They'll no let me buy a pint!' he explained to a bunch of old boys at the next table. 'Whit ye complainin fir?' they asked. 'Any chance we can join yis?' another joked.

He glanced about the pub, trying to remember the last time he'd been in such good company. He felt he could stay here all day. He looked down at the two whiskies sitting in front of him, wondering if he'd be able to finish them. It had been a while since he'd enjoyed himself like this. They were a couple of good lads, Paul and Davie – home for the holidays. They worked in Ayr and were making good money, so they said; something to do with computers.

'So whit about this joke then?' asked Paul.

Archie had heard a comedian doing Scouser jokes on the telly the previous night and he was trying to remember them. Davie was taking it in good fun and had heard most of them himself.

'Oh, aye, that's it,' recalled Archie. 'Whit dae ye call a Scouser in a semi-detached?'

'I've 'eard this one,' said Davie.

'A cat burglar!' said Archie.

Paul spat his pint out; some flowed out of his nose.

Davie looked at Paul wiping the lager from his nose. 'It's not tha funny,' he said. 'Ere y' are: wha d' y' call a Scouser in a suit?'

Archie and Paul shook their heads.

'The accused,' he said.

It had been some night at the club. Usually they wouldn't let you in if you looked like you had a drink in you. But it was nearly Christmas, and she knew the bouncer. Besides, she never had any trouble in passing for eighteen; Jaqui was the one who needed a bit of work to make her look older. It had worked tonight: Jaqui had copped off in the kebab shop – stood winching a guy who looked like the wee bloke from Boyzone.

Siobhan reminded herself to give Jaqui a good slagging tomorrow. She could imagine her face as she told her the way she'd been carrying on, saying how beautiful the wee guy was in front of the whole queue. The guy loved every minute of it. Siobhan wondered how long it would be before he saw Jaqui's true colours. She only went into the kebab shop to get something to eat – she'd drunk that much she felt sick. She was probably bent double in a shop doorway right now, with the poor guy holding her up by the collar, wondering what the hell he'd let himself in for. She was all mouth, Jaqui – couldn't hold her drink. Siobhan realised she wasn't much better herself tonight: she was steaming.

The taxi turned into her street and she looked up at the living-room window for signs of life. It looked like they were all in bed. She knew her mammie would wait up for her though. Siobhan couldn't see what the point was. She only went straight to bed anyway. It wasn't as if they sat having a meaningful conversation. She'd told her mammie a million times not to wait up, but she said she worried about her and couldn't sleep till Siobhan was in. Siobhan knew the real reason: she wanted to catch her with a drink in her so's she could nag her about the evils of alcohol, or about the way she was dressed. She could just imagine: '*Ye cannae walk oan ice in they high heels, Siobhan! An that skirt – it's like a pelmet: y'll catch yir death ay cauld. Here, put this woolly hat oan an tek that glitter aff yir face – ye look like y've goat frostbite, hen!*' Everyone tonight had told her she looked georgeous. Her poor auld mammie didn't have a clue.

Siobhan paid the taxi driver and opened the door. Now came the tricky bit, keeping out of her mammie's way when she got in. Just take a deep breath as you walk past; don't let her smell your breath.

She got out the taxi and adjusted her short skirt. She

took a step forward, almost falling flat on her arse on the ice and laughed to herself.

Pure affronted.

Nobody about: just as well.

She went to put her key in the close door.

Already open.

One of the neighbours must be having a party. Maybe she'd get an invite? She opened the door and walked into the close.

Dark: the bulb had gone again. There was glass on the floor. Someone must have smashed it.

He stepped out of a dark corner of the close before her eyes could readjust to the blackness.

Oh fuck.

Oh no, *please* . . .

He put his hand across her mouth and pinned her against the wall. She could smell the drink on his breath. His nose traced her neck and down to her shoulder. He breathed deep, taking in the smell of her perfume, pushing himself up against her. She knew that familiar feeling digging into her thigh from the slow dances: he had a hard-on. But this was no slow dance.

'Awright, Siobhan,' he said.

It wasn't the same being in a club without Malkie. Still, he'd be in Liverpool now with his brother, checking out the fanny, probably. The boys said they'd give Malkie a month then he'd soon get tired of it and come back. Scobie thought different. He knew that was probably the last he'd ever see of him. Scobie looked about the dark club, trying to figure out if he was below ground or above it. The place was full of people milling about, going places. From the bar to their friends, to the bog, to buy fags, up to dance, back to their seats, up again, back to the bar, another pish. For fuck sakes, he wished they'd all mellow out. He glanced at an air vent in the ceiling and wondered how much ganja it would take to pump through the air-conditioning system that would slow these hyper-bastards down. He couldn't remember being in here before – couldn't even tell you the name of the place if you paid him a million quid. He leaned against the bar, eating crisps, occasionally turning his head to eye the talent on the dance floor and watch the laser above the DJ booth bounce off the mirrorballs to fill the room with thousands of thin red beams. He was sure they tickled you when they hit you. He smiled and watched the red dots dance about, tickling the palm of his hand.

The DJ seamlessly mixed in 'Forever Young'. Scobie hadn't heard it for ages. That was the thing about Christmas: DJs could pull out any old shite and people would dance to it. He used to dance to it himself a few years back with Malkie, Shug and Chic. It was like their anthem at one time. He fancied a dance now and considered getting on the dance floor, but the notion soon left him when he remembered he was too wasted and would end up looking like an arse.

He'd had a couple of spliffs before he went out, and

another in a pub bog before they came in here. He'd put a bit too much skunk in it and had to stand on the toilet and breathe the smoke out of the window so's no one got a whiff.

Chic and Shug were into Agro Dave's speed so Scobie was left to smoke the whole joint himself. Waste not want not. He didn't want to risk taking a spliff into the club and he was fucked if he was going to flush it down the lavvy pan.

Chic kept telling him to leave the blaw alone, have a wee bit of whizz, but he saw what it did to the other two: made them talk a lot of shite, then they complained they couldn't get to sleep at night. Fuck that. Anyway he hated speed: gave him palpitations and made him think he was having a heart attack. A wee bit of blaw did him. Straight from the earth. Mother Africa. None of this designer shite.

He swigged at his pint of heavy and swung his head round to take another look at the barmaid. Not bad. Long black hair, a bit pasty-faced for his liking, but not bad. Looked like one of those Goths dressed all in black like that. He eyed her cleavage and guessed she was wearing a Wonderbra. Great invention. Must have been a man who invented that; like a baker putting freshly baked rolls in the window: look but don't touch. He sniggered to himself as the word 'baps' came to mind.

Imagine tackling one of those Wonderbra fuckers tonight, trying to get the bastard undone. No chance. Tonight he couldn't find his arse with both hands.

Then the paranoia hit him: what was he doing here? Who was he out with? He remembered: Chic and Shug. So where the fuck were they? He looked across to the dance floor and spotted Chic dancing, his white shirt shining like a beacon under the UV lights – he looked like the Persil Boy. Scobie calmed down when he saw him, realising he'd just drifted off on another tangent again. It started coming back to him: Shug had been eyeing the young bird with long blonde hair, short black skirt and the legs that went up to her neck: the model. Chic kept telling Shug to grab her for a dance. Scobie thought Shug must have left with her because he hadn't seen him for a while.

Chic reappeared back at the bar, sweating and wafting the front of his shirt up and down to cool himself off. He took a swig of his Beck's. 'Seen Shug?' he asked, looking about.

'Naw, man.' Scobie slowly looked about the club and munched his crisps, then offered Chic the packet.

Chic pushed them away. 'Whit huv ah telt ye?' He finished his beer. 'Thirsty as fuck, man,' he said. 'This whizz is awright.'

Scobie shrugged as if to say, 'I wouldn't know about that.'

'Ye want a wee bit? It'll wek ye up.'

'Ah'm awright,' said Scobie, nodding in time with the music, trying to look like he was into it. What he really wanted was a quick visit to the hamburger van, then a taxi home to his bed.

Chic pointed at Scobie's pint. 'Ye want another wan?'

'Naw,' said Scobie.

Bundle of fun, thought Chic, bundle of fucking fun. He waved to the Goth barmaid. 'Beck's please, darlin.' She flashed him a white toothy smile that could match only his own under the UV lights above their heads. Chic put a fiver down on the bar next to Scobie. 'Git it oot ay that, will ye? Ah'm away the bogs a minute.' He sniffed twice and raised his eyebrows, letting Scobie know he was going to do the last of the whizz. 'Then ah'm gonnie git intae hur knickers.' He nodded over at the girl he'd been dancing with, then headed off to the toilet.

'Is that all?'

Scobie swung his head round. The Goth barmaid was talking to him.

'Eh?'

She nodded to the Beck's that sat on the bar in front of him. He didn't remember ordering that? She took the fiver off the bar, rang up the drink and returned with the change.

'Oh, right . . . sorry, ah wis dreamin,' he said.

She held the change out for him. He stared at her.

'Something wrang?' She went to put the change on the bar.

Scobie realised he was staring. He couldn't help it. It was those eyes. Dark. Piercing. Black. He wanted to ask if they were contact lenses, but what came out was: 'Thanks . . . keep the change.' He smiled at her. She smiled back and his eyes dropped down to her teeth.

Fangs.

Pointed incisors.

A fucking vampire – here in Glasgow?

She saw the look on his face. He realised she knew that he was on to her. The teeth were a giveaway. How the fuck did she expect to go unnoticed when it was so obvious what she was? He looked about at the crowd. Young girls tossed their hair back and laughed, exposing bare white necks. Guys leaned in close to one another, talking in each other's ears so no one else could hear. Busy plotting. Their next victims? He'd seen this scene before: any minute now shutters would come down over the doors – the bouncers and the DJ would turn into vampires.

He tried to remember the name of the club he was in but the *Titty Twister* was all that came to mind. He scanned the crowd: nobody else was bothering. The fools – didn't they know what was going on? Surely there were more of the bastards in here! He felt someone staring at him and he turned back towards the bar. The Goth barmaid was looking at him strangely. She put the money in a glass behind the bar and walked off to serve another customer.

Scobie pulled his shoulders up, making his neck less visible and stood against the wall, holding Chic's beer tightly in case he got jumped. Although, he realised, what protection a bottle of Beck's would give him against the undead fuck only knows. He hoped Chic would come back soon so he could persuade him to leave before things got out of hand. He didn't like coming to discos any more; there were too many weird people about. That vampire bird just put the fucking tin lid on it. Besides, everybody knew that dope and discos didn't mix. It was totally the wrong drug. This wasn't his idea of entertainment. He preferred a quiet night in with a good quarter of skunk and an Evil Dead video compared to this shite any day.

Shug stood at the sink in the Halfway bogs, washing the blood off his knuckles. He could still smell the shit. He examined his shirt: there was some on his cuff.

'Fuck. Dirty wee cow.'

He remembered being out in the town, ages ago, meeting up with Evelyn and her pal Angela. Shug was looking for a place to crash after a run-in with Big Hugh. Mick was out with his mates and Evelyn said Shug could stay at theirs if he promised to make sure he was in bed before Mick got in. That way Mick wouldn't be pulling faces. They jumped in a taxi and got back to Evelyn's. Then he met her: SIOBHAN THE BABYSITTER. Only fifteen, but fit as fuck. Shug had a drink in him. Kept pouring her drinks. They were having a good laugh. He was taking the piss out of her for being a wee lassie, too young for this and that – said she was under-age: too young for sex.

She said, 'How d'ye know ah already haven't?'

That shut him up. He sat and stared. She burst out laughing.

Definite come-on.

That was ages ago. Surely to fuck she must have turned sixteen by now?

Tonight, the last thing he expected when he put his hand down her drawers was a handful of shit. He vowed to stick to women his own age in future.

Stupid wee lassies were all the same: all talk until you got them in the clinch, then they shite themselves – literally.

It was pure disgusting. He'd ended up slapping her with the shitty hand, catching his knuckles a cracker across the roughly plastered wall.

He looked up at the mirror and checked his reflection. He dried his hands, wrapped some bog roll over his knuckles and went back through to the bar.

Someone laughed out loud. Shug instantly knew who it was. He glanced across to where the laughter came from – over by the pool table. Aye, he was right: heads were turning away, avoiding his eye. He thought he recognised that stupid fucking laugh. That big basta was in again. Shug eyed him with contempt. Better no let him catch me though, he thought. He'll kick mah cunt in. Shug went back to the bar and swigged at his Beck's.

'Made a cunt ay in front ay the boays: game ay pool – went wrong laist week. Nay need fir that though. No in frontae Chic an Scobie . . . fat basta.' He swore that was the last time he'd smoke blaw – especially the shite Scobie handed him that afternoon. It totally fucked up his game and made him look a right cunt in front of: **Big George**.

George must have known Shug was stoned out of his nut because he kept giving him laldy every time he went to take a shot, then backing off, saying he was only having a laugh. He knew it was putting Shug off. Shug got to the point where he was so angry he couldn't remember if he was on striped balls or not. Chic was away to the bar and Scobie wasn't any help – he was totally off his tits and couldn't remember his own address.

Shug decided to go for the stripes. He pocketed the ball and George clapped his hands together.

'Two shots!'

'Eh?' said Shug.

'Two shots tae me – ah'm stripes.'

Bastard.

George stepped up to the table and pocketed the remaining two balls, then the black, walking off with the fiver Shug had bet him. Shug only found out when Chic came back from the bar and told him that *he* was on stripes: the big cunt had been taking the piss because they were that stoned they couldn't think straight. It was too late to do anything about it now.

Shug swigged his Beck's. He heard them laugh again and knew they were still laughing about him. He hated that fat bastard. The Big Yin they called him. Who the fuck did he think he was, Billy Connolly? Been shaggin the barmaid in here for a couple of weeks. What she saw in him fuck only knows. Now the dick couldn't keep away from the Halfway since she gave him a ride. He was in here every day in case someone nipped her.

Paranoid cunt.

Shug looked over at him again: the-ten-pie-eating basta stood with his mates, laughing about fuck all and looking over at the bar every five minutes just to make sure she was still there. His mate nudged him and handed him the cue. George walked up to the pool table, leaned over and went to take his shot.

A bloke at the bar cracked a joke. The barmaid laughed. Big George turned his head away from the pool table and looked at the bar. His face dropped. Shug saw it and grinned.

Jealousy.

A weakness.

Nice one.

Siobhan sat on the floor of the close and pulled off her knickers and tights. She retched at the smell and burst into tears: a mixture of fear and relief. Thank Christ for the shits.

Saved by a bad kebab.

She walked out of the back door and dumped the tights in a neighbour's bin, hoping to fuck her mammie had gone to bed.

Evelyn and Jamie were curled up on the couch watching the TV. She looked down at him: her wee boy. How fast he'd grown. It seemed like only a year or two since he'd been born. She looked across at his christening photo on the mantelpiece, remembering the trouble they'd had trying to get him christened, because she and Mick weren't members of the chapel. They had to go for a talk with the local priest to convince him they weren't atheists. That was Mick's theory anyway.

Father Reilly. He enquired about her faith. She told him she was as good as Catholic, being married to Mick. Father Reilly eyed Mick with disdain, knowing he'd long forgotten what the inside of a chapel looked like and wondered what kind of Catholic that made her. They knew they'd been caught out. He told them to start coming to chapel; that was the first step.

Mick assured him they'd go, but they'd just been busy lately, what with work, and more recently because of the baby. 'Bring the baby,' said the old priest. He had an answer for everything. There were already five couples, long-standing members of the chapel, waiting to get their babies christened. Evelyn and Mick had no chance. By the time they'd totted up enough bonus points from attending mass Jamie would be at least five.

Evelyn sighed as they got up and thanked him for seeing them. He said he'd see them again – in chapel on Sunday. Mick thought the old bastard had more chance of seeing his arse. They argued all the way home. It wasn't Mick's fault, it was his religion.

She managed to talk him into it and for the next two weeks they attended mass. Jamie's pram sat in the aisle, with everyone who passed casting him admiring glances and asking his name. On the third week they turned up to find a new priest taking mass. Instead of the craggy features of Father Reilly glaring down at them there was the youthful Father Monaghan, a handsome Italian-looking guy in his twenties. Father Monaghan explained to the congregation that Father Reilly had been hit by a bus and had a broken leg. Ya dancer, thought Mick. Father Monaghan said a prayer for his speedy recovery. Take yir time, thought Evelyn. During the prayer Mick and Evelyn glanced at each other and grinned, each knowing what the other was thinking.

After mass Evelyn collared the priest and introduced herself and Mick, expressing their concern for poor Father Reilly – such a nice old man. Evelyn asked how long Father Monaghan would be covering for him.

'At least a month,' he said. He looked down at Jamie, wrapped up in a blanket in Evelyn's arms. 'What's his name?' he asked.

'Jamie,' replied Evelyn.

'Hmm . . . means "Jacob". Did you know?'

Evelyn shook her head.

'I much prefer Jamie' he said. 'Jacob sounds like a cracker, doesn't it?'

Evelyn laughed at his joke.

She never laughs at my jokes, thought Mick. Evelyn smiled at Father Monaghan and flicked her hair away from her face. She's flirtin wi hum! thought Mick. She fancies a priest . . . that's sick!

Evelyn told the priest that they'd hoped to see Father

Reilly today about the christening in a couple of weeks. Time was drawing near and she knew Father Reilly already had five babies to christen. They needed to know so's they could make alternative arrangements. But it would be a shame, this being their chapel and all.

Father Monaghan put his finger into Jamie's palm and Jamie's little hand curled round it. 'We can always make it six.' He smiled.

The day of the christening everyone turned out: Evelyn's mum, dad, Shug and a couple of distant aunties and uncles. Mick's side took up half the chapel. Evelyn watched with tears of joy in her eyes as the young priest held Jamie aloft and christened him 'James Michael Donnelly'. The mass continued while the parents and babies were led through a side door and the babies were paraded in front of the Sunday school kids. Most of the fathers took off and went outside for a fag, but not Mick; he didn't want to miss a thing. The Sunday school teacher told the kids that these wee babies had been baptised in the name of Jesus and they should welcome them into the world. She asked them to sing 'Shalom'.

Evelyn had a lump in her throat as these tiny people welcomed the new babies into the world with this lovely Jewish song. She cradled Jamie in her arms, listening to these angelic wee voices singing their welcome to the babies. She looked across at Mick standing by the door and could see he was fighting back the tears. She smiled at him. He tried to smile back but his lips were twitching away, doing their own thing. It was a moment she'd never forget. Two hours later at the party it was back to reality when Shug tried to bottle Mick's cousin because he said he was noising him up.

Her wedding wasn't much better. Big Hugh started a fight with Mick's da, saying he'd paid more than he had for the wedding. Mick's da pointed out, as far as he was aware, Evelyn and Mick had had to cough up most of the money themselves in the form of a bank loan. He reminded Big Hugh that he'd been out of work for years and was in no position to pay for anything. Big Hugh took offence at this, mainly because it was the truth, so he swung at Mick's da and missed. They both ended up rolling round on the carpet, throwing rabbit punches until someone split them up. Then the name-calling started: Fenian this, blue-nose that. Both men as bad as each other. It put a dampener on the rest of the night, emphasising to the guests of both religions that this was a mixed marriage and, although they were all there to wish Evelyn and Mick every happiness, nobody really saw it working out.

Evelyn looked up at her wedding photo on the wall. She'd be damned if she'd prove that lot right. This was the first time in seven years she and Mick had been apart. And the reason: their family coming between them, yet again. She leaned across to the phone table, picked up the receiver and started to dial Mick's mother's number. She paused, then replaced the handset. She'd give Mick time to cool down first. Maybe call him in the morning.

Day Three

Evelyn rolled up the sleeves of her dressing-gown and stood at the sink to wash the breakfast dishes. She looked out into the back close and saw another rat running out from the bins. It frightened the life out of her putting out the rubbish – she always got Mick to do it. They'd been on to the council loads of times about the rats. They'd put poison down but she was sure they were getting immune to it. It was hopeless phoning again, especially at this time of the year; everybody would be finished up for the holidays.

She looked at the pedal bin, overflowing with beer cans. She'd get Shug to take the rubbish out later. She didn't see the need to tell him about the rats, he'd find out sooner or later. She smirked to herself as she thought of the big shitebag tearing back up the close stairs.

She watched the rat squeeze itself effortlessly through the wafer-thin gap under the door of one of the coal bunkers. It must be full of them in there, she thought. Nobody used them for coal any more: most of the flats were now central-heated and the locks on the coal-bunker doors were broken. Some of the neighbours put their bins in them but Evelyn didn't even know which one was supposed to be hers. They were all full to the brim with rubble anyway.

Once Mick had been out for a walk with Jamie in the buggy. As they turned into the back close Mick heard a cough coming from one of the coal bunkers. He opened the door and found a tramp sleeping in it. Jamie was only two at the time. He asked Mick, 'Who's dat?' Mick told him it was Santa, having a wee kip before Christmas.

A few days later Evelyn had been out shopping. She was laden with bags of messages and was walking Jamie on his reins. Rather than having to hunt for the close key she decided to walk round the back way. They turned into the back close to find a rat lying on the ground in front of them. It was huddled up with its paws stretched out in front of it and its sides were heaving in and out like a dog about to be sick.

'Bunny rabbit!' shouted Jamie.

Evelyn grabbed hold of him and tried to guide him round it.

He struggled and tried to pull away from her to see the rat. 'Want it!' he shouted.

'It's no a bunny rabbit,' she said, pulling him towards the close. 'It's dirty.'

He spun round on his reins, trying to get to it. 'Want a bunny rabbit!' he screamed. 'Ah want it!'

He fell to the floor in a tantrum. She pulled him up with one arm by the reins and tried to manoeuvre him and the messages into the close. He struggled and started screaming. She grabbed him round the waist and carried him upright. He battered his heels against her shins.

She lost her rag. 'Yir no huvin it, ye spoilt wee basta! It's a rat, no a bunny rabbit!'

'Want it!' He continued to thrash, holding his arms up in an attempt to try and slip out of his jacket. She grabbed hold of him and carried him like a surfboard as she stormed up the stairs.

When Mick got home from work she told him what had happened. He went out the back and it was still there in the same position. It had stopped breathing. Poisoned.

The following day he shovelled it into a carrier bag and took it up to the council offices. He dumped it on the desk, telling the girl he had a two-year-old kid who was playing out the back and tried to stroke it. The girls behind the counter looked at him like he was mad, and smirked at each other till he tossed the bag at them, then they screamed and ran to the back of the room. He warned them if the council didn't do something about it – today – he'd shoot the fucking rats with an airgun and be back here with more of them, every day till the council got their finger out of their arse.

One of the girls picked up the phone and said she'd see what she could do. Within an hour a bunch of blokes appeared and started hauling the back close apart, pulling rubble and rat carcasses from the coal bunkers. Evelyn had never seen Mick so wound up before. Usually it was 'anything for a quiet life'. Until it came between him and his family, then he was like a madman.

She turned away from the window and smiled to herself, shaking her head at the thought of Jamie: thinking Santa Claus was a tramp and a rat was a fluffy bunny. The innocence of kids – saw the good in everything at that age. It's a pity we have to grow up, she thought. Then your problems really start.

She looked over at Shug, sitting smoking at the kitchen table, wearing just his black Adidas tracksuit bottoms. His bare feet were flecked with the black fluff off his cheap socks that gathered in between his toes. The soles of his feet were sticking to the vinyl floor tiles. Evelyn could still picture him when he was as innocent and impressionable as Jamie. A far cry from what sat in her kitchen now.

He set fire to a cigarette packet, burning his fingers in the process before putting it out in the ashtray. Evelyn put another dish in the drainer and glanced at his knuckles: burst and bloody, probably from the previous night's fighting.

'Whit time did you git in at?' she asked, picking up a cloth and drying the dishes.

'Dunno, nae watch. Ah'm no intae time.'

'De ye want somethin tae eat?'

'Nah, ah'm no hungry.'

'JAMIE? ARE YOU READY YET?' she shouted to the bedroom as she clattered a couple of plates into the cupboard.

'Fuck sakes, Ev, turn it up, eh?'

'Sore heid?'

'Aye, a wee bit; rattlin they fuckin dishes disnae help either.'

'Fightin, wis ye?' She indicated his knuckles.

'Dunno, cannae remember. Ah wis pished.' The comedian laughed at his own wit.

She shook her head, disgusted. Jamie came in, dressed and ready for school. He'd managed to put his tie on over his shirt collar. Shug saw it as a chance to change the conversation.

'Wee Man!'

'Hiya.' Jamie smiled.

'Mere, Wee Man, let's fix yir tie.'

'Whit dae ye want fir yir breakfast?' asked Evelyn, putting the last of the dishes away. She opened the cupboard and looked at the cereals.

Jamie stood in front of Shug getting his tie fixed. 'Whit is there?'

'Coco Pops or Frosties?'

'Coco Pops.'

'Yir Uncle Shug can get it fir ye. That's if he's no goat the shakes, that is.'

Shug held his hand out steadily then shook it uncontrollably. Jamie laughed then noticed the bloody knuckles; he held Shug's hand still to get a better look, then looked up at him, shocked.

'Shhh . . .' said Shug. 'Power Rangers.' He punched the air. 'Pam! Pam!'

Evelyn placed the box of Coco Pops on the table and went into the living-room to get her purse and bag. Jamie sat down at the table. Shug poured the Coco Pops into a bowl then added some milk with his cigarette still in his hand. Some ash fell into the cereal. Shug scooped it out quickly and spooned it on to the table. He looked round to see if Evelyn had noticed, then handed Jamie the spoon. Jamie looked at it, disgusted.

'It's awright, it'll no herm ye.' Shug took the spoon off him and stirred the cereal. 'See. It's away. Eat it.' He handed him the spoon again.

Jamie ate slowly, pulling faces. 'Urg.'

'Eat it, or ah'll no take ye the gemme at New Year.'

'Mah da sais ah cannae go the fitba till ah'm bigger,' said Jamie.

'Aye, well he's no here, is he?'

Evelyn came back in with her bag, catching the last part of the conversation. 'Who's no here?' she asked.

'Santa,' said Shug.

'Uncle Shug's gonnae tek me to the fitba,' said Jamie.

Evelyn pulled a bottle of perfume out of her bag and squirted it about her neck. 'He's no goin tae any gemme, ah'v telt ye, he's too wee.'

'Aye, sure yir no, are ye? You an me, eh, Wee Man. Let's git intae these Fenian bastards . . .' He started singing as though he were at the match. 'Hullo, Hullo, we are the Billy Boys, Hullo, Hullo . . .'

'HAW YOU!' she shouted. 'SHUT IT! I'm no huvin that carry-oan in mah hoose.'

Carry-on? Had the woman no respect for tradition?

'Jist cos you married a Tim!' he said. 'Aye, where is he noo, eh? Leavin ye wi the wean. If ah see that cunt ah'll . . .'

Evelyn went over to the sink and emptied the water from the bowl. A couple of spoons rattled into the sink. She picked up the dishcloth and gave them a quick wipe. 'You'll do nuthin,' she said. 'Y've done enough . . . an dae ye mind no talkin like that in front of Jamie!' She dried the spoons on the Lake District tea towel.

'Ach, he hears worse than that at school, don't ye, Wee Man? Anyway, whit dae ye mean ah'v "done enough"?'

'Whit dae ah mean? *Whit dae ah mean?* It's nae wunner he left. Ah'm surprised he husnae killed ye!' The spoons clattered as she threw them into the cutlery drawer.

'Are you sayin it's aw mah fault or somehun?'

'Aye, it's yir fault. We were awright till ah sterted lettin ye stay here. Ah don't know whit ah wis thinkin ay, the way *you* carry oan. Even when ah sterted goin oot wi Mick, it took ye a year tae even sit in the same room because he wus a Catholic. But ye don't mind eatin his food an livin unner his roof when mah da chucks ye oot! Dae ye?'

'Aye, aye, awright!'

'Anyway, ah telt ye laist night – yir no stayin. Ah cannae mek a go ay mah marriage wi you here. Y'll huv tae find somewhere, today, or ah'm changin the loacks!'

'Whit?'

Conversation over. She turned to Jamie. 'Ye finished, son?'

'Yeah . . . yuck!' He threw the spoon in the half-finished cereal.

'Bit it's Christmas,' pleaded Shug.

'I don't gie a fuck if it's Chinese New Year.' She put her coat on, annoyed with herself – now *she* was swearing in front of Jamie. 'Ah want ye oot. Ah'll throw ye oot if ah huv tae!' She put Jamie's hat and coat on him. 'Ready?'

'Wait.' Jamie ran into his bedroom.

Shug wasn't giving up without a fight. 'Oh aye . . . y'll throw me oot, will ye? Well ah'd better stert sellin tickets then cos that'll be worth seein.'

Jamie reached under the mattress and pulled out a creased card and a quarter-bottle of whisky wrapped in Christmas paper. He bent the card back into shape then put it, along with the bottle, into his school bag. A large empty whisky bottle he'd been keeping his change in sat on top of his set of drawers. It was a great idea of his da's to give him that bottle. He'd brought it back from work after cutting a money slot in it for him. A couple of his da's pals had put their change in it to start him off. His da said it was a good way for him to save up for Christmas presents, although he always gave him the money to buy his ma's, and she'd always buy his da something, then give it to Jamie to wrap up and say it was from him. It was a great secret. They never did find out.

Jamie ran back to the kitchen.

'No! No me – a team,' said Evelyn.

'Oh, so y've goat a team noo, huv ye?' Shug laughed.

'Aye. An dae ye know whit: they'd gie ye a kickin an turf ye oot ay here jist tae wipe that smile aff yir face. Yir no liked roon this area, Shug. Mek yirsel useful an git packed – gie us all a brek, eh?' She looked down at Jamie. 'Moan, son.' They walked out of the room.

'Cow,' sneered Shug.

Evelyn and Jamie walked past the shops in the direction of his school.

'Mum, where's mah da?' he asked.

'He's at his work, son,' she said, trying to be nonchalant.

'Aye, ah know . . . but?'

She looked down at him, trying to figure it out, how to word it. God love him. He knew what was going on – he wasn't daft. She stopped walking.

'Whit is it, son?' she asked.

'Where did he go laist night?'

'Tae yir Grannie Donnelly's.'

'Why?'

She started walking again. Jamie followed. 'Tae look after hur,' she said. 'She wisnae well.' She hated lying to him, but it was only a wee white one, she told herself.

He looked up at her, puzzled. 'Could Granda no look after hur?'

'Aye, but he needed a bit ay help fae yir da.'

'Oh . . . Is she better noo?'

'Aye, ah think so.'

'So mah da'll come hame fae hus work tonight then, won't he?'

She hoped he would, but knowing how thick-skinned Shug was she'd probably need an army to get him out first.

'Oh, look, is that yir wee pal Liam up there wi hus mammie?' She pointed up ahead, trying to distract him.

'Aye.' Jamie spotted Archie leading some kids across the road. Archie waved to them as they walked off towards school, then crossed back over and nodded a 'good morning' to a man out walking his dog.

Jamie started dragging Evelyn along the street. As they got near the crossing he stopped and pulled out the card and present from his school bag.

'Mum, hoad this fir us please.' He handed her the bag and ran towards Archie.

'STOAP RUNNIN. Y'LL FALL OWER!' she shouted after him.

Archie turned as he heard Evelyn's voice, and saw Jamie running at him.

'Archie!'

'Jamie, son,' he laughed, 'yir the furst boay ah'v seen who cannae wait tae git tae school! They're usually doggin it.'

Jamie grinned from ear to ear as he held the present up to him. 'Archie, Happy Christmas!'

'Is that fir me?' He was embarrassed. 'Oh, hey, son, ye shouldnae huv bought me a present.'

'It's whisky!' blurted Jamie.

'Is it! Oh, lovely.'

'Yir no supposed tae tell whit it is,' said Evelyn. 'Y'll spoil the surprise.' She smiled at Archie. 'Mornin, Archie. Happy Christmas.'

'Happy Christmas, love.' He indicated the whisky. 'An thanks.'

'Oh, no guilty, that's nothin tae dae wi me. He did that aff his ain back; he's been savin his poacket money fir weeks.' She smiled, remembering Mick's embarrassment at having to go to the Paki's the other day with pockets full of twopences to buy it for him.

Archie looked down at Jamie. 'Whit? Nae sweets?'

Jamie grinned.

Archie was moved. He opened up the home-made card and read it proudly. 'To my pal Archie, Happy Christmas, love from Jamie . . . an three kisses as well! Ah, that's briwyint that; thanks, son.'

Evelyn noticed he was moved as she saw a tear appear in his eye.

Archie shook Jamie by the hand, then, realising this was too formal, bent down and kissed him on the cheek. 'Happy Christmas, pal. Ah hope all yir wishes come true. Yir a wee smasher.' He pinched his cheek and looked up at Evelyn. 'Isn't he?'

'Aye, he's no a bad boy, are ye, son?'

Jamie tried to suppress the big grin taking over his

face: his gesture of goodwill had just made him a hero in his mother's eyes. She crouched down, adjusted his coat and kissed him on the nose, covering it in lipstick. She tutted, brought out a hankie, wet it and roughly wiped his nose.

'Mu-um!' he protested.

'Ah'll git ye at three, right?' she said. 'We'll go an see yir gran fir an oor, then we'll go tae McDonalds.'

'Right.' He kissed her back on the nose. 'Yir freezin.' He pulled her collar up as though *he* were the adult. He took Archie by the hand and they walked off. Evelyn watched as they waved goodbye and stood at the crossing, chatting like old friends. She smiled to herself at how lucky she was.

The traffic echoed under Central Station Bridge. Mick paced about outside the café. He knew it had been a mistake going back to his ma's last night. She gave him that pitying look when she answered the door and ushered him into the living-room. His da didn't say much either, barely looked up from his paper. Mick knew what was going through his mind though.

He'd lain on the bed in his old room. It was now the spare room, although it hadn't been decorated since he moved out. It was like they were keeping it as a shrine to him, hoping he'd come back or something. Well, this was only temporary. He looked up at his old football posters. Cuttings of Mo Johnstone were plastered here and there: 'Shock as Rangers sign Catholic'; 'Souness in death threats'. One from an English paper read: 'Souness I Bigotry 0'.

That was his favourite.

He remembered one September weekend when he went to Blackpool with a couple of mates. One of the boys suggested a trip to Liverpool to watch the Derby. After hitting a few pubs in the town they got on the bus to Anfield. On the bus they were greeted with an unusual sight: Liverpool and Everton supporters were sitting next to each other, wearing full colours but laughing and taking the piss out of one another.

These guys travelled to the match together?

Mick and the boys sat and watched: gobsmacked. Imagine that happening with Rangers and Celtic? Never in Glasgow. Never in a million years.

They got off the bus and walked towards the ground, silent. They all knew what the others were thinking: there was a cancer eating away at the west of Scotland. Best just to ignore it; maybe in time it'll go away. It was never mentioned again.

He glanced through the café window, trying not to be seen. The blue Formica tables and brown padded seats looked inviting as he stood outside in the cold. A nice hot coffee and a chance to make it up with the missus was what he really wanted. Chances were they'd start arguing because he'd gone and walked out on her and Jamie: something he swore he'd never do. He sighed and strode off, then stopped as he changed his mind. He turned back round, opened the café door and went inside.

The place was empty, apart from a couple of early morning shoppers and an old man trying to warm his hands on a mug of hot tea. The waitress, Marie, was in her fifties. Marie was tired of clearing up other people's crap and her face showed it. Worry lines had permanently etched themselves on to her cheeks and mouth. Her laughter lines had turned into crow's feet in her mid-thirties. There was no winning. She looked at the table and took a cloth out. Spilt sugar, butter portions stuck to the seats. Wee bastards. She'd speak to the owner about letting schoolkids in; they were more trouble than they were worth. If her own boys did that she'd tan their arses.

Mick sat down at a nearby table.

Marie glanced up: just another customer. 'Mornin, ah'll jist git these plates oot ay yir road. Can ah git ye anyhun?'

'Aye. Mah wife.' He smiled at her.

She looked up at him, recognising the voice. 'Mick! God, sorry, love – ah didnae see ye. Ah don't think she's oan the menu but ah'll see whit ah kin dae. She's on hur brek; dae ye want a wee cuppa?' She walked behind the counter.

'Aye, awright – coffee please. So, how ye keepin, Marie?'

'No bad; yirsel?' She put a cup under the espresso machine and it gurgled into life.

'Ah'm awright.' He fiddled about with the salt cellar.

Marie had already heard Evelyn's woes this morning

and knew everything wasn't rosy in the house of Donnelly. She came out from behind the counter with the coffee. 'There ye go,' she said, placing it down. 'Ah'll jist get hur.'

Evelyn was sitting in the staff-room, wearing her light blue uniform, permanently stained with small flecks of coffee and tomato sauce. She turned the page of the newspaper and looked at a picture of Raquel Welsh in an evening dress. How old was she? Older than her ma. God, the difference was like night and day. Great to have money, she thought, sipping her tea. It was all right when it was just her and Marie working, they could take regular breaks. If they wanted a quick fag and it was quiet then the other covered – no problem. It was a different kettle of fish when that wee bitch Lynne was working. Didn't smoke, didn't drink, did everything by the book. She was never late and always found a reason to stay behind, long after her shift had finished. Evelyn and Marie couldn't get out the door fast enough when theirs finished. There was a want about that lassie Lynne: something missing upstairs.

Marie popped her head round the door. 'There's someone in tae see ye.'

'Ah'm on mah brek.' She eyed the TV page and took a drink of her tea. 'Ah'll see them when ah come oot.'

'Mebbe he'll no be there when ye come oot.'

Evelyn put the paper down. 'He?'

Marie smiled and nodded.

'Mick?' said Evelyn.

Marie grinned and nodded excitedly.

Evelyn jumped up and tidied her hair in the mirror. 'Why d' ye no say?'

'Ah jist huv! Moan, there's nuthin wrang wi ye – yir beautiful. Away oot there an see yir man.'

'Wait a minute' – she searched in her handbag – 'ah'll jist put some lipstick on.'

Marie grabbed her by the arm, spun her round and ejected her from the staff-room. 'Oot, ah sais!'

Evelyn came flying out of the room and into the corridor. She scowled at Marie and adjusted her uniform. Marie playfully pushed her along and pinched her on the arse. 'Wahey!'

'Stoap it you!' squealed Evelyn.

Marie always knew how to cheer her up. They'd worked together for the past three years. Evelyn had always worked since leaving school and prided herself that she'd never been out of a job for longer than six weeks in all that time. That was until she had to pack in her job at the hairdresser's when she became pregnant with Jamie.

Jamie was two when she decided to go back to work. She thought she was going cabin crazy and needed to get out of the house more, get her life back. The hairdressing shop she'd previously worked at had closed and she had no formal hairdressing qualification to speak of. She went for a couple of interviews and they all told her the same thing: the only way she could get back into hairdressing was as a junior. She felt a bit daft, starting at the bottom again, especially at her age when all the other juniors were only about sixteen.

She was about to give up when she saw the advert for the café. Mick didn't want her to work, and said he earned enough, but she was sick of having to watch what she spent all the time. She said she didn't want to end up like her ma, and wanted to be able to buy decent clothes for Jamie whenever she felt like it. She already had a nursery place organised for him and knew it would do him the world of good to be with other kids his own age. He was starting to get a bit of a handful and Evelyn reckoned that his tantrums were down to frustration: he was going as mad as her and needed more mental stimulation than he was getting looking at four walls. Mick had no argument and had to give in. Besides, she pointed out, the job was only part-time. If it didn't work out . . .

Jamie took to nursery like a duck to water and Evelyn hit it off with Marie straight away. Mick did a bit of grumbling at first but soon changed his tune when Evelyn brought her wage packet home. Chinkies and carry-outs weren't a thing of the past any more, neither were decent clothes. Evelyn was back in the workforce now and providing for her family again.

Mick sat at the table, looking depressed. Evelyn walked over to him, hoping he'd come here to sort things out. She wanted him back. They were a family. As far as she was concerned she'd given Shug his marching orders and they could all get back to normal.

'Hi, Mick.'

He looked up. She was standing in front of him like a shy schoolgirl. 'Er, hiya.' He clumsily jumped to his feet and went to give her a peck on the cheek. Evelyn, unaware of the impending kiss, sat down: he ended up kissing fresh air. Embarrassed, he checked to see if anyone saw him before sitting back down again

'How are ye?' she asked.

'No bad . . . how are you?'

'Awright, ah suppose.'

'How's the Wee Man?'

She shrugged and played with a piece of silver paper from a cigarette packet. 'He's awright. He seems awright. Ye can never tell wi kids though, can ye? He husnae shut up aboot you since ye walked oot. He wants tae know whit's goin oan; so dae ah.'

She looked up at him from her piece of paper: he was choked. She didn't like seeing him upset. She started to fill up and looked out of the window for a diversion.

Outside, the thunder of lorries and buses cut through the smell of the grease and exhaust fumes. Inside there was an embarrassing silence.

'Ah'v telt Shug tae go,' she said. 'He'll be oot th'day.'

'Good.' Mick sat back and relaxed in his seat.

'So, are ye gonnae come home?' she asked.

'Aye, when ah know he's definitely away.' He took a mouthful of his coffee and pondered the worst-case scenario. A homeless Shug would be an accident waiting to happen and Mick would get the blame for turfing him out. Shug would probably end up sleeping in the bus station and get stabbed. Fuck him, thought Mick. *He* wasn't responsible for his life.

'He'll be away tonight . . . hoanest.' She twisted the piece of paper and awaited his answer. 'Tomorrow at the latest.' She cringed.

Mick smiled sarcastically and slowly shook his head. It was the same old shite. He put the cup down in the saucer and looked up at her. 'Look, ah'll mek it easy on ye. How aboot if ah stay at mah ma's another night? It'll gie us a bit ay breathin space and gie dickbrain a chance tae find somewhere tae crash? Besides, ah'v hardly seen hur, huv ah?'

She tossed the piece of paper in the ashtray and looked at him as if to say, 'An whit aboot me?'

'Oh, come on Ev, don't be like that. Ah'll only huv tae go back over there fir the presents th' morra anyway.'

Evelyn looked puzzled. 'Why, are they no comin for their Christmas dinner noo?'

Mick shrugged his shoulders. 'They think they'll be in the way, wi us no gittin oan. Mah ma says they'll come over an see the Wee Man next week.'

'Great,' said Evelyn sarcastically. 'Anyway, you've changed yir tune, huven't ye? Ah thought they drove ye mental?'

'Aye, they dae . . . but ye cannae pick yir family, can ye?' He sipped his coffee again.

That was true. Who in their right mind would want a brother like Shug. It made sense; they did need a bit of breathing space. 'Aye, awright,' she said, 'but jist mek sure yir back fir Seturday, eh?'

They looked at each other and smiled with relief. Evelyn grabbed his hands and squeezed them.

'God sakes, Mick, it's only bin wan night, bit ah miss ye. D'ye realise we've never spent a night apart since before the wean wis born?'

He took one of her hands, kissed it and held it against his cheek. He sighed; relieved some normality had resumed in their relationship. 'Ah know. This is stupid, this, but ah hud tae leave – ah couldnae think straight – ah thought ah wis crackin up.'

'It's awright, it's awright.' She tried to calm him. 'Jist forget it – ye don't need tae explain.'

'But ah want tae. Ah shouldnae huv left yis; ah'm tryin, but ah jist cannae huv um stayin aw the time. Ah cannae live in the same hoose as yir brar. Ah tried, ah really tried mah best, but he's drivin wedges between you, me, an the wean!'

'I know, shhh, it's awright. He's leavin.'

'I mean he's pished oot hus boax most ay the time an willnae speak tae ye. When he's no pished he's speedin an ye cannae shut the basta up! Whit would happen if the wean goat his hons on some ay hus gear an swallied it? Eh? Fuck sakes! Ye cannae git a sleep fir the cunt cos he's up aw night. Teachers comin tae the hoose, sayin the wean's fallin asleep in school, askin if there's anyhun wrang. Fuckin right there's somehun wrang! Arseholes comin tae the door fir um, sayin he owes them money . . . ah'm sorry, Ev, but ah cannae live like that; mebbe you kin but ah cannae. An ah don't want mah wean brought up like that either!'

He looked up – she was quietly crying.

'Ah'm sorry, Ev, ah'm sorry.' He turned away, disgusted with himself.

'It's awright' She looked across to the counter to see if Marie had noticed her crying. She was too busy cleaning. Besides, she wasn't nosey, Marie; never stuck her nose in where it wasn't wanted but was always on hand to give you advice if you needed it. Evelyn dried her eyes, 'It's mah fault,' she said, shaking her head.

'It's no yir fault. I know ye feel soarry fir um when yir auld man throws um oot: ah kin understoan that – he's yir brar. But kin ye blame yir auld man? It's no aw hus fault. Ah mean, yir ma's no fit fir aw that carry-oan wi they two ye know.'

She pulled a pack of cigarettes out of her overall pocket and lit one. There was plenty of time to give up in the New Year. Her nerves were too jangled to think about it just now. 'Ah know, ah know.' She blew the smoke into the air. It filtered through her fringe and hovered like a blue cloud above their heads. 'Ah jist wanted tae help um though. I thought that if he stayed wi us noo an again, goat away fae mah da, he'd mebbe calm doon, get himsel a joab, a nice girl . . . ye know?'

'A nice girl?' Mick sat back in his seat, shaking his

head at her naivety. 'Fuck sakes, Ev, he's goat eyes like a rapist! He frightens the shit oot ay women. He's a psycho. Ah jist cannae stick um. Ah cannae stay in the same hoose as um, an you widnae let me turf um oot. So whit could ah dae? It wis either hum or me . . . an you chose yir brar.'

She flicked her ash in the ashtray and looked him in the eyes. 'Ah didnae *choose*. Ye cannae ask someone tae *choose*.'

He could see she was getting uptight. He hadn't come here for an argument – he was trying to sort things out for God's sakes.

'How would you have liked tae huv bin in mah position, eh?' she asked.

He looked back at her. He hadn't really considered that.

'Anyway,' she said, 'ah'v telt um if he disnae git oot he's gettin a doin fae the boys who drink in the Half-way.'

'An ye think that'll scare um intae leavin, dae ye?' he asked sarcastically.

'It should dae; there's aboot ten ay thum after hus blood. He'll no go back in there in a hurry!'

'Why?'

She'd been holding this back. It would just have proved his point about Shug, and he'd say, 'Telt ye so.' He was bound to find out sooner or later though. 'Well, ah didnae want tae tell ye this, bit' – she drew on her cigarette, thinking how to tell him – 'ye know how he's goat an uncanny knack ay stertin a riot in an empty room?'

'Aye?' His eyes narrowed and he leaned forward.

'Well, ah finds oot oan the bus comin intae work this mornin, doesn't ah? Ah met Nancy. She tells me he wis in the pub spreadin rumours aboot the young barmaid – ye know, the wee quiet wan? Sayin that she wis huvin it aff wi this wan an that wan. He kept windin up hur man – the Big Yin.'

'George?' asked Mick.

'Aye, George. So, George gets really pissed aff an jist snaps. He goes mental an throws wanna they big stools ower the bar at the lassie.'

'Fir fuck sakes!' He stared at her, unable to take it in.

'Ah know. Then everywan goes mental, laying intae the Big Yin wi pool cues an boatils. Then the Big Yin's pals jump in an aw. Two bloks go flyin through the windae. There wis polis, ambulances, gless, blood, you name it, a major battle.'

'An where wis Shug?'

'Got oaf hus mark dint he?' she sneered, wiping some ash off the table with her hand. 'Typical. The big shitebag winds the whole place up an then pisses aff!'

'Sick basta! How's the lassie?'

'Ah heard she's no too good. Ah tell ye, Shug wis tekin a risk hopin tae stay wi us – ower the road fae the pub! Whit if someone wis tae see um comin an goin?'

'Ah know.' Mick ran his fingers through his hair as he thought of the consequences. 'Knowin Big George he'd have trashed the place tryin tae find um. Wi a wean in the hoose an aw, it disnae bear thinkin aboot.' He shook his head at the very thought.

Evelyn stubbed out her cigarette. 'Well if Shug sterts his carry oan aboot leavin' ah'v a good mind tae tell George where he is.' She looked at him. He was still thinking – taking it in.

She glanced up at the clock, realising she'd had twice as long as usual for her break. It was a good job she wasn't on with Lynne. She looked across to Marie and gave her a nervous smile that said, 'I'll no be a minute.'

Marie stared back with a pleading look in her eyes as a crowd of early morning shoppers came in: first port of call after Argyle Street, en route to Sauchiehall Street, via the Buchanan Galleries. If New York was 'the city that never sleeps' then Glasgow was 'the city that never stops shopping'.

'Look,' said Mick, 'don't tell um anyhun. George'd kill um. Ye couldnae live wi that oan yir conscience, could ye?'

'No, but . . .'

'Jist tell Shug ah'm gien um a chance cos he's yir brar. Tell um that ah know the Big Yin an hus pals, an if he's no oot the hoose by th' morra ah'm gonnae grass um up tae them.'

She glanced across again at Marie, trying to cope. 'Aye, awright. We're gettin busy, ah'd better go.'

'Okay.' He kissed her gently on the lips. 'Ah'll see ye th' morra. Gie the wean a kiss fir us, eh?'

'Aye.' She smiled. 'See ye th'morra.'

She got up and went back to work. Mick walked out feeling ten feet tall.

Jamie watched Miss Jackson scribbling on the board. They were learning all about the poor black babies in Africa. He looked across at Anna Doyle sitting in the next row. She was poor. She didn't have a da. He looked at her grey socks, splattered with paint from yesterday's lesson and knew that her ma would let her wear her socks for more than one day at a time. His ma always made him put on clean socks every day, though he never knew why – his feet didn't smell.

He looked at Anna's long black hair, tied up with an elastic band. The other girls called her a 'tink' and pulled the band from her hair. She'd cry when she put it back in again, saying it was too tight and it was pulling her hair out. If the band broke she'd have to get Miss Jackson to give her a new one out of the drawer.

One day Jamie saw Miss Jackson give Anna a card with coloured elastic things for girls' hair wrapped round it. Anna wore them to school for a few days but the other girls still pulled them out and threw them away.

Sometimes Anna's pal, Wee Mary, would brush Anna's hair in the playground and put the elastics in for her. There would always be a load of black hair left on the brush. One day Mary pulled the hair off the brush and the wind blew it into Bernadette O'Neill's face.

Bernadette went 'Yeurghh!' and threw it at her pal. They kicked the hair about the playground like it was a black hairy jobbie. Bernadette picked it up and put it in Liam's pocket, but he didn't bother until she told him whose it was and he went 'Blearghh!' and pulled it out and threw it away. Anna stood in the playground and just looked at him like she was sad, but she didn't cry.

Wee Mary was poor as well. Her ma died when she was a baby and she lived with her gran now. Mary always smelled of chip fat. Mary and Anna got free school dinners and would get pushed out of the dinner queue by Bernadette O'Neill and some of the other girls who called them 'smellies'. One day Wee Mary punched Bernadette in the eye and Bernadette went greeting to Miss Jackson. Miss Jackson took Mary into an empty classroom to tell her off, but Mary was smiling when she came back out again. Jamie didn't think she got told off at all.

The next day, Mary's gran had to come and see the headmaster and Jamie saw her going into his office. When he walked past the headmaster's office on his way to his classroom he could smell chip fat.

Miss Jackson tapped and scraped the chalk on the blackboard while Jamie sat in a world of his own, staring at Anna's socks. He looked up at Anna's face and saw her looking back at him. He smiled, caught out, expecting her to say 'Pan Watcher'. That's what you said if someone was staring at you. She never said anything. She smiled at him like he was her pal. He looked about to see if anyone was looking at him but they weren't. He smiled back.

Liam never spoke to Anna because she was a smelly, but Jamie always said 'Hiya' when he saw her in the street. He never spoke to her in school though, in case Liam or the others saw him.

Ever since Jamie told his ma that they called her names, his ma always asked about her. He wished he hadn't said anything now because she asked him all the time and it got on his nerves.

His ma always said that Jamie should play with her, as she didn't have any friends. It was a shame, not having a da. He remembered seeing her in the Paki's one day. She didn't have enough for a loaf and the Paki let her off with ten pence. Jamie asked her where her da was and she told him that he had an argument with her ma and the police came. When she came home from school the next day her ma told her he was away and he wouldn't be back.

Jamie felt sick as he remembered his ma and da having an argument the other night, his da walking out without eating his tea. He knew his da wasn't at Granny Donnelly's. They'd been arguing because Uncle Shug was always at their house. Sometimes Jamie would wake up in the morning and Uncle Shug would be asleep on the couch with the telly on and his da would be going mad.

Maybe Uncle Shug was going to move into their house and his da would stay at Granny Donnelly's? He hoped not: that meant he'd only see his da on a Sunday when he went to visit his gran. He didn't want that. He wanted his da to live at home with them.

When he finished school today he'd remember to tell his ma to phone him up and tell him to come straight home from his work. Jamie didn't want to be called a smelly.

'Promise ye'll no tell anyone.'

'No way – yir gonnae huv tae tell someone.'

'Ah don't huv tae dae anyhun.'

'Aye ye dae . . . he'll jist dae it again.'

No answer.

'If you don't tell someone, ah will.'

'No y'll no' – ah'll top masel.'

'Will ye fuck. Ah mean, look, he's probably oot there right now; gonnae dae it again . . . some poor lassie.'

'Gies wan ay yir fags.'

'Ye don't smoke.'

'Ah dae noo, mah nerves are shattered.'

Jaqui pulled out a cigarette. She lit it and handed it to Siobhan. 'Are ye sure it wisnae Bobby Turner?'

Siobhan looked across the schoolyard at Bobby playing football. 'Ah telt ye, it wisnae hum. Ah'd know if it wis Bobby. Ah know hus voice.' She drew on the cigarette.

Jaqui watched as the smoke went in Siobhan's right eye. She blinked and rubbed it. 'He could put on a voice, ye know,' said Jaqui.

Siobhan stared across the schoolyard. She looked

confused as she tried to remember. 'It wisnae hum. This guy wis bigger – skinnier. Ah'v met hum before, somewhere. Ah don't know . . . Look, jist forget it.'

'Jist think aboot it, will ye.'

'There's nuthin tae think aboot: ah wisnae *raped* – ah shat mah drawers. There's shit up the walls in the close. Mah da wis goin hus dinger! Blamin some old jakey – he'd fuckin die aff if he knew it wis me!'

'It wisnae yir fault.'

Siobhan drew on the cigarette and coughed. She threw it on the ground and stubbed it out with her heel. 'Like ah sais, forget it.'

Archie sifted through the pick and mix at Asda, shoving sweets into a bag. He wasn't accustomed to buying sweets for kids. He realised this was the first time in years that he'd actually bought something for someone else. He'd no one to buy for and no family apart from his sister in Australia.

He always wished Jean and he had been blessed with a child. He made out it didn't bother him that she couldn't have any, but inside it hurt. He knew it hurt her too; he saw it in her eyes every time she held a baby.

Still, they'd had some good times over the years. But that was all over now. Sometimes he felt as if he were just going through the motions; filling time until his number was up. He checked himself. What was he thinking? He had his job, his health and a couple of good mates . . . and then there were the kids.

The checkout girl weighed the bag. 'Six eighty please.'

Six eighty for a bag of sweets? He considered taking it back. No, it was going to be worth it.

Shug walked along Clyde Street, trying the doors of parked cars. He stopped at a white G registration Escort then walked around the car checking the bodywork. He looked at the driver's window: WARNING CAR ALARM. He rocked the car from side to side.

No alarm.

He pulled out a long, thin icing spatula and slid it down between the window and the bodywork. He often thought about what he'd say if he was pulled up with it: 'Er, ah'm a professional cake decorator, officer – hoan-est.' He preferred the spatula to the screwdriver – you could get done for carrying a screwdriver: offensive weapon. But a good brief could laugh a spatula out of court.

Click

Open Sesame.

Whistling 'Whistle While You Work,' as though he were one of the Seven Dwarfs happily going about his business, he jumped in the driver's seat and surveyed the situation inside the car: a bright yellow Krooklok cov-ered the handbrake and gearstick. No problem.

He unscrewed the top off the gearstick, took off his shoe and tapped the Krooklok from the underside with the heel. It slid off. He removed it from the handbrake and threw it on the passenger seat. Still whistling, he replaced the gearknob, then gave the steering wheel a couple of sharp turns to break the steering lock. He took the Krooklok and hit the ignition barrel a couple of times with it until it broke from its mounting, then wiggled the wires till they snapped off it. He touched the ignition wires together.

Nothing.

'Hmm . . . Deid.'

He pulled the bonnet catch and got out of the car, lifted the bonnet and looked inside.

'Ya sneaky basta!'

These cunts were making it harder for him to make a living. Who, in their right mind, would take the HT lead off the starter? Probably some dozy tart working in an office, taking pish advice from her da.

'Aye, hen. Tek this lead aff an the bastas cannae tek yir motor – it goes dead. Immobilises it, y'see.'

Bollocks.

He pulled two HT leads out of his pocket, fitted one, and then dropped the bonnet. He jumped back into the car, touched the ignition wires together again and the car started first time.

He drove up to the lights and waited for them to change. He turned on the radio, opened the glove compartment and pulled a handful of tapes out on to the passenger seat.

Mick trudged up the metal staircase in Tower Records. Lou Reed's 'Vicious' blasted out from the ground floor.

He wondered if the staff were trying to educate customers in their own personal taste in music, or if it was just a ploy to get you to buy a CD that they'd found boxes of lying about.

He turned the corner on to the first floor and looked about at the thousands of videos. You could get anything here. The most obscure shite on the planet and they'd have it in stock. He located the comedy section and wandered over, pausing for a moment to look at a boxed set of *Fawlty Towers*, then remembered he'd taped them all off the telly the last time they'd been shown.

This was weird: out shopping in daylight. He'd managed to slope off work early, saying that a wisdom tooth was giving him serious gyp and he needed to see a dentist before Christmas. His gaffer eyed him suspiciously for a few moments before okaying it. It wasn't as if Mick was one of these fly bastards, coming up with every excuse under the sun so they could take off for a swallay. His gaffer knew he wasn't like that.

'Lucky cunt,' said a workmate as Mick put his bag over his shoulder and closed his locker.

'Ah'm in fuckin agony here,' he said, trying to play it up, rubbing his jaw.

'Aye, right.' His workmate smirked back at him.

Ah, fuck it, thought Mick, there's mair tae life than work, plus, if he spent any more time in that place he might as well take his bed in.

He cast his eyes over the comedy section. Evelyn loved *Father Ted*. Mick had already spent most of his wages on presents for her and Jamie, but Evelyn could do with a laugh. That's what was missing at the moment: laughter. He loved to hear her laugh. He could just imagine them curled up on the couch on Christmas Day. She'd be in hysterics. Jamie would have an empty can of lager and be going 'arse!' making her worse. He smiled to himself. He was a comic that boay. Aye, they could all do with a good laugh.

Shug drove fast down Union Street, window open, jungle blaring from the radio. One by one he checked the tapes.

'Pish!' He threw it out the window.

'Pish!'

And another one.

'Pish!'

And another.

In the distance the lights were changing to red: he put the boot down.

Mick came out of Tower Records and walked to the lights at Jamaica Street. He started to cross.

Jungle.

The roar of an engine.

Pulled back by the jacket.

'Fuckin hell!'

A white Escort flashed past, just missing him.

The inside of the garage was like an Aladdin's cave spray-painted with oil. Seventeen-year-old Lee sat inside a Sierra, clocking the speedo. He wiped the sweat from his brow and glanced at his reflection in the rear-view mirror. His short brown hair was flecked with white paint from the bonnet he'd sprayed this morning. His eyes were bloodshot and itchy, and encircled with oil from his hands from where he'd been rubbing them. He looked like a panda. He told Harry, the owner of the garage, that the paint irritated his eyes and that they should be wearing goggles, but Harry said he never wore them. If Lee needed goggles he could go and buy them himself.

It wasn't the apprenticeship Lee had envisaged, but he'd learned more in the past year than he could at any major car plant: like how to take the etching off windows, the number off a chassis, and how to do a dodgy MOT.

Lee's old man had been round all the garages a few weeks before Lee left school, asking the owners if they had any jobs going. He told Lee that if he was as interested in cars as he said he was then he wouldn't mind starting at the bottom like everyone else. He'd have to make the tea and do a bit of running round for the other mechanics, but you had to start somewhere. Lee knew his old man meant well and was only doing it so Lee wouldn't end up drinking Buckie on the streets like his older brother Stevie. Stevie was only twenty-four and he looked like a jakey. Couldn't go a day without a bevvy.

What Lee couldn't figure out was: out of all the

garages his old man went round, why Harry was the only one who agreed to take him on. Lee remembered his old man coming home with a tie for him, saying, 'Ah've goat ye an interview th' morra.'

'The interview' was in the dingy office of Harry's garage, sitting at an oil-stained table covered with iron filings. It consisted of a couple of questions about the combustion engine, while Harry slurped cold coffee from a chipped mug covered in oily fingerprints, and scoffed a Mars Bar. He asked Lee what he would do if he drove through a puddle and the engine cut out. Lee told him. Basic stuff, thought Lee. Harry scrunched up the Mars Bar wrapper and threw it on the floor. 'Joab's yirs if ye want it.'

That was as good as a handshake and 'Welcome aboard, young man' coming from the likes of Harry.

When Lee got home his old man was over the moon. Stevie took Lee to one side to warn him about Harry: said he'd heard he was a dodgy bastard who'd done time for ringing cars. He also said he'd been charged with manslaughter, although he couldn't remember what the circumstances were exactly – thought it might have been an apprentice he got into an argument with. He told Lee if he knew what was good for him he wouldn't take the job. Lee knew Stevie was winding him up and decided to take it anyway.

After working with Harry for a week Lee started thinking that Stevie might have been right. He saw Harry chase an old boy out of the garage, threatening to wrap a tyre iron round his head if he didn't come back with the cash to pay for his new exhaust. 'Fuckin cheques!' said Harry. 'Ah telt um cash. Auld cunt should use wan ay hus cheques tae buy himsel a fuckin hearin aid!'

Harry had a bastard of a temper and Lee spent most of his time trying to keep out of his way. He could put the fear of God into Lee with just a look, and a day never went by without Lee thinking he might get the sack. If the truth were known he hated him, the greasy bastard. 'Harry the Greek' people called him. Lee never called him that – knew what would happen if he did. He didn't even know if he *was* Greek, although he did have jet-black hair streaked with grey, arms like a gorilla and eyes as black as coal. When Lee talked about him to his mates he always referred to him as Lucifer.

Harry's favourite scam was to fit a car alarm, then go out to the owner's house a few days later and nick their car. Only last week a tidy wee bird with a Peugot came in to get an alarm fitted. Harry took the keys off her and told her to come back in a few hours. Lee knew what his game was and told him it was shite what they were doing – the poor wee lassie had most probably put herself in debt to buy that car. Harry said he couldn't give a fuck: the insurance would see her all right.

He sent Lee out to a nearby ironmonger to get the girl's key copied while he fitted the alarm to her car. Hours later she came back, all smiles, thanking Harry for doing such a good job – she felt much safer now.

Harry gave her a one-year guarantee for the alarm and filled in her name and address on the guarantee form, stressing that the 'guarantee' was for parts and labour in case the alarm malfunctioned; it wasn't a guarantee that her car wouldn't get nicked, ha-ha. If a good car thief really wanted it no alarm in the world could stop them. She smiled and nodded her head. He took a copy of the form for 'his records' and, unknown to her, a copy of her key for his amusement. He waited a couple of days, then gave Shug's pal, Chic, the key, and the address. Chic went to the girl's house and found the car parked in the street. He turned off the alarm with the spare key fob then drove it back to the garage. The next day Harry stripped the car down and put the alarm back in its box for the next sucker who wanted one fitted.

Lee didn't particularly like what he was doing, but it was a job. He knew the money wasn't great but he could earn fifty quid a time on top of his wages for running nicked motors over to Stranraer. He handed them over to a young Irish bloke called Dermot who took them on the ferry to Ireland. Dermot never said much, just, 'Howyeh. Got the keys?' Dermot's boss acquired logbooks of write-offs and called the garage once or twice a week to place an order. 'A Volvo 340DL, H reg, grey if you have it.'

Harry would put out the feelers with a couple of wide-os he knew and within a day or two, hey presto, a grey Volvo would disappear from Glasgow city centre, soon to be given a new lease of life on the Emerald Isle.

* * *

Harry was under the bonnet, replacing the camshaft. 'Seen more than its fair share of taxiing, this basta,' he said.

Lee heard him mumble something but didn't want to ask what.

The sound of loud music came from outside the garage. Harry was getting agitated. He almost cut his hand with the spanner as it slipped from his grasp. 'Lee!'

No answer.

'LEE!'

Lee popped his head out the driver's window. 'WHIT?'

'TURN THAT SHITE AFF!'

'THE RADIO'S NO ON!'

'WHIT?'

'IT'S NO ME! He pointed to the front doors.

Harry kicked open the large red, paint-chipped doors. They wobbled on their hinges and swung back at him, threatening to smack him in the face. He pushed them apart again and stormed outside, shaking his head in disbelief as he surveyed the scene.

Shug was standing on the front seats of the Escort with the top half of his body sticking through the sunro of. He was dancing to Afrika Bambaattaa's 'Pupunanny' and sounding the horn.

'PUPUNANNY – GONNAE STICK IT UP YIR FANNY! – HARRY, MAH MAN! WANNA BUY A MOTOR?'

'Fuck sakes, Shug! Keep it doon, eh?' said Harry,

annoyed at Shug's blatant disregard for discretion. He looked about the street. 'Bring it in,' he said, and walked back into the garage.

Lee looked up from the speedo and saw Shug driving the Escort in. 'Aw fuck, ah hate that basta!' He slid down the seat so as not to be seen.

Harry closed the front doors and walked around the car, inspecting it. Shug got out and paced about after him, a bit on edge.

'No bad, eh? Whit dae ye reckon: two fifty? Eh?' He pulled out a cigarette packet, saw it was empty, crumpled it up and threw it on the floor.

'Fuck off!' said Harry. 'Two fifty. How long ye hud it?'

'Aboot hof an oor. Any fags, Aitch?'

'Don't smoke.'

'Fuck sakes, a mechanic that disnae smoke, whit's the world comin tae? Well c'moan, how much?'

'Gies a minute, eh?' He looked at the bodywork.

Lee was slumped down in the driver's seat, carefully adjusting the numbers on the speedo: 'Fifty-three thousan miles. No, make it fifty-three four hunnert an twenty-wan: mair convincin.'

'Haw you!' Shug's head popped up at the driver's window. Lee jumped out of his skin and dropped the speedo in his lap.

'Fuck sakes! Shug.'

'I hope yir no clockin that, ya wee basta. That's a criminal offence, ye know.'

'Is it? Shit, ah'd better stoap then, eh?'

'Giz wanna yir fags.'

'Ah don't smoke.'

'Don't smoke whit?'

'Ah don't smoke fags . . . an ah don't smoke dope.'

'AH DON'T SMOKE DOPE AN AH DON'T DO COKE!' Shug drummed on the car door. 'C'moan, Wee Man, away ower the shoap an git us some, eh?'

'Piss aff! Ah'm no yir slave.'

'No yet yir no.'

'Ah'm busy.'

Shug ducked down. Lee heard him rummaging about and wondered what he was doing until he saw him come back up with a blowlamp. Shug reached into the car and turned the gas on, then put his lighter next to it. 'An ah'm mental,' he said.

Lee clocked the manic grin. 'Aye awright, awright.' He got out of the car.

Shug handed him some money. 'Club.'

Lee reluctantly took the money and went out. Shug looked over to Harry.

'Moan tae fuck, Aitch man, ah'v no goat aw day.'

'A hunnert.'

'Whit? Fuck off, ye could sell that fir a grand!'

'Yir erse. Ah'm the wan tekin the risk here, no you. Ah'm the wan who hus tae strip it doon an sell aff the parts tae make any money. It could be months afore ah git mah money back.'

'Aye aye, awright, a hunnert an fifty.'

'Hunnert an twenty.'

'Gies it, ya robbin basta'.'

Harry smirked to himself as he handed over the cash.

Shug came out of the garage, counting the money, making sure Harry hadn't stiffed him. You couldn't be too careful, there were thieves everywhere.

Lee came round the corner with the cigarettes. Another couple of hours working with Lucifer then he'd be finished. Away home for a bath, then out to see his girlfriend Liz. She nearly gave him it last week but was put off by the smell of turps from his hair. He knew he'd have to use turps again tonight to get the paint out. He remembered Stevie had a selection of baseball caps at home. Lee reminded himself to nick one and start wearing it to work. It was getting beyond a joke, this: it didn't matter how much shampoo he used he always ended up smelling of turps for the rest of the night. Baseball cap and goggles: essential equipment if he was to have a sex life. He smiled to himself as he turned the corner, thinking about what Liz would say if he came to bed wearing them.

'Whit you laughing at, ya mad cunt?'

He looked up. Shug was walking towards him, stuffing a handful of notes into his pocket. Lee warily handed him the cigarettes and change. 'Nuthin,' he said.

'Yir no right in the heid, son,' said Shug. 'Go oan, fuck aff back tae yir hole, ya greasy wee basta.' Shug indicated the garage. As Lee went to walk past Shug growled like a vicious dog and stuck his neck out at him. Lee flinched and hurried past. Just for the fun of it, Shug went to chase him and tried to kick him up the arse, but Lee dodged out of the way and ran for the safety of the garage, slamming the big red door behind him.

'Wee wanka.' Shug laughed to himself and walked off up the street.

It was amazing what fifty pounds could get you in Glasgow: two bottles of Buckie, three Doves and half a dozen jellies.

The Savoy was heaving. Ultrasonic's 'Appreggio' was building up to a thundering climax. Shug had just necked his second Dove. He was coming up; big-style.

Indian Warrior.

Woo-hoo, ya fucker.

Fuck *Dances With Wolves*. Dance like a maddie, ya bam.

The sweat ran down his back. He spotted a babe with long, brown shining hair. She looked like an Indian squaw: beautiful. Every flash of the strobe was like the paparazzi snapping her. He watched, wide-eyed, as she tossed her long hair high in the air.

FLASH.

The job in Liverpool had turned out to be great. Malkie's brother, Al, met him at Lime Street Station and gave him a lift back to his flat, flung his bags in the door and took him straight out on the piss. It had been the first time they'd seen each other since their mother's funeral.

Al had paid for the whole thing as he was earning decent money now, but Malkie's embarrassment at being skint only added to his grief. Whit kind ay son cannae afford tae bury hus aen ma? he thought. It was at that point he swore to do something about his life. His ma and da had scrimped and scraped all their days. Malkie didn't want to end up like them.

He sat with Al in the quiet pub, catching up on old times. By the end of the night Malkie had had a bit too much to drink and started crying about what a shame it had been for their parents: worked all their days to give him and Al everything and now they were dead with nothing to show for it. 'Whit a fuckin life,' he said, rubbing his watery eyes. Al reminded him that their parents had two sons to be proud of. Malkie said the only one they had anything to be proud of was Al – he'd done something with his life.

'So huv you noo,' Al reminded him. 'Yir gonnae work fir me. Ah'm gonnae show ye the ropes an git ye sterted. In a couple ay years y'll huv yir aen place – you wait an see.'

Malkie managed a smile at him and shook his head. 'Ah'm a waste ay space.'

Al finished his beer and stood up to get another round in. 'No yir no. Mah ma an da never thought that, an neither did I; so, dae us a favour, eh? Stoap yir greetin an prove us aw right.'

The next day Malkie started work at AL'S BAR

* * *

Al didn't show any favouritism. That was just the way Malkie wanted it.

The staff were a good laugh and Malkie found himself getting on well with them. From the minute he arrived he had his eye on Joanne, one of the barmaids. His first night there and she was cracking Scotsman jokes. She sidled up next to him at one of the lager taps, put a pint glass under the tap and looked him in the eye: 'Ow can y' tell a Scotsman's name?' she asked.

Malkie shook his head.

'Put yer and under is kilt . . . an if e's gorra quarter-pounder e's a McDonald.' She pinched his arse, laughed and walked away.

Malkie stood with his glass overflowing lager into the drip tray. Fucking come-on if ever I saw one, he thought. She was a goddess in her twenties. He couldn't take his eyes off her – until he found out she was engaged to one of the bouncers. The lucky bastard.

His first night behind the bar the place was jumping. A DJ mixed away in the corner. Bodies crammed together with their arms pressed against their sides. Guys tried to drink from bottles of beer without elbowing the person next to them every time they raised their arm, while the girls had it worked out and always drank through straws. Malkie felt as though he kept getting in the way of the other barstaff behind the cramped bar, tripping over the crates that lay on the floor because they didn't have the time to restock the shelves. He quickly learned to lip-read scouse as the music was so deafening, and he found himself trying to keep pace with the stuff the DJ was playing, serving drinks at the speed of light, but he soon slowed down as the nights went on. He'd only just got here but loved it already. A few nights ago, he thought, ah wis windin up the crowd in Finlays . . . could huv bin fuckin kilt.

He thought about Scobie and Chic: they weren't bad cunts – he'd keep in touch . . . maybe. No, he'd definitely give Scobie a phone. He was harmless – *sound* as they said down here. But he knew it was only a matter of time before the police nabbed Chic. He was becoming too gallus. Malkie was sure as fuck not going to tell Shug where he was staying. Before he left, Shug had been asking for his new address but Malkie kept flannelling – couldn't find a pen, all that shite. In the end Malkie promised he'd phone him when he got settled. Shug said he'd be straight down there – always fancied 'the Pool'. Fuck that, thought Malkie. He hoped he'd seen the last of him.

Malkie pushed his way through the crowd towards Al, who was standing near the dance floor. Malkie raised the two bottles of beer level with his face to stop them from getting knocked out of his hands and edged slowly through the mass of swaying bodies.

His crotch brushed against a young girl's arse. She was wearing what looked like a short silver nightie. She never batted an eyelid. He imagined the feel of the silk fabric as he hoisted it up over her hips. He considered going back to have another shot at rubbing up against her. Al watched him and laughed – brotherly telepathy.

Malkie looked over at him and indicated the girl while pursing his lips together as though he were in pain. Any more of this and he would be: or at least his dick would, trying to escape the constraints of his jeans.

So this was actually it: Cream. He'd heard the CDs, bought the T-shirts; now here he was in the club, checking out the fanny. Ya dancer.

He handed Al his beer. 'Is it like this aw the time in here?' asked Malkie.

Al bobbed in time with the music and looked about at the talent. 'Aw the fuckin time, mah boay, aw the fuckin time.'

Malkie's eyes followed a girl as she bent down to pull up her knee-length boots. The front of her flimsy top was no match for her tits, giving Malkie and Al more than an eyeful. 'This place is fuckin hoachin wi fanny,' said Malkie.

'Telt ye it would be,' said Al, scanning the dance floor for prey.

A skinny blonde with a sunbed tan, wearing a white vest and shorts, sidled up behind Al and winked at Malkie. Malkie smiled back, thinking he'd scored, until she put her arms around Al and slipped her hands inside his shirt. She made a point of looking Malkie straight in the eye while she did it.

Al turned round and grinned like a loon when he saw her. 'Becky? Awright, doll – how ye dein?'

'I'm fine, luv, ow are you?' she said, eyeing Malkie. 'Oo's yer mate?'

'He's mah wee brar,' said Al. 'Jist doon fae Glesga – he's workin at the pub wi me!' He turned to Malkie. 'Malkie, this is Becky. She's pals wi Joanne fae behind the bar.'

Malkie shook her hand. 'Oh, right. Nice tae meet ye.'

Becky eyed him a bit too long, making Malkie remember his potential trouser trouble if she kept looking at him like that. 'Nice t' meet yer . . . Malkie. We're all over there if y' wanna come over.' She pointed to the other end of the dance floor.

Al looked at Malkie for an answer.

Malkie grinned back at him. 'Ah'm there, dude,' he said.

Becky took Malkie by the hand and led him through the crowd. He turned and caught Al's eye. Al's grin said it all: Malkie was in there. 'Ya fuckin stoatir,' Malkie mouthed at him. Al laughed and pushed him on through the crowd.

Day Four

Punters spilled out of the clubs and headed, like sheep, straight to the kebab shops to get fleeced. Shug had followed *The Squaw* to the taxi rank at Central Station. She didn't want to know him. Minnie ha-ha? Minnie ***boo-hoo***, more like – miserable cunt.

He couldn't push it as he'd been getting eyed by a couple of wide-os at the back of the queue, so he swiftly fucked off to the Queen Street rank instead.

That was two hours ago – almost an eternity. He'd already been home, collected some of his stuff and got a taxi to Evelyn's. Right now he was butt-naked in her spare room, dancing in front of his miniature strobe. His hands moved about in front of it as though he were controlling it.

'Mum . . . Mum . . .'

Evelyn could hear Jamie's voice above the music as she woke up. He was standing at the side of her bed, rubbing his eyes. She looked at the alarm clock: 04.50. She turned on the bedside light and lifted him into her bed.

'Moan, son, you sleep wi yir mammie.' She got out of bed and went out of the room.

She opened the door to Shug's room, squinted in the strobe light and turned on the main light switch. Shug was oblivious and continued to dance. She angrily hit the stop button on his ghetto-blaster and the music stopped. So did Shug; he turned to face her. The strobe continued to flicker.

'FIR FUCK SAKES, SHUG! DAE YE KNOW WHIT TIME IT IS?'

'Whit?'

'Ye woke the wean up! Is there somehun wrang wi you? It's four in the mornin!'

'Ah cannae sleep . . .'

'How no?'

'Ah'v hud three Eckies.' He grinned, picking up a bottle of Beck's. 'Moan, Ev, dae ye want a boatil ay beer? Huv a dance wi us . . . moan.' He turned the music back on again and started dancing.

Evelyn picked up the ghetto-blaster and threw it on the floor, then and marched over to the strobe, ripped the plug out of the wall and hurled that on the floor too. The glass smashed and a couple of pieces landed on the carpet as the strobe bounced across the floor and hit the wall.

'That's it, ya basta', she said. 'Ah'v hud as much as ah kin take ay you. If yir no oot ay here by the time ah git back fae mah work, yir fuckin deid!'

He stared at the ghetto-blaster in disbelief. 'Ya broke mah cassette, ya bitch! Look at it.'

'Ah'v tae git the wean up fir school in three oors!' She tried to compose herself. 'If we don't git a sleep because ay you, ah'll come back in here an ah'll knife ye, ya cunt! Noo git tae yir fuckin bed an keep the noise doon!'

Jamie came in, looking scared, holding on to her leg.

'Ah cannae,' said Shug, 'ah'm still buzzin!'

'Huv ye no goat anyhun ye kin take tae come doon?'

'Aye, jellies . . . somewhere.' He looked about the room.

'Then find them, take the loat – an die, ya basta!' She looked at him, disgusted. 'Yir jist like mah da – an erse.'

He took great offence at this. 'Am ah fuck. Mah da's a drunken auld basta.'

'Aye, an yir a drugged-up, *young* basta.'

She picked Jamie up and walked out, slamming the door behind her.

Shug located two jellies that had rolled out of his jeans and ended up by the skirting board. He leaned over, picked them up and took them with a swig of beer. He reached for his Walkman and put it on. Fast tinny music came from the headphones as though there were bees in his head. He nodded in time with the sounds, picked up the strobe and set about fixing it, taking the broken glass away from the bulb and cutting his finger in the process. He sat and watched as the blood dripped on to the carpet.

* * *

Ten-year-old Evelyn was playing on the swings, in the park, with her friend, Janet. Shug was eight, sitting in a sandpit with Scobie who was building himself a sand-castle with a broken plantpot. Shug sat behind him, playing with a box of matches. He looked across to the hut as the park keeper came out with a litter-spike and a large bag for the litter. He took off his cap and wiped his sweaty brow. He'd been sitting in his hut for the best part of the morning, drinking tea and listening to the radio, slowly baking away as the sun heated up the hut's tin roof. His son, Wee George, had come by earlier to drop off sandwiches and a large wedge of cake. He thought a brisk walk round the park with the litter spike would soon sharpen his appetite, but he had no intention of doing all the work himself.

'Right, who's gonnae gie's a hon cleanin up this park then?' the park keeper shouted to the kids.

Evelyn knew the routine. 'Me!' she shouted back.

'Me an aw!' shouted Janet.

They ran over to him. Two small boys followed, curiosity getting the better of them.

Scobie was up for it. He turned to Shug. 'He gies ye sweets fir pickin up papers wi a stick.'

'Ah know,' said Shug, uninterested.

The park keeper smiled over at Shug and Scobie, revealing a couple of missing teeth. He handed the kids little home-made pointed sticks for picking up the litter and took off his dusty brown jacket, flinging it over the chair inside the hut.

'There ye go. Noo ye know whit tae dae, don't yis?'

'Aye.' Evelyn and Janet demonstrated by stabbing the grass with the sticks.

The two boys looked puzzled.

The park keeper stabbed at a crisp packet for their benefit. 'Look, like this. An be careful. Nae hittin each other wi em, right?'

The boys nodded and copied him.

'That's the gemme, boays. An when we've cleaned the park up' – he reached into the hut and came out with a large bag of sweets – '*Dah-dah-dah-dahhh!* Bit yis don't git thum if ye don't mek a good joab ay it. The mair papers ye pick up, the mair sweets ye git. Right?'

'Aye,' said Evelyn.

'Right. Okay,' said Janet.

He looked over at Shug and Scobie. 'Whit aboot yir brar an his pal?' he asked Evelyn. 'Dae they no want tae help?'

'Nah, mah brar's twisted.'

'Aye, it's mair sweets fir us, isn't it?' Janet grinned.

Scobie wanted in, badly. 'Moan. Ye comin?'

'Na! Ah'm no pickin up shite.'

'It's no shite, it's jist ice-cream papers.'

They watched as the kids walked off in the distance. Scobie looked between them and Shug; he couldn't decide whether to go or stay. 'It's dead easy . . . moan.'

'He's a dirty auld man.'

'How is he?' Scobie kneeled in the sand, watching the kids.

'Gien oot sweets tae kids. Yir no supposed tae tek sweets affay strangers.'

'He's no a stranger, he's the parkie. Anyway, yir Evelyn aywis teks sweets aff um fir pickin up the rubbish.'

'Aye, an if ah telt mah da he'd kill hur. He'll kill hum an aw fir gien hur them.'

He set fire to Scobie's laces and laughed. Scobie turned round and saw his shoes on fire.

'Aya!' He spun round and quickly put his feet under the sand. 'Shug! Stoapit will ye?'

'Ah'm bored,' sighed Shug. 'Dae ye want a fag?'

'Aye. Huv ye goat wan, like?'

'Aye, ah pinched it aff mah da.' He pulled a crumpled cigarette from out of his sock and looked about the park.

'Yir no gonnae smoke it here, are ye?' asked Scobie.

'Nah.'

'Well where then?'

They both looked about.

'Parkie's hut!' said Scobie.

'He might be in there,' said Shug, his brow furrowing.

'He's no. He's away ower there' – he pointed away in the distance – 'pickin up the rubbish. He'll be away fir ages.'

'Are ye sure?'

'Aye.' Scobie got up. 'Moan.'

They walked along to the hut and stood outside.

'You first,' dared Shug.

'Nah, you. Yir the wan wi the fag.'

'So! Yir the wan who sais he's no in. Oan ye go then . . . shitebag.'

Scobie slowly opened the door and peered inside.

A cigarette burned in the ashtray. A half-finished cup of tea, a flask and a newspaper sat on the battered table.

The park keeper was pissing into a metal bucket in the corner of the hut. He breathed a sigh of relief and scratched his head again.

Scobie sniggered. 'He *is* in there.'

'Whit's he dein?' asked Shug.

'A pish!'

Shug giggled and peered into the hut. Scobie swiftly moved to one side and shoved him in.

The park keeper heard them: he turned round, still peeing. 'Haw you! C'mere!'

Shug about-turned and tried to run out, but before he could make it Scobie, still laughing, shut the hut door on him.

Whack!

Scobie froze as he heard the thud. The door vibrated as Shug's head made contact with the other side. Scobie hadn't expected that. He stood, wondering what to do.

Inside the hut Shug rebounded off the door and landed on the bare wooden floor, dazed.

The park keeper winced – that must have hurt like

hell. Shug looked up at him, scared; blood running from a gash across his forehead.

The park keeper's eyes widened with fear as he saw the blood pouring from Shug's head. He remembered his army training: don't panic. Stem the flow. He reached for his handkerchief and moved across to Shug. 'Jesus Christ, son, hoad oan the noo . . .'

Shug looked at the park keeper's groin and screamed in terror. The park keeper, stopped in his tracks, wondered what was wrong. He followed Shug's field of vision: he still had his cock out. He quickly zipped up his trousers, shook open his hankie and hurried over to try and stop the blood. 'Yir awright, son,' he tried to calm him, 'yir awright.' He pressed the clean white cotton hankie firmly against Shug's head, applying pressure. Shug struggled, thinking the park keeper was trying to lever his head off.

Scobie backed away from the door, laughing nervously. Inside the hut he heard Shug scream.

Suddenly the hut door was wrenched open and a hysterical wild-eyed Shug, with a gash across his head like an open mouth, flew out the doorway and ran at Scobie like a train, splattering him with blood. The park keeper came out of the hut with blood on his hands, holding the red and white hankie. The boys screamed and ran for their lives.

The park keeper stood at the door of the hut, looking at the specks of blood in the grass. He wondered if he should go up to the phone box and call the police or an ambulance. He hoped the boy would be all right. His own boy was about the same age and he hated to think that he could have an accident like that with no one about to help him. He looked across the park. The boys were still running and were already some distance away. He decided to leave it. The next time he saw the wee boy's sister he could always ask after him.

Big mad Hugh walked towards the hut with Shug in tow. Shug's head had been professionally bandaged: a wee trip to the Royal. He pulled the door open. The park keeper sat at the table, reading. He lowered his newspaper and looked at Shug, then at Big Hugh.

'This hum, son?' asked Hugh.

'Aye, that's hum,' said Shug.

Big Hugh pulled an open razor from his back pocket and walked into the hut. Shug stood outside and watched the door slam shut. He pissed in his pants as he heard the park keeper scream in terror.

Shug sat bolt upright in bed; sweating like a pig as the front door slammed. He could hear Jamie running along the hall. He looked at the clock: 16.10. He rubbed his face, sighed and lay back in bed, reaching for his fags. The bedroom door opened and Evelyn stood in the doorway with an incredulous look on her face.

'Haw you! Are you takin the pish oot ay me or whit?' she snarled.

'Whit?'

She pointed a threatening finger at him. 'Ah telt ye tae be oot ay here by the time ah goat hame. Dint ah? Eh? Dae ye want me tae pick up that phone? Dae ye? Cos that's aw it takes – wan phone call an yir history, ya basta.'

He hated it when she lost her rag, she was a total nightmare. 'Aye, aye. Gies a chance, will ye? Mek us a cup ay tea, eh? An ah'll git mah stuff thegether.' He climbed out of bed.

'Y'd better!' She glared at him for a second then turned on her heel and stormed out of the room.

He sat at the kitchen table in his usual seat, smoking, drinking a cup of tea. He was on a comedown from the Eckies and in a right mood for an argument: where the fuck was he supposed to go?

Jamie sat across from him with a huge bag of sweets, ignoring him. Evelyn put a ready-made lasagne in the oven, picked up a cup of tea and a copy of *Chat* magazine from the kitchen table and walked past them on her way to the living-room.

'Moan, son,' she said to Jamie, 'put them away. Yir dinner'll be ready soon.' She looked down at Shug. 'An you, drink up an piss aff!'

'Gies a chance tae wek up, eh?'

'If I wis tae wait fir you tae wek up ah'd be drawin mah pension, ya basta. GIT OOT, AH SAIS!' She stormed out before she lost it completely.

Shug looked at Jamie's sweets. 'Gies wan.'

Jamie glanced at him and continued to eat them.

Shug nodded at the bag.

'Gies a sweet, Wee Man.'

'Na!'

'C'moan, yir ma'll no gies anyhun tae eat . . . jist wan.'

'Na!'

Shug made a grab for the bag. 'Gies wan, ya wee basta.'

'MUM!'

'Awright, awright . . .' He let go. 'Who bought ye aw the sweets, yir ma?'

'Na!'

'Yir gran?'

'Na!'

'Granda?'

'Na!'

'Na! Na! Na!' he mimicked. 'Who then?'

'Archie.'

'Who's Archie?'

'Mah friend.'

'He mist be a gid pal, eh? There aboot a fiver's worth there.'

Jamie put a small jelly snake in front of him. He picked it up and ate it.

'Is he in yir class, this Archie?'

Jamie laughed. 'No. He disnae go tae school; he's too auld.'

'How auld? Is he as auld as me?'

'Aulder.' He popped a sweet in his mouth

'Aulder than me?' he asked suspiciously. 'An he gies ye a big bag ay sweets? Whit fir?'

Jamie shrugged and peered into the bag. Shug stared at the table as the realisation struck him. You didn't have to look far to find them; they could be a neighbour's husband, your uncle . . . even your da. That was how they went about their sick little business: befriended kids, gave them sweets, gained their trust then started touching them up. Told the kids it was their little secret. If the kids cried they used a bit of psychology on them: told them the police would come and they would be taken away from their mammie and daddy, that they wouldn't be a family any more and it would be all their fault. They didn't want that, did they?

Shug had to find out more. He tried speaking to Jamie about it as though he were asking what his favourie film was.

'Hus this Archie . . . er . . . ever touched ye? Y' know.'

Jamie was uninterested. He shrugged again, still eating.

'Wee Man, hus Archie touched ye?'

'Aye,' said Jamie, getting fed up with the questioning, 'he's touched mah hon – he holds mah hon, doesn't he? He's the lollipop man.'

'The lollipop man?'

'Aye, at oor school.'

Now it made sense. In almost every child abuse case

you read about the child was abused by a relative, neighbour, or friend of the family. Shug fought to stop his anger getting the better of him and tried to play it cool.

'Hus he tried tae touch ye anywhere else? Tell me!'

'Na!'

'Hus he ever tried tae kiss ye or anyhun?'

'Aye,' said Jamie nonchalantly, 'he gied us a kiss this mornin.'

'Whit?' The dirty bastard! While they were all happily going about their business the Wee Man was being pawed by some child molester and they couldn't even see what was going on? That's how they operated, these cunts – like thieves in the night. He thought they'd escaped all that, and yet here it was happening all over again. There was no way out: they were everywhere. 'Jamie, son,' Shug asked, 'hus he ever shown ye hus wullie?'

Jamie burst into uncontrollable laughter at the very thought.

In a blind rage Shug threw his cup across the kitchen. It bounced off one of the units and smashed on the draining board. The tea arced in the air for a second as though it were trying to follow the cup, then gave up the chase and splashed all over the floor tiles instead.

Jamie stopped laughing and jumped back in his chair.

Shug leaned over the table, picked him up and shook him violently, spilling the sweets out of the bag.

Jamie started to cry with fear.

'TELL ME,' shouted Shug, 'HUS HE TOUCHED YE? IF HE'S TOUCHED YE AH'LL KILL UM!'

'MUM! MUM!'

Evelyn came racing in and pulled Jamie away. She slapped Shug hard around the face but it had no effect: he barely flinched.

'WHIT IS WRANG WI YOU? WHIT HUV YE DONE TAE UM NOO?'

'Niver mind whit *ah'v* done tae um. Whit's that auld basta bin dein tae um, eh?' He pointed at Jamie. 'Yir supposed tae be hus fuckin ma an ye cannae even keep an eye on yir aen wean.'

'Whit are you talkin aboot? Whit auld basta?'

'That lollipop man!' He indicated over his shoulder with his thumb as though Archie were in the next room.'He's bin touchin up aw the weans. Yir wean as well!'

'Whit?'

She stared at him, open-mouthed. The stupid bastard: away with the budgies. She pulled Jamie closer to her. He held on to her leg and hid behind her.

'Archie is a lovely auld man who wouldnae hurt a fly, niver mind a wean. I don't know whit yir oan, Shug, but if ye don't gie it up, it'll kill ye. It's drivin ye mental.' She picked Jamie up and held him close. 'Jist dae us a favour an leave the noo, eh? Before ye dae any mair damage.'

'Damage?' he sneered. 'Ah'v no even sterted . . .' He went to stroke Jamie's hair as if to say cheerio. Jamie pulled his head away and buried his face into Evelyn's shoulder. Shug scowled at them both and walked out.

Shug bounded down the close stairs, carrying his bags. The close door slammed shut behind him. Evelyn stood at the window, cuddling Jamie, looking down into the street. They watched Shug stride out of the close and set off up the street without a backward glance.

If Scobie had known it was Shug at the door he'd never have let him in. The business in Findlays was enough to convince him the cunt wasn't right in the head. It was all right being stoned out of your nut while they went about winding people up, but in the cold light of day Scobie was starting to realise that the whole thing was getting a bit out of hand. It was too dangerous.

All he wanted was a quiet life. Malkie had pissed off to Liverpool, Chic had his bird and the baby and Scobie had his wee routine – no complications. He came and went as he wanted, with no one to hassle him. He ate when he liked and occasionally he'd meet up with Chic and the boys; but lately the thought of that was becoming less and less appealing. The last person he wanted to see tonight was Shug.

Wee Trish the art student was crashed out in his bed, wrapped up nice and cosy in his king-size duvet, wearing just a pair of skimpy white drawers. She'd appeared about nine, bursting with energy as usual, asking if he could give her enough for a couple of joints as she was going up the Uni. He'd put on a Peter Tosh album and rolled her a couple of skinny spliffs. She was totally hyper as usual, looking through his vinyl collection and talking shite while knocking back the bottle of Newcastle Brown she'd found lying in the fridge. He skinned up a fat little puppy full of skunk and shared it with her. They sat talking about what Glasgow bands they'd seen lately. After a couple of draws she'd got the giggles about Scobie's odd socks and completely forgot about the Uni.

Half an hour later she was into some serious sex. Scobie, being as wasted as he was, and desperate to savour this long-awaited moment, took his time and tried to make it last for ever; God knows when he was going to get another chance like this, he thought. He prolonged it so much she fell asleep on him. He'd woken up to find Trish sprawled out underneath him and Shug hammering on his front door. This threatened to fuck up his night completely. He weighed up the situation: Trish was lying underneath him. A couple of hours had passed and they were now both in a better state to get it on, but there was no way he could with ***'Scobie!'*** being shouted through the letterbox, putting him off.

He wished he'd never answered the door to that bastard, but it was a dead giveaway that Scobie was in. He cursed himself for leaving all the lights on and the album on repeat play. He answered the door and Shug bounded in.

'Bout fuckin time, man, whit kept ye?' He walked into the living-room and sat down on the couch.

'Er, ah wis asleep.'

'Y'll niver guess whit happened tae me.'

'Tell us in the mornin, eh? Ah'm fucked.' Scobie scratched his head. He didn't want to get into it. Besides, he knew it would be an epic story. Nothing normal ever happened to Shug. He handed him a sleeping bag, made his excuses and went back to his bed, cuddling up to Trish. He wrapped his arms around her, wondering what to do about his nutter of a mate.

Things change. People change. He knew they'd grown up together but now it was time to try and sever the ties. His ma always said he was easily led, and Scobie had been led by Shug all his life. He could never win an argument with the bastard either. Shug was right and that was that. It was as if Scobie didn't have an opinion, couldn't think for himself.

He remembered back in school. It was in fourth year, a free period where the class were left to amuse themselves. Shug came in and sat at the other end of the room. He was laughing and joking with some of the others. He looked over at Scobie and started singing 'My Old Man's a Dustman'. The other boys all laughed as if they were in on some sort of joke. Scobie didn't know what they were laughing at until later on when one of the boys told him that Shug was in the town yesterday and saw Scobie's old man sweeping up. Mah da . . . a bickie man? thought Scobie. Nah, he works in a factory . . . somewhere.

He thought it was a load of shite until he realised that

he hadn't seen his old man for months and it could actually be possible. When he asked his ma if it was true she confirmed it. It was half the reason they split up after he was made redundant: she didn't want to be married to a road sweeper.

The singing continued in school until Scobie snapped one day and swung a fist at Shug. The class cheered Scobie on as he got the better of him, slamming his head into a desk. A teacher came and split them up but both Scobie and Shug knew who would have won the fight if the teacher hadn't intervened. They started speaking a few days later and the whole thing was never mentioned again. Shug never apologised. Scobie soon realised that Shug wasn't a mate. No mate does a shitty thing like that to you.

Scobie had always had a good relationship with his old man. At least he had a job, a wage coming in and a bit of dignity. Not like Shug's da – the jakey old cunt.

Scobie cuddled up to Trish, trying to figure out why he ever hung about with Shug. Entertainment, he supposed. Shug would do anything for a dare at school. He was the class clown and Scobie thought it was cool to be his mate. But Shug always took the piss out of him whenever he had an audience. He was a wicked bastard really and had got worse over the years. Scobie thought about some of the stuff that they'd done to people in the past. If Wee Trish knew what a shite he'd been she'd have nothing to do with him. He'd rather have an easy life with a nice bird like Trish – no complications.

He breathed in the clean fresh smell of her hair and looked across at their reflection in the mirrored wardrobe. They looked good together. He could get quite used to having Trish about. It would be a nice change. He disentangled himself from her and lay back, staring at the ceiling. He liked his time of the night, when he'd lie here, stoned, thinking deep thoughts. Dope helped you do that – figure out the answer to the universe. The problem was, he could never find a pen to write it down and an hour later he'd forgotten what it was he'd been thinking about.

He wasn't sure if it was spiritual awakening or just plain old common sense that struck him; something that had evaded him for years, but he knew it was time he made a New Year's resolution. A bit of advice his old man once gave to him was, 'Treat people the way you expect to be treated yourself.' Now he knew why people always treated him like a cunt.

He'd been watching *Oprah* yesterday. She was talking about making a fresh start for the New Year – getting rid of your emotional baggage. Shug was the first bit of baggage he wanted rid of. Scobie knew he'd have to come up with something good by the morning. There was no way he wanted *him* staying over Christmas.

Shug pulled the sleeping bag up, turned on his side and tried to get comfy. He looked about the room, noting the similar décor between this place and Scobie's ma's old tenement next door to Shug's. As a kid he'd spent more time playing there than in his own house.

He looked across to the bathroom; Scobie had left the light on. Shug couldn't be bothered getting up to switch it off, so he lay staring at the light shining through the crack in the door.

He'd left it too long. Now he was sweating – doing the shitty walk. He walked up the close stairs the way Elvis used to walk on stage when he was obese. Leaning forward, arse in the air.

Just a few more stairs. Oooh . . . Turtle's head. Touching cloth. He looked into the living room. His ma was staring out of the window, smoking. He shuffled across to the bathroom and tried the handle. The door was locked.

'Who's that?'

'Da, ah need—'

'Away oot an play.'

'Da, ah need a jobbie . . . *quick*.' He started dancing on the spot.

His ma pulled him away. 'Moan, son, away fae the door.'

'Ah need a jobbie.'

He could hear Evelyn quietly sobbing in the bathroom. He looked up at his ma.

'Yir da's gien Evelyn a bath.'

'Ah'll only be a minute,' said Shug.

'Away an ask Mrs Scobie can ye use her toilet. Tell her

ah'm waitin oan a plumber.' She walked back to the window and stared into space, nervously dragging on a cigarette.

Mah da niver gies me a bath, thought Shug. He walked to the front door.

Evelyn cried again.

Maybe the soap was in her eyes.

Day Five

The minute the news report came on and they mentioned 'William Drake' Evelyn remembered his name from reading about him in the papers. He was a paedophile due to be rehoused. As long as it wasn't anywhere round here, she thought. She reached for the remote and switched over. A cartoon came on instead. There were always people in the news doing horrible crimes to wee kids. She didn't want to know what they did to the child; she could imagine. It was a sick world where humans behaved worse than animals. What on earth would possess someone to use a child for their own short-lived sexual needs, then, as if that weren't the ultimate sin in the face of humanity, take the poor child's life so as to save their own skin and not be caught. She went sick to the pit of her stomach every time she thought about Jamie being snatched off the street by one of these people.

Whenever she read about another case she always said a quick prayer asking that the child didn't suffer, that God would take away any pain from the poor wean.

All this business with Shug suspecting Archie had her thinking. She knew it was a load of rubbish the minute she talked to Jamie about it. She explained to him why Shug was so angry: that he loved Jamie and thought someone was hurting him. She made Jamie promise that he'd tell her if anything ever happened; he wouldn't be taken away, nothing nasty would happen to his mammie and daddy – that was just a horrible story that these bad men made up so they could go on hurting wee girls and boys.

Jamie knew about these people – he'd been told in school, but Archie was his friend and he'd also warned him about bad men and women.

Evelyn satisfied herself that all was well and this was all down to Shug going off the rails. That's what was wrong with him: he'd been brought up in the same mould as his da. People had to be put in wee boxes: Catholic, Protestant, Celtic, Rangers, English, Paki, Chinky, Darkie. Shug was always looking for a cause and, like his da, would only have to look at a newspaper to find one. 'Fuckin English bastards comin up here an tekin oor joabs.' In the past she'd reminded him that half of the Rangers team were English. 'Good players but,' came his reply, his nose buried in the sports section. He had a way of justifying everything: the law according to Shug.

It was all starting to make sense now. It obviously affected Shug more than it did her. It was just another one of those things they never spoke about, even though they both remembered it like it was yesterday. She knew she was as bad as her mother: in denial. So what? It suited her to forget about it – what's done is done. She had enough problems in her daily life without dragging up the past and adding to them.

Jamie wandered in with a bowl of cereal, gave her a smile that said 'morning' and sat next to her on the couch.

She sipped her tea and thought about her ma, how her life had turned out. She had no happiness left any more. The only thing that brought a smile to her face was seeing Jamie. Evelyn knew she should make the effort and take him up to see her more often, but she was busy with work and . . . She knew it was just another excuse – she could work in a wee visit round her shifts; she was only part-time and her ma only lived ten minutes away.

She knew what the problem was: she didn't want to see *him*. Every time she went to see her mum she phoned first and casually brought the conversation round to ask if her da was in or not. If he was out on the pish then he'd be away for hours and Evelyn could visit and be away by the time he got home.

'Ah'v no missed them again, huv ah?' Hugh would ask Irene.

Evelyn felt guilty, but she was only doing what any mother would do: she was protecting her boy. She knew Hugh was a sick old bastard and if she ever caught him with his filthy hands on her son she'd do time for him.

In the past he'd held Jamie as a baby and played with him, but only under her close watch. She remembered only last year feeling sick as Hugh came up behind Jamie and wrapped his arms round him. It brought it all back. Hugh smiled at her, happy to be spending some quality time with his grandson. Evelyn forced a smile. She knew the hug was in all innocence but she wasn't prepared to take the slightest chance. He'd betrayed her trust as a child – he could quite easily do it again.

She sipped her tea, trying to work out when Hugh had last seen them . . . eight months, as long as that? She knew it upset him, especially when he was drunk, but she knew half his upset was remembering what he'd done to her. You can't run away from your head, she thought. She hated to think what horrors were in her da's. There was no forgiving what he'd done, and by keeping Jamie away from him she knew that in some small way she was paying him back. So what? He deserved ten times worse than anything she could ever do to him.

Mick hadn't a clue what had gone on in the past and she saw no reason to fill him in. She didn't want to be seen as damaged goods. They never had a problem with sex. She wasn't a nympho, but she'd been with a couple of guys before Mick.

Andy Clarkston He was one of them. She remembered what a charmer he was when she started seeing him. He had his own business and his own flat. She saw Andy as her escape from her ma's house. She moved in with him and thought she was in love until he started to demand sex all the time. It reminded her of her da.

Andy had some strange ways. He'd make her have a

shower before she got into bed, then another shower after they had sex. Weird. Sometimes, if they did it more than once, she was never out of the bloody shower, and he'd be standing outside, holding his towel, waiting his turn.

All the tins in the cupboard had to have the labels facing the same way and he'd make her sit on a plastic sheet in the car. There was definitely something odd about him.

It wasn't long before the arguments were happening round the clock. Andy started getting violent, grabbing her arm and throwing her down on the couch while he shouted about the tins or other petty rubbish. When she complained that she couldn't live like this he told her to leave. She did, only too gladly. She didn't know whatever happened to Andy but she pitied the poor lassie he ended up with.

Mick was different. He never forced her to do anything. She was the one who had had to drag him off to bed in the end. They'd been going out for two months and he'd only ever kissed her. She justified seducing him, to her pal Angela, as her way of finding out if he was gay or not. She was glad she did – six months later they were engaged.

She was happy she'd ended up with Mick, although they always swore they'd never have any secrets from one another. She knew she was still living a lie, but this was one secret she'd rather keep to herself. She'd managed to switch it off, blot it out like it never happened, as though it were a scary film she'd seen but would avoid if it ever came back on the telly again.

She imagined how upset Mick would be at the thought of her as a wee girl, having to deal with all that. He always smiled at pictures of her as a girl; said he wished he'd known her back then and would have loved to have been her childhood sweetheart. Romantic fool. He always said that if they ever had a little girl he'd want her to be just like Evelyn as a girl. So cute, with her long brown hair in ringlets.

She remembered her ma would spend hours on her hair . . . until Hugh started to interfere with her and that's when all the brushing and putting it up in bunches stopped. Irene let Evelyn's hair grow into a matted mane until it was impossible to get a brush through it. Thinking back, her ma must have been trying to make her little girl less appealing to him. Hugh had always commented about how wee lassies should have long shiny hair. It must have driven him mental when Irene took Evelyn to the hairdresser's and had it all cut off. Now that Evelyn was a women, she realised her ma was only using what she could to hurt him back, even if it meant using the kids.

She looked up at the clock: they'd have to get a move on.

'C'moan, son, turn that aff, ye don't wannae be late on yir laist day, dae ye?'

'Right, ah'm comin.'

He picked up the remote and turned off the TV, lifted

the cereal bowl up to his face and slurped the milk from it. He jumped down off the couch and took the bowl to the kitchen. Evelyn followed him with her cup and put it in the sink. She realised she'd made herself feel depressed thinking about all this – she'd have to put it out of her head. She was damned if she was going to let that stupid brother of hers drag this business up again after all this time. She'd worked hard at putting her past behind her and getting on with her life. She'd had to: there was no such thing as Childline when she was a wee girl.

Shug stood in the swing-park next to the school, drunk and swigging from a bottle of Buckie. He thought about that daft cunt Scobie this morning – couldn't get Shug out of the flat fast enough so's he could be alone with that wee ride of a student. He'd taken Shug to one side in the kitchen and told him he didn't want him staying any more; he wanted to spend more time with his new bird. Said he'd give him a call in a couple of weeks and they could go out for a drink. Shug told him where he could shove his drink. That's mates for you. Birds were ten a penny but mates were mates. He always was a dozy cunt, Scobie. All he needed now was some stupid wee tart telling him what to do. Shug thought he'd give him two weeks, tops, then he'd soon come crawling back.

He looked across to the other side of the road. Evelyn and Jamie were walking down the street in his direction. As they got nearer he turned his head away and slid behind a tree to avoid being seen. A group of school children ran past and lined up at the crossing. He peered round the tree, watching Evelyn speaking to Archie for a minute before moving on.

He watched Jamie and Archie talking. He strained to hear their conversation, but couldn't for the noise of the traffic.

Jamie joined the group of kids at the kerb. He said something cheeky to Archie, which made Archie shake his fist in mock annoyance.

Shug furrowed his brow, tried to lip-read.

Jamie said something else, cheekier still, and laughed.

Shug craned his neck, anxious to hear.

Archie tried to suppress a laugh and act as though he were shocked. He bent down and playfully put Jamie across his knee, pretending to spank him in front of his friends. Jamie and his friends squealed with laughter.

Shug stared ahead, raging. 'Fuck sakes! He's touchin his erse . . . broad daylight! That's shite, that man, fuckin shite!' Somebody had to do something! Archie put Jamie back down and led the kids across the road. Shug turned away again as Jamie passed by, unaware, and walked off to school with the other kids. As Archie turned to cross back over the road Shug stepped out from behind the trees, jumped the railings, pulled out a Stanley and walked up behind him. He was just about to malkie him when a young woman drew up in a car and sounded the horn, attracting Archie's attention. Shug put away the blade and watched Archie give her directions. He decided to leave it. There was a time and a place: a change of tactics was called for, but he'd have to move fast. He jumped the railings, picked up his wine and walked off across the swing-park in search of a phone.

Shug was watching *The Kenny Everett Show* and laughing at this mad wee guy with a beard, dressed up like a woman. Evelyn came in from the kitchen with a cup of tea and placed it down on the coffee table in front of Hugh. She went to sit over by Shug on the couch but Hugh put his leg out, blocking her path.

'Ye no gonnae sit by yir auld man, hen?'

Shug looked across at her. She glanced at Hugh uneasily.

'Ah'm awright ower here, Da.' She pointed to the space next to Shug.

'Twelve years auld an yir too auld tae sit wi yir da awready? That's oot ay order that, Evelyn.'

She nudged his leg away and tried to walk between him and the couch. Hugh leaned forward and gave her arse a playful smack. It stung through the thin cotton dress she was wearing. She gave him a smarmy smile, not letting him know he was getting to her. She sat down next to Shug and watched the TV, aware of Hugh's eyes staring at her. She didn't want to look over at him but couldn't help herself. She wanted to ask him what the hell he thought he was looking at. She hated him.

She glanced over. He was staring at her legs.

She looked away from him, and fixed her gaze on the flowery pattern of her thin white cotton dress. It was short. Too short to be wearing when he was about. She'd forgotten. Her ma would have told her to take it off if she'd been here; said something about the colour, she could see her knickers through it – anything but let her wear it about the house, but her ma was away to work and would be gone for hours. Evelyn had only put it on because it was so hot lately.

'Shug, son, away doon the Paki's an git us some fags.' Big Hugh reached in his pocket and pulled out a fiver.

Shug looked at Evelyn. She glared at him as if to say, 'Don't you dare.'

'Ah'm watchin this,' said Shug.

'Whit ye watchin this crap fir? Away and git us some fags ah sais!'

'Ah'll go,' said Evelyn, eager to get out of the house.

'Naw, darlin, you stay where ye are. Ah want that lazy bastard tae go.'

This was always how it worked. He manipulated Shug into going down the shops. When Shug got back the door was locked. Then Evelyn wouldn't speak to him for days for leaving her alone with that dirty bastard. Well, it wasn't going to happen again, thought Shug: he knew *his* game only too well.

'Ah'm no goin,' said Shug. He looked at Evelyn; they were both aware of the consequences of saying 'no'.

Hugh stood up. 'Did ah fuckin hear you right?' He bounded over, knocking the coffee table with his tea over. He grabbed Shug by the hair and lifted him to his feet. 'Y'll fuckin go if ah huv tae drag ye there masel!'

'Ah'll go wi ye!' said Evelyn, getting up. Hugh pushed her in the chest, knocking her back down on the couch again. The colour drained out of her and she looked up at him with fear etched across her face.

'Yir goin nowhere,' he said. 'He's gonnae git me fags an that's it – end ay story!' He dragged Shug by his hair towards the hall. Shug clung on to the living-room doorframe with tears in his eyes. Evelyn saw the look on his face: pure defiance. A grown man pulling his ten-year-old son out of the door by his hair so he could have sex with his own daughter? This wasn't right. They all knew it. It was time someone made a stand.

Hugh pulled harder on Shug's hair: a clump came away in his hand. Shug yelled out in pain. Hugh grabbed him by the collar of his T-shirt and hauled him through the doorway.

'Da, leave hum! Please?' cried Evelyn.

'You shut yir fuckin mooth an sit doon on that couch! Ah'll deal wi you in a minute.' He flung Shug up the hall. Shug burned his elbows on the threadbare hall carpet as he landed against the front door. Hugh walked up and stood over him, glaring. The look was usually enough to make the wee bastard understand who the man of the house was.

Shug lay on his back, rubbing his sore head. He gritted his teeth and aimed a kick at Hugh's groin. Hugh doubled up as the size five Doc Marten made contact and grabbed his balls in agony. Shug sat up against the front door, waiting, expecting the lights to go out any minute and to wake up in the Royal. He watched Hugh take his hands away from between his legs and put them on his hips as he bent over to get his breath. Shug decided he was as good as dead anyway so he aimed another kick, just to make sure.

'Aya!' Hugh cried out. He grabbed his balls again and kicked Shug up the arse. Shug saw it coming and arched his back, trying to make the kick less painful. Hugh leaned against the wall. It was worth the pain, thought Shug. Now he could leave the house quite safely. Evelyn would be all right. There was no way that bastard could do anything to her with swollen balls. Shug knew the pain and how long it lasted. He'd been kicked in the balls at school a number of times and knew that all you wanted to do was sit with your head between your legs until the pain went away. Even walking was painful for at least half an hour.

Shug got up on his feet and looked at Hugh with his head bowed and his hands resting on his knees. He could hear him taking deep breaths. They all knew what this was about. It had gone on far too long. Shug opened the front door. 'Ah'm goin the polis aboot you – ya dirty cunt!'

Hugh looked up, puzzled. Was he bluffing? 'You go anywhere an ah'll tek yir fuckin heid aff yir shoulders!' They stared each other out while Hugh contemplated his next move. 'Want tae end up in a hame, de ye?' Hugh grinned. He knew that would put any notions of blowing the whistle out of the wee bastard's head. Evelyn slowly approached from the living-room and stood at the doorway, watching anxiously. It was always the threat of the home that scared them. Hugh looked at her worried face, then at Shug. 'Both ay yis? Eh? Cause that's whit happens. Y'll be split up – wan ay yis wi wan family, the other wi somewan else – that's if yir lucky, cause maist ay they weans never git oot the hame till they're grown up.' Hugh watched Shug studying Evelyn's face, knowing there was no way he wanted to be split up from his sister. 'Y'll niver see yir ma again,' said Hugh. He looked at them both.

Stalemate.

'Aye, ah fuckin thought so,' said Hugh. He straightened up and threw the fiver at Shug. 'Noo away an git mah fags.' He turned round to Evelyn. 'An you, mek me another cup ay tea.'

Evelyn was still in her staff uniform making the dinner. It had been a bastard of a day at work and she was still in a stinking mood. Lynne had grassed her and Marie up for the length of time they'd been taking for their breaks and the boss had hauled them both in to the office. He told them the holiday was over and if they didn't get their fingers out they would be for the high jump.

Evelyn took Jamie's fish fingers out of the oven and put them on a plate, contemplating dosing Lynne's tea with laxatives tomorrow. She was a wee shite anyway. 'JAMIE! DINNER!' she shouted.

Jamie sat on the floor in his room, playing with his Power Rangers.

She put the dinner on the table. 'JAMIE! AH SAIS YIR DINNER'S READY!' She listened for a reply: there wasn't one. She lost her temper, threw the tea towel down on the kitchen table and stormed off to the bedroom.

Jamie sat, oblivious, playing with his toys. Evelyn appeared in the doorway.

'Am ah talkin tae masel?'

'Whit?' he asked, still playing with his toys.

'Niver mind whit! Yir dinner's gettin cauld.'

'So?'

'*So!* Git in there an git it eaten!'

He pressed the button on one of his Power Rangers figures: its head changed in a split second from a man into a Power Ranger 'Na.'

'Ah'm gonnae count tae five . . . an if yir no in that kitchen by the time ah dae—'

The front doorbell rang.

'JAMIE! DAE YE WANT ME TAE SKELP YIR ERSE?'

'AH'M NO HUNGRY!' he shouted back angrily. He threw down his toy in defiance and scowled at her: a tantrum was on the cards. She tried to keep her cool.

The doorbell rang again.

'Ye sais that ye wis hungry when ah asked ye.'

'WELL AH'M NO NOO, AM AH!' he growled: a frightening impression of Shug.

She tried to diffuse the situation with a softer approach. 'C'moan son, it's fish fingers an chips: yir favourite.'

He pulled a face as though she had just told him it was a dog turd. 'Fish . . . PISH!'

She lost her cool and marched into the bedroom. She grabbed his wrist, picked him up with one hand and smacked his backside with the other. 'GIT YIR SKINNY WEE ERSE IN THAT KITCHEN AN GIT IT EATEN – NOO!'

She half dragged, half frog marched him into the hall. He started crying and defiantly dug his heels into the carpet. As they got near the front door the doorbell rang again.

'AYE, AYE!' she shouted to the door.

He broke free of her grasp, threw himself dramatically on to the hall floor and started sniffling and sobbing. She opened the door without looking to see who it was: too harassed. She looked down at Jamie, acting like a drama queen. 'GIT UP, YA WEE BASTA!'

'Mrs Donnelly?' came the woman's voice.

'Aye!' Evelyn turned to face the door.

Two women stood in the doorway, surveying the scene in the hall. One was large with a dark, greasy, outgrown perm; quite well dressed. The other stood behind her. Thin with short straw-like hair: possibly one of the prison officers from *Prisoner Cellblock H*.

The larger woman held up her ID. 'Mrs Donnelly, I'm Irene Gribben, this is Jean Paterson. We're social workers. We've been asked to—'

'*Whit?*'

Jean flashed her ID. 'Social Services, Mrs Donnelly. Can we come in, please?'

Evelyn realised how it must look. She was standing shouting at a sobbing child. She tried to put it right. She bent down to pick him up. 'Aw Jamie, son, c'moan an . . .'

Jamie squealed and turned his body away from her, acting as though she were a demon. He got up and ran along the hall, crying, to the safety of his room. Evelyn had her back to the women as she watched him run away. She scrunched her eyes closed and gritted her teeth.

'*Fuck*,' she mouthed silently.

The room was deadly quiet. Evelyn sat nervously smoking on the edge of her two-seater leather couch. The social workers sat on the couch opposite her.

She fidgeted uneasily, licked her finger and tried to remove a food stain from her work skirt. The social workers continued to stare at her: the waiting game.

'Look, ah don't want ye tae get the wrang impression,' said Evelyn, 'Jamie's jist a wee bit tired an crabby, that's aw. He widnae eat his dinner, an ah jist loast the place wi um, that's aw there is tae it. Ah don't hit um, he's no a battered child if that's whit ye think!'

She shakily drew on her cigarette and flicked the ash

into the ashtray, then adjusted the position of the ashtray in a feeble attempt at making the place look tidier. She glanced about. The room was tidy, but she felt like they were zooming in on every speck of dust and coming to the conclusion that she was a terrible mother for allowing her child to live in this pigsty.

The social workers continued to stare. Irene said, 'We realise that it must be difficult for ye, bringin up a child oan yir own' – she indicated Evelyn's uniform – 'havin tae work all day . . .'

'Ah don't work *aw* day,' said Evelyn, a little too defensively. 'Ah droap Jamie aff in the mornin an ah pick um up again when ah finish. Mah shift finishes at hof two. Ah'm niver late fir um. Anyway, who sais that ah'm oan mah aen?' She flicked her ash into the ashtray again and tidied a couple of magazines on the table.

'Mrs Donnelly' – Jean leaned forward – 'we're not trying to say that you can't cope, or that you're a bad mother. It's nothing like that. There's not really any delicate way to put this, but the reason we're here is we received a phone call about Jamie . . .'

'Whit dae ye mean?'

'The person told us that Jamie was being abused and we have to follow any—'

'*Whit?*' Evelyn wasn't sure if she'd heard her properly. Had they the right house?

'Our procedure is that we have to follow up any—'

Evelyn was stunned. 'Abused? Who? Who sais that ah abuse mah wean?'

'Mrs Donnelly! Please, let me finish. It was only a phone call – it's nothing to get excited about. You must appreciate that we have to follow these things through, and we wanted to speak to you about it first.'

Evelyn tried to light another cigarette but the lighter wouldn't work – even after five or six attempts. Frustrated, she threw the cigarette down and started to cry. She was losing it. Her body was starting to shake. Sobbing and frightened, she looked up at them.

They had the power. It could go either way.

Judge and jury.

Their decision. This was wrong – totally wrong.

She lost it: 'Don't tek mah boay. Please, don't tek um. Ah huvnae done anyhun tae um, honest, ah wouldnae hurt um.'

Irene looked at Jean as if to say, 'Here we go again.' She went over and sat next to Evelyn, calmly pulled a cigarette out of the packet and handed it to her. She took out her own lighter and gave Evelyn a light. 'Shhh . . .' She put her arm around her. 'C'moan, hen, nobody's gonnae tek Jamie away. Don't be silly noo. Dae ye want a wee cup ay tea?'

'Aye.' Evelyn dried her eyes and nodded. Always the waitress, she got up to go and make it herself.

'No, no you.' Irene laughed. 'Jean, away in an mek the lassie some tea, eh?' She motioned towards the kitchen.

'Eh?' Jean was a bit slow on the uptake.

Irene fixed her with a stare and darted her eyes towards the kitchen door.

'Oh, right.' Jean took the hint and went to interrogate Jamie.

'Look,' said Irene, 'Evelyn, isn't it?'

Evelyn shakily took a deep breath to calm herself. 'Aye.'

'Evelyn, calm doon and ah'll explain aboot this phone call . . .'

Jamie sat at the kitchen table, quite happily eating his dinner and reading a comic.

Jean came in, looking about the white, tiled kitchen. 'Hiya Jamie, I'm Jean.' She checked there was water in the kettle and switched it on, admiring the expensive cordless model and wondering if it would be appropriate to ask Evelyn where she bought it.

'Mah Auntie Jean?'

'Have you got an Auntie Jean?' She took a good look at the cooker and the tiles behind it: spotless.

'Aye, she stays in Govan. Bit ah'v niver seen hur afore.'

'Never? Why not?'

'Mah mammie sais she's a witch.'

'Oh . . . er, where does your mammie keep the teabags, son?'

He jumped down off the chair and went over to the worktop, took down a container and prised the lid off to reveal the teabags.

'Thanks.' She took them from him. 'Guess where I was today?' She wiped her finger along the worktop then looked at it for signs of dirt. Finding none, she nodded her approval.

'Where?' he asked.

'Your school.'

He shook his head as if to say, 'No you weren't.'

'I was. And I was speaking to your teacher as well.'

'Ah bet ye wisnae. Whit's hur name then?'

'Miss . . . Jackson! I'm right, aren't I?'

'Aye.'

The kettle clicked. Jean put a couple of teabags in the pot sitting next to the kettle and poured in the water.

'She said that you were a good boy in school. That's good, isn't it?'

'Aye.' He climbed back up on his chair and picked up his comic.

'I know someone else's name that you know,' she said, 'and it begins with a . . . A.'

'Who?'

'Archie, the lollipop man.'

'Oh, aye,' he replied, uninterested.

'Is Archie a nice man, Jamie?'

'Aye, he's mah pal.'

She poured herself a cup of tea, took it over to the table, pulled out a chair and sat down beside him.

'Jamie, can you tell me about your pal, Archie?'

Evelyn had stopped crying, but her blood was still boiling.

'So, let's get this straight,' said Irene. 'You think that the person who called us was your brother?'

'Ah *know* it wis ma brar – the sick basta.' She tried to suppress her anger.

'Well, even if we knew the name of the person we widnae be able to tell ye. It's always treated as confidential. In this instance the caller widnae leave a name, and the person who took the call said that they couldnae git much sense oot ay hum.'

'Aye, that'll be Shug awright.'

'And that he seemed a wee bit confused.'

'Confused? Ha!' She drew on her cigarette, 'Mental mair like. Dae ye know where he's goat this stupid idea fae? Jist because auld Archie gied Jamie a bag ay sweets – this is in the middle ay the street, wi me standin there an aw. That's an offence, is it? Noo the auld feller's gonnae git labelled a child molester?'

'Of course no,' said Irene.

Jean came in with the tea. Irene continued with the amateur telepathy by flashing her an 'anything?' look. Jean scrunched up her nose and shook her head.

'Ah mean,' said Evelyn, 'whit kind ay world are we livin in when someone like mah brar kin point the finger at an auld man like Archie an stert a witch hunt?'

Jean laughed at the audacity. 'Evelyn, this isn't a witch hunt, this is as far as it gets.'

'Oh aye, ah bet,' said Evelyn. 'Ah suppose this is how the Orkneys thing sterted, is it?'

Jean stopped laughing. The comment was a bit too close to home.

'Ah'v known Archie for years,' said Evelyn. 'Ah trust

um. Ah'd go so far as tae say ah'd probably trust um wi mah boay's life. He'd dae anyhun fir that boay; there's no way he'd herm um.'

'We know,' said Jean, 'but we just have to make sure. We're sorry if we scared you.'

Irene picked up her bag. 'Whit we dae noo is we go back tae the office an tell oor boss that we've visited you and Jamie, and everything's fine. This jist gets filed as a malicious phone call an that's the end of it. It won't be necessary to contact yir husband.'

'Ah hope no.' Evelyn stubbed out her cigarette. 'Cos if he finds Shug after this . . . he'll kill um.'

Irene and Jean got up and walked into the hall. Evelyn followed and opened the front door for them. Irene pulled out a card. 'If you do get any mair trouble fae your brother, you can reach us at this number. We should be able to help.' She handed it to Evelyn.

'Aye, thanks. Bye.'

They walked out. Evelyn closed the front door. She looked at her hands: shaking like a leaf. 'That's it, Shug! That's fuckin it!' She tore up the card.

Senga McDade waddled in from the kitchen, carrying two coffees and a plate of rolls. The room was full of cigarette smoke. She glanced in the mirror: her roots were beginning to show through her short peroxide hair, which was now looking more yellow than the colour it had been dyed a few weeks ago. She never considered it could be the nicotine that constantly engulfed her. She made a mental note to have her hair done again next week.

'Betty, open wan ay they windaes, will ye,' she said.

Betty hauled herself up off the floor and opened the window. She caught her breath after her exertion and looked out into the street. 'There a young boay hangin aboot oot there. Mebbe it's the boay that phoned.'

Senga was uninterested. 'Aye, mebbe.' She plonked her enormous bulk down in the armchair and stuffed a roll in her mouth.

She was fast becoming a local hero. Her following was growing. New disciples were being indoctrinated daily, almost hourly. With every television appearance and news report her popularity rose.

At the age of forty-four and after two failed marriages, she had finally found her calling: she was to rid the world of paedophiles.

'Put it oan again, eh Senga?' Betty pointed to the video.

'Ach, see you.' Senga laughed, spitting a piece of chopped pork on to her chin.

Betty pressed *play* and the video came on.

'. . . With the release of convicted paedophile, William Drake.'

Drake was part of a Glasgow paedophile ring that had preyed on young boys in the late 1980s. When a boy had been found dead it didn't take the police too long to round up the gang. If they'd rounded them up a bit earlier the little boy would still be alive today.

Resources.

Manpower.

Bullshit.

Drake was now up for parole and due to be rehoused in Drumchapel.

Betty smiled to herself as Senga came on the screen, surrounded by mothers and toddlers waving home-made banners. A reporter shoved a mike under Senga's nose. Betty knew the words off by heart. She mouthed them along with her hero on the TV.

'There is no way that the people ay Drumchapel are gonnae ston fir this! We want that pervert oot! Wherever he moves tae we'll hound him. He'll no be able tae settle. No in Scotland anyway.'

There was a knock on the door.

'Betty,' said Senga.

Betty was in a world of her own. What she would have given for three wishes:

She wished the reporter had asked *her* the questions.

She wished it was *her* whose name had appeared in the *Daily Record*.

She wished it was *her* who'd dreamed up DAP: Drumchapel against Paedophiles.

She could start her own group. Aye, great idea . . .

'Ach . . . Betty?' Senga elbowed herself out of the chair and dragged her bovine frame across to the door. She opened the front door and saw Shug standing in the street, shivering cold.

'Er, Senga McDade?'

'Aye?'

'Ah spoke tae yir pal before oan the phone – ah'm Shug. Ah goat yir number aff a bloke ah met in the pub. Ah hope ye don't mind, like?'

'Oh, aye – moan in, son an git a cuppa tea.'

Mick sat in silence, eating his dinner. He looked across at his da. He'd been shovelling steak pie into his gub for the last ten minutes, without once uttering a sound or looking up from his plate. His thick spiky grey hair moved backwards and forwards as he chewed. Thin, silver-rimmed specs were perched on his nose. His eyes stared through them, never leaving the plate to look up. Mick knew what he was thinking: should have stayed at home and sorted it out with the missus, not come running to his mammie. If only they knew the half of it.

He looked across at his ma.

Frail and timid. She caught his eye and gave him the smile that mothers give their kids when they haven't seen them for a while. He wondered if she was happy or not, now that he was back home for a couple of days. She was usually glad of any conversation. *Silent Witness* didn't have a look-in with the old boy for company. The only time he'd spoken tonight was to say, 'Pass the salt please.'

He was a man of few words, his da, until he had a drink in him, then it was 'The troubles in Ireland this and the troubles in Ireland that.' Mick looked at his da's tattooed forearms: a shamrock, Eire and Celtic. Silly old cunt had never even been to Ireland. They'd been to Majorca – twice. The closest they'd ever been to Ireland was the Isle of Man. He remembered going on holiday as a kid. His da had been in a few pubs in Douglas and suddenly decided to take them on a bus trip to see 'something special'. They went to Port Erin. His da pointed across the sea at Ireland and told Mick, with a tear in his eye and passion in his voice that was where they came from. Mick thought they were looking at Scotland and his da wanted to go home.

His da wasn't a violent man but he'd been in a few scrapes over the years when drink had got the better of him. He always had an opinion which he would defend to the death . . . until someone came up with a better one, then he'd completely change his tune and agree with them instead. He followed the crowd, that was his problem. Unable to form an opinion unless it was tried and tested or steeped in hundreds of years of religious shite.

His da was a bigot, although he refused to believe it. His so-called 'mates' down the bowling club were bigots as well and he couldn't even see it. Cronies, the lot of them. Feeding each other with stories about their arguments with low-life Protestant neighbours who kept parking cars in front of their doors. Crime of the century.

Mick's da had an ongoing vendetta against their next-door neighbours, a quiet young couple called Robert and Alison. Mick got on okay with them and would talk to Robert whenever he came to visit his ma and da. Mick's da hated Robert because he drove a removal van, which, although it was never in front of Mick's da's front door, at certain times of the day would block out the sun and plunge the living-room into complete darkness. His da used to go mental, saying that orange bastard was costing him a fortune in electricity.

The minute Robert and Alison moved in Mick's da had them sussed. 'Protestants,' he sneered.

'How d'ye know?' asked Mick.

'Ah kin tell.'

'Whit, ye sayin: they look like Protestants?'

'Ah seen them oan Sunday, goin tae the other place.'

THE OTHER PLACE was his da's way of saying church. As far as he was concerned Protestants didn't practise religion, not his religion – the *true* religion. Whoever they prayed to wasn't the same God that he did. They could be worshipping the devil in there for all he knew.

By marrying Evelyn Mick knew he'd turned out to be a disappointment to his old man. He'd have had a better reaction if he'd told him he was gay. Mick didn't give a damn: the old bastard could like it or lump it. He knew his da always had high hopes for him, settling down with a nice Catholic girl; 'keeping the bloodline pure' his da called it. Mick said he was a 'fucking Nazi' and told him that's how Hitler started.

'Ye don't know fuck aw, dae ye?' said his da, shaking his head at him.

Mick's da never did come round to the idea of him marrying Evelyn. He did come to the wedding, but only after months of the ma trying to persuade him.

They'd been watching *The Jazz Singer* on TV. Laurence Olivier was playing Neil Diamond's old Jewish da. When Neil Diamond told him he was getting married to a non-Jewish girl the old boy started ripping his clothes – a Jewish sign of mourning. He looked Neil Diamond in the eye and cried that he had no son.

Mick's ma looked across at the da, watching the film, squirming uncomfortably in his armchair. 'Who dis that remind ye ay?' she asked scathingly, getting up to make herself a cup of tea.

'Whit?' He looked at her like she was mad as she walked into the kitchen. She'd made her point though. She left him alone to sit and stew for the rest of the afternoon. He sat and thought, realising he'd been a bit pigheaded. He decided to speak to Mick later and tell him he'd come to the wedding. It wasn't right to bear a grudge. Mick was only a young man and we all make mistakes.

Mick sat picking at his dinner. The sound of his father's knife, scraping off the plate irritated him, went right through him. Why did he have to eat like that?

He looked at his ma and da, sitting eating, gazing at their food. He wished one of them would say something – break the silence. He couldn't take this. He felt himself squirm, almost too embarrassed to speak. But should he speak? Surely it was expected of him? He was the guest.

Maybe his parents just had nothing left to say after thirty years of marriage. Would they appreciate the distraction? Fuck knows, but this silence wasn't right. It was bizarre.

He looked about the room for something to talk about. The old standard lamp in the corner had been there for as long as he could remember. He thought about asking his ma how long she'd had it. His da's fish tank lit up the far wall with an electric blue glow. Its pump whirred away, sending thin jets of bubbles up to the surface that the fish swam through like it was some sort of game. He thought about asking his da about the strange-looking fish with yellow bulging eyes, but decided against it, remembering years ago when the old boy and his ma went to Blackpool for a week. He'd left Mick strict instructions on how to feed the fish. Mick was seeing Donna Brannen at the time and had spent the week shacked up in her flat shagging her silly. He arrived home the day before his ma and da to find only two of the bigger fish left in the tank. He couldn't figure it out until he saw the assortment of fish heads lying at the bottom. The two fish swam past him as if to say, Well, whit did ye expect, leavin us tae starve, ya basta? We hud tae eat somethin! When his da got home and saw what had happened he glared at Mick then punched him on the jaw and stormed out of the room.

Mick looked out of the window, wondering if he should ask about the neighbours, but then realised his old man probably still had a feud going with one or two of them, so he knocked that idea on the head as well. No, silence it was. Much less hassle.

At least it was different in the work's canteen. Everyone had a paper. You had to have one – it was your guard. A couple of times he'd forgotten to buy one on the way to work, only to find he had to make conversation with a complete and utter wanker at lunchtime. He knew better than to get caught out like that again.

There was a procedure you followed: you got your meal, sat at a table, said 'Awright?' to whoever, then opened the paper. You ate your dinner and read it, cover to cover. You could make it last an hour if there was a dick sitting opposite. If the dick spoke to you, you made a big deal of lowering the paper and going 'Whit? Aye,' until he got the message. The only other time you lowered your paper was when someone with half a brain voiced an opinion on what was on telly last night, which supermodel they would most like to shag, or the state of play in the Premier League. Those were the three subjects: nothing else.

He wished he had a paper now. But he knew the old boy would take offence – call him an 'ignirint pig'. He looked about at the décor: hadn't changed in years. A crucifix hung on the wall, a holy picture nearby. The crucifix gave him the willies – reminded him of his mortality: the finality of death. Some people looked forward to it. His gran was a prime example: treated death like an old pal who'd soon be chapping at her door. She'd open it up with a cheery grin: 'Right, son, be wi ye in a minute – I'll jist get mah coat.' Maybe the older you got the less it scared you. He glanced at his da. Sometimes he found himself acting like him lately. He could walk into a room without even knowing what the fuck he went in there for.

He looked down at his meal: hardly touched. Whenever he argued with Evelyn he always lost his appetite. This was nuts: he had to break the silence before he went fucking bananas.

'Ah met Auld Geordie the other day,' said Mick. 'He was in tae see some ay the boays like.' That was his da's starter for ten. The old boy used to like Geordie.

'Oh, aye,' said his da, uninterested, chasing the last of the peas round the plate with his fork.

'Aye,' said Mick, 'he wis askin fir ye . . .'

'Hmm . . .'

Fuck. It was like drawing teeth. He tried again. 'Some boay, Geordie, eh?'

'Good plater. One of the best,' said his da.

It suddenly occurred to him that his da's conversation was nothing like what he did for a living: riveting. He turned to his ma instead.

'So, Ma, ye goat aw yir Christmas shoppin in yet?'

'Aye.'

'Good.' This was going slightly better. There was a pause while she took a deep breath.

'Ah goat Jamie . . . one ay they . . . things – that game oan the telly he wanted . . .'

There was something wrong – something in her voice.

Mick looked at her face. She was welling up. What was all this? She looked up at him from her plate; stared right through him.

'God knows when ah'll see hum, tae gie hum it – the wee sowl.' She started to cry.

Mick felt sick. What was wrong? His da clanged down his knife and fork on his plate.

'Now look whit y've done!'

'Whit? Ah'v no done anyhun! Ma, whit's wrang?'

She pulled a crumpled paper hankie from her sleeve and tried to stem the flow of tears. 'Ah'll never see mah grandson again!' she blurted, getting up and hurrying out of the room.

Imagine that: actress of the year goin to yer ma.

'Oh, fir fuck sakes!' said Mick, pushing his plate away.

His da pointed a finger an inch away from Mick's nose. 'An ye can pack that in fir a stert aff – swearin! Ye didn't use to swear until ye . . .'

Mick shoved his da's finger away. 'Whit? Took up wi that loat? Is that whit ye wis gonnae say?'

'Ah wisnae gonnae say anyhun; ye never listen anyway.'

'Aye, too right. Whit wis the laist pearl ay wisdom ye gimme? When ah telt ye ah wis getting merried? Whit wis it? "Merry that lassie an yir merryin trouble?" '

'Aye, well ah'v bin proved right, haven't ah? Ah bet y've stopped goin tae chapel as well.'

'Aw, fuck aff. Yir as bigoted as the rest of them doon there!'

'Whit huv ah telt you aboot yir language in this hoose?'

'Well next time yir tekin confessions, "yir eminence", gies a shout, eh? Ah'll bring mah fuckin rosaries. Ah'm goin oot.' He got up and walked out of the room, slamming the door behind him.

He went to take his jacket off the hook in the hall. Upstairs he could hear his ma sobbing. He wanted to go up, put his arm round her, tell her she was over-reacting and that things were going to be fine between him and Evelyn, and that this wasn't the start of a separation. It was just a daft argument that had got out of hand. But the old boy would hear them and be up the stairs like a shot, shouting and bawling; it'd only make things worse. Mick thought it best to leave it. Let them calm down. He decided to go up to the Glass-house, his old local. It was only a ten-minute walk from here. He'd have a couple of pints and maybe meet up with a few old mates. He took his jacket off the hook and slung it on. The lining tore again as he put his arm in the sleeve. 'Ah, fuck it!'

Shug sat in the car, waiting. He looked across the dark car park as something glinted in the distance: a passing car headlight reflected off a roadsign.

The trip to Senga's hadn't entirely been a waste of time. It wasn't as if Senga was unsympathetic to his cause, just a bit wary.

A couple of months back, a young woman visited

Senga, saying her uncle used to touch her up when she was little.

'Right, Betty.' Senga put on her coat and sprang into action.

Betty knew the drill. She rounded up the group and they were round there in no time.

Banners were waved.

Stones thrown.

Windows smashed.

Police called.

Press called.

Pervert named.

Big mistake.

The poor man was innocent. After lengthy questioning the young woman had no choice but to come clean. The uncle had simply owed her mother money and had no intention of paying it back. She'd decided to teach the uncle a lesson he wouldn't forget in a hurry. The local vigilantes were hot news and they could brew up a nasty storm for him.

The uncle was never charged. The young woman was. But the papers had already jumped on the nonce bandwagon and named him as a molester – big-time. When his name was cleared they couldn't be bothered to print a retraction.

Mud sticks.

Welcome to Drumchapel: twinned with Salem.

Shug had spent the afternoon trying his best to paint a nasty picture of evil Archie, but Senga was being cautious. She didn't want to end up with egg on her face a second time, so she suggested going through the proper channels. She phoned the school: closed for the Christmas holidays. She phoned the council: their Christmas holidays had started way back in November, so all she got was a recorded message and some jingle-bells.

Betty was tempted to get out the burning torches and have Shug lead the way. Senga told her to back off – she would review the situation in a couple of weeks. The kids would be quite safe over the Christmas holidays. They wouldn't be coming into contact with the old pervert.

Betty kept up the act as she walked to the front door with Shug; making sure Senga's living-room door was closed before she showed Shug her true colours.

He looked across the car park again as he started to make out Betty's shape in the dark. Here she was, right on time. A gang of people followed close behind. No Senga.

Archie stood at the stove, stirring a pot of soup. He walked over to the worktop and turned on the radio.

A brick came flying through the window, knocking the pot off the stove and splashing him with scalding hot soup.

'Jesus Christ!' He ran his hand under the cold tap and looked at the broken kitchen window. The wee bastards – what were they up to now? He lifted up the blinds to see if he could see them. That was strange: no kids. An angry mob had gathered outside his house. A man was pointing at him.

'There he is noo!'

Somebody threw another brick. Archie ducked for cover as the blinds took the brunt of it. He ran into the hall and picked up the phone. He dialled 999 as more bricks came smashing through the window.

'Police please!' he shouted as he cowered under the stairs.

Betty stood across the road from Archie's house, leading the angry mob of mothers, children and irate-looking men in a chant.

'OOT, OOT, OOT, CHILD MOLESTERS OOT! OOT, OOT, OOT, CHILD MOLESTERS OOT!' A group of mothers waved banners.

A young bloke with cross-eyes and an expression like a startled gerbil lit a Molotov cocktail and flung it towards the window: it landed on the roof and burst into flames. The burning petrol ran down the slates and into the plastic guttering, melting it in seconds.

Round the back of the house, Shug stood on a wheelie bin and reached up for the phone wire that went from the telegraph pole into Archie's house. He looked up as the burning petrol ran down the slates. Dozy cunt, he thought. Fuckin miles aff. He pulled out his Stanley and cut through Archie's phone wire, then slunk back into the shadows to observe the fun as the shouting, banner-waving crowd moved closer to the house.

Mick was heading to the Glasshouse when he heard a window smashing and a cheer go up. He walked to the end of the street and looked over to see what the noise was about. Someone's front bedroom window had been put in. A crowd stood watching – doing nothing about it. There could be weans in there, thought Mick. What's going on? He hurried down the street, towards the crowd. A thin young woman with ginger hair pulled severely back into a ponytail was holding a little girl by the hand. They stood at the top of the road, watching. Mick went over to her.

'Whit's happenin?' he asked.

'Wanna they paedophiles hus moved in tae that hoose doon there. Ah'm no huvin the likes of that stayin roon here – ah'v goat a wee lassie tae think about.' She pulled the little girl closer to her.

Mick looked across at the house being targeted. There was something familiar about it. 'Ah know a bloke who stays in wan ay they hooses – Archie, a lollipop man.'

'Aye, that's hum,' she said, 'the lollipop man – he's the pervert.'

'He's no a pervert,' said Mick. 'Fir fuck sakes!'

He pushed past the angry crowd outside the house, lifted up the letterbox and looked inside. 'Archie? Archie, are ye there?' His eyes readjusted to the dark: he could just make out Archie, sitting huddled under the stairs, frightened.

'Archie, it's Mick!' he shouted. 'Mick Donnelly. Wee Jamie's da – it's awright!'

Shug glowered as he watched Mick. What was that interfering cunt doing now? His ears pricked up as he heard the police siren and he started moving to the safety of the back of the crowd.

Mick could hear the siren getting closer. 'Archie, the polis are comin – it's gonnae be awright, man. Jist sit tight!'

Senga wid be proud ay me, thought Betty as two pandas and a van came screeching round the corner. The van stopped half across the road, in front of Archie's place. A craggy-faced sergeant slowly got out of the car, put his cap on and walked over to her, while surveying the damage to Archie's window. His back-up got out of the van and started to move the crowd away.

'All right, Betty, whit's goin on?' the sergeant asked wearily.

Betty sniffed and adjusted her coat. 'Whit dae ye think? We're protectin the community.'

'Yir makin an erse ay yirsel. Has Senga put ye up to this?'

'Senga's goat nuthin tae dae wi it!'

He looked across to the house. 'Drake doesn't live there, ye know?'

'Ah know that – ah dae check ma facts. Archie Prentice, lollipop man, he's a paedophile.'

'An ye know that to be a fact, dae ye?'

'Aye.'

The mothers and toddlers stood on the other side of the road, trying to make out what Betty was saying to him. She turned and glanced at them. At least some people could see sense. All she needed now was the press; where the hell were they? They were missing all this.

The sergeant watched his officers as they tried to more away the crowd. 'An where did ye get this info fae?' he asked.

'A reliable source,' said Betty smugly. She'd seen someone say that on a film once. She looked up at the sergeant, awaiting his next question. If she spun this out long enough the cameras were sure to arrive. She looked about to see where they were. They always arrived on time for Senga.

Mick looked about the Glasshouse. Some atmosphere: there was more life in a jakey's string vest. A couple of guys played darts, another bunch were getting into the dominoes. Two old boys on the next table were playing cards; Mick was sure one of them had nodded off while looking at his hand. Still, it was safe here, not the kind of place you'd expect to get glassed in, despite its name. Archie had calmed down. He finished his whisky and placed the glass back down on the wine-stained table.

'Ah jist cannae understoan it,' he said. 'Why wid anyone want tae dae such a thing?'

Mick took a swallow of his pint and shook his head. 'We live in sick times, Archie. The whole world's gone mad . . . Anyway, it's mah roond – anothir Grouse?'

'No, ah'd better no, ah'd better be aff.' He looked at his watch. 'It's gettin late.'

'Ye don't huv tae git up fir yir work, dae ye?'

'Oh aye, that's right' said Archie. 'Two weeks ah'm aff fir; how could ye forget that.'

Maybe the old boy was tired, thought Mick. It had been a long night. 'Listen, if ye want tae git aff ah'll come hame wi ye – mek sure ye git hame awright.'

Archie waved his hand, the way old boys do after they've had a couple and they're not scared of anybody. 'Yir awright, son. The polis said they're gonnae keep an eye on the place anyway.'

'Aye, but ye niver know.'

'Ah'll be awright.'

'Well if ye change yir mind . . .' He pointed to Archie's empty glass. 'Same again?'

'Aye. Thanks, son.'

It was way past closing time. Archie and Mick came out of the pub into the crisp night air. Archie wrapped his scarf around his neck and fastened his jacket, the whisky keeping him warmer than any winter coat could.

Mick decided to jump a taxi to the Halfway and see if he could get a lock in. He fancied a good swallay to settle his nerves after all that carry-on tonight. He'd offered to drop Archie off, but Archie wouldn't have it, said it was taking Mick out of his way and he could get a taxi himself.

They waved goodnight and set off in opposite directions. Mick turned round. 'An don't forget that taxi!'

Archie gave him the thumbs-up, but had no intention

of getting one; a five or ten-minute walk, that's all it was; besides, the fresh air would do him good.

The lights went off in the pub.

Archie walked about ten yards then realised he needed a slash. He turned to go back to the pub but saw that it was in darkness.

He trudged off into a nearby alleyway, pulled down his fly and breathed a sigh of relief. It was then he heard the footsteps approaching.

'Haw you!'

Day Six

Old Mrs McFarland led Coco past the duck pond. He stopped and watched as the ducks slipped about on the ice. She pulled on the lead; Coco followed her, through the gate and into the park. She let him off the lead and he ran into some bushes. Moments later Coco came out with a scarf covered in blood, ran over to her and proudly dropped it at her feet, then ran back into the bushes again. She picked up the scarf and followed him.

The doctor walked along the corridor, reading from a clipboard. He'd be glad to get out of here: just one more hour and he'd be off. A young junior doctor, about to start his shift, followed him, pulling on his white jacket.

'Just the usual wankers starting the festivities early,' said the doctor. He opened the door of the room and ushered the junior doctor inside. 'And this poor old bastard. Keep an eye on him tonight, will you. Brought in this morning, critical, serious head injuries.'

'Whit happened?'

'We don't know for sure. Attacked by someone in a park? Maybe a gang.' He consulted his notes. 'Blood/alcohol high. In shock, continually drifting in and out of consciousness, some internal bleeding, numerous lacerations to the body, mainly on hands and arms. Fending off an assault from a knife, it looks like – lost quite a lot of blood. You know the score: next twenty-four hours are the most crucial. I'm waiting on the results of a scan to determine if the blows to the head have done any permanent damage.'

'Muggers – bastards.'

'Hmm, maybe.' He flipped over the page. 'Hypothermic too – temperature's up now though . . . Oh, yeah, surgery: had to remove the genitals, what was left of them – badly mutilated.'

'Fir fuck sakes!'

The doctor tapped the junior on the chest with the clipboard. The junior took it off him.

'That's not all,' said the doctor, raising his eyebrows. 'I can't be absolutely sure' – he looked about, making sure they weren't being observed – 'but the lacerations on the chest actually look like a word.'

'A word? Whit word?'

The doctor pulled back the dressing on Archie's chest. The junior leaned forward to get a better look. He felt the vomit rise in his throat as he made out the word ***BEAST.***

Day Seven: Christmas Eve

Shug sat on the back seat of the top deck of the bus, fiddling about, pulling stuff out of a carrier bag. He took out a hypodermic syringe, a needle and a packet of joke fake blood capsules. He emptied the capsules into a small bottle of mineral water, shook it and filled the syringe with the dark red water before putting it back in the bag.

He got off the bus, made his way across the road, dodging the traffic, and peered through the window of the chemist shop.

A high counter and a metal grille covered the dispensary: the owners occasionally expected trouble. The pharmacist stood at the counter, serving a small elderly woman who was dwarfed by the old cast-off fur coat she was wearing. Shug walked into the shop and looked about the shelves. The pharmacist gave the old woman her change. She slowly counted it before putting it in her purse. She picked up her prescription off the counter, turned round and shuffled past Shug and out of the shop. Shug approached the counter.

The middle-aged pharmacist smiled at him: slicked-back hair and a Colgate smile. 'Yes?'

'Huv ye got anyhun fir AIDS?' asked Shug.

'What?' The smile soon dropped.

'Aye, ah'v got AIDS an ah cannae git tae sleep at night fir aw the worry an na, no?'

The pharmacist wasn't sure how to play this one. If it was a joke it wasn't a funny one. 'Has your doctor or the hospital prescribed anything for you?' he asked.

'Aye, Tamazepam.'

'Have you got your prescription?'

'Aye, here it's.' Shug pulled the syringe out of the bag.

The pharmacist was horrified. He took a nervous deep breath, crept uneasily along the counter and pressed an alarm button, hoping help would soon be on its way.

Shug moved closer to him, threateningly. 'The doctor sais ah kin huv as many as ah like; an he sais that if ye don't gies em, ah kin stick this in ye.'

'Look, we don't actually stock a lot of Tam—'

'Don't gies it, eh?' He threw the carrier bag at him. 'Fill the bag or y'll get mah virus, ya basta.' He came nearer with the syringe.

The pharmacist started to panic. 'Okay! Okay, I don't want any trouble, hang on . . .' He quickly unlocked a cabinet and began taking plastic containers out, putting them in the bag. When the shelf was empty he lifted the bag on to the counter and backed off.

'Thanks very much!' Shug snatched it off the counter. 'Very kind ay ye!'

The pharmacist breathed a sigh of relief as Shug made to leave the shop.

'Oh, by the way, pal' – Shug turned round and pointed the syringe at him – 'Happy Christmas.'

He squirted the fake blood all over his face and white coat; the pharmacist froze, horrified. Shug laughed, watching his expression changing to a mixture of fear and anger. Suddenly the guy roared, picked up a cosh from behind the counter and charged after him.

'*Fuck!*' He'd overstayed his welcome. Shug made a run for the door but the pharmacist caught up with him and hit him hard across the back with the cosh. Shug let out a cry, spun round and plunged the needle into the pharmacist's arm. As the pharmacist screamed with terror Shug pushed him away from the door and ran out of the shop.

Moments later a police car pulled up. The dazed-looking pharmacist came out of the shop and wandered about, thinking what the hell he was going to tell his wife when he got home: went to work with a packed lunch, came back with a death sentence? Two policemen leaped out of the car. The larger of the two chased after Shug; the other clocked the blood and the syringe lying on the ground. He stayed with the pharmacist, not wanting to get too close.

Evelyn and Jamie were in the Disney Store. On a large video screen Jiminy Cricket was looking up at a twinkling wintry sky, singing 'When You Wish Upon a Star'. The staff grinned inanely at Evelyn every time she caught their eye. She wondered if these kids had been sheltered from the real world – if they'd managed to breeze through life without coming into contact with drugs, alcoholism and child abuse. Maybe they'd had the same kind of life as her and Shug but hid it behind a permanent smile?

She looked at her watch and picked up her shopping bags. 'C'moan you, we'd better move it if we're gonnae catch that bus.' They walked out of the shop and into the mall. 'We've still tae git yir da's yet.'

'Whit'll we git um?' asked Jamie.

She looked over to Boots the Chemist. 'Er . . . after-shave. Moan in here a wee minute.'

They entered the shop and went over to the gents fragrance counter. She started sniffing the aftershaves, squirting Jamie with a tester and trying to smell him. He pulled a face and tried to wipe it off.

'Don't ye like that wan?' she asked.

'Na!' He spat on the floor.

'Jamie! Stoap that.' She looked about to see if anyone had seen him. Kids, you couldn't take them anywhere – what a showing up. 'D'ye think yir da'll like this? Smell.' She held a tester under his nose.

Jamie sniffed at the tester. 'No bad . . . Mum?'

'Whit?'

'Is mah da comin back?'

'Aye, he's comin fir hus Christmas dinner th' morra.'

'Aye, ah know. But is he comin back fir good?'

'Aye.' She held two aftershaves up. 'Which wan?'

He pointed to the blue one. 'Is Uncle Shug comin back?'

'No.'

'Whit? Never? Where's he gonnae live?'

'Jamie, son, don't you worry about yir Uncle Shug – he'll be awright.' She handed a bottle of aftershave to the consultant. 'This wan please.'

Evelyn looked through the rain-soaked window of the bus. Jamie sat beside her, his eyes closing with tiredness. She looked down at him as he yawned.

'Whit dae ye want fir yir dinner?'

'Dunno . . . anyhun.'

'Anyhun? You?'

'Aye?'

'Yir a fussy wee bugger, y'll no eat anyhun ah gie ye. Whit dae ye want?'

'Anyhun, ah sais!'

'Fried squirrel?'

'Aye.' He smiled.

'A badger's bum?'

He looked up at her, grinning. 'Aye, wi chips.'

She looked out of the window and gathered her carrier bags together. 'Next stop's oors.'

He jumped on to the seat opposite, wiped the window and looked out.

'Whit are ye dien?' she asked.

'Ah'm gonnae gie Archie a wave when we get tae the crossin.'

'He'll no be there, son, he's aff fir Christmas. Moan.' She got up. 'This is oor stoap.'

Shug sat in a booth in the dingy café, drumming his hands on the table in time with the jukebox. He'd given the polis the slip and left him coughing and wheezing somewhere near Curry's. The fat cunt couldn't catch a cold. A waitress came over, carrying two slices of buttered bread on a plate and put it down in front of him.

A skinhead walked into the café. Shug knew him as Woody. He held the door open for his mate who had an Oasis haircut. Someone must have kidded the guy on he looked like Liam Gallagher and he believed them. 'Liam' stoated off the doorframe as he came in, out of his tree. He was wearing head-to-toe Adidas: the traditional dress of the shoplifter. Woody spotted Shug and walked over to him. Liam followed.

Shug looked up. 'Awright, boays!'

The guys sat down at the table. Shug handed Liam the carrier bag. He delved in and pulled out a couple of the Tamazepam containers, ripped the plastic seal off one and checked the jellies. Satisfied with the goods, he nodded to Woody who pulled out a wad of money and handed it to Shug.

'Nice wan, Shug.' Woody got up to leave. 'See ye.'

Liam put the carrier bag into a holdall, winked at Shug, and gave him a high five. The guys went towards the door.

Shug poured sugar over the bread 'Aye! See yis, boays,' he shouted after them. 'Happy Christmas an'a.' They walked out of the café. 'Ya pair a dicks.'

He sat nodding in time with the dance track playing on the jukebox as he ate his magic piece.

Jamie was asleep in bed. His Christmas stocking hung nearby. Lisa Stansfield's 'All Woman' drifted in from the living-room. It was one of Evelyn's favourite songs. The first time Mick heard it he said it reminded him of her.

She took offence, saying, 'Who's no a lady?'

He shook his head, saying, 'Naw, naw, ah didnae mean it like that.'

'So yir sayin ah'm scum?' she said, folding her arms and turning away from him.

There was no winning with women. He told her she had it all wrong. He was glad she wasn't one of these posh birds – just normal working class. It was nothing to be ashamed of. He was glad they were who they were. He told her to remember that: 'Yir aw woman,' he said, taking her face in his hands and kissing her gently on the lips. That was the closest thing to a compliment from Mick Donnelly.

She hoped romance was in the air tonight. The room was lit by just a couple of candles flickering on a table set for two. She came in from the bedroom, looking beautiful but a bit harassed struggling with the new shoes she'd got in the Frasers sale along with her new black sequined dress. She stood in front of the mirror, admiring herself, secretly chuffed at the thought of Angela's boyfriend having to pay fifty quid for the same dress last week. Evelyn couldn't believe her luck today when she saw it had been reduced to twenty-five. She knew the Frasers sale always started around Christmas Eve. She smiled to herself, hoping Angela's arse looked massive in it. It served her right. She'd seen it first. She leaned forward in the mirror and put on her lipstick, pressing her lips together and wiping the corner of her mouth.

The front doorbell rang. She straightened out the front of her dress and went to answer it. As she opened the door all she could see was a mass of Christmas paper and the top of Mick's head.

The presents lowered. He stood smiling at her, dressed smartly, grinning from ear to ear.

'HO HO HO!'

'Where's yir key?' she asked.

'Ah'v only goat wan pair ay hons!'

'Sshh! He's asleep.' She stood to one side to let him in. He kissed her on the cheek.

'Ah'v missed hum. Ah'm away intea see um.'

'Don't wek um up. We'll niver git um back tae sleep if he knows yir here.'

He dumped the presents under the Christmas tree in the corner of the room, sliding them along the pine needles that had fallen from its branches. He took off his coat, watching the tiny white tree lights as they slowly blinked in sequence. He loved this time of the year.

Evelyn came over and looked down at the pile. 'Bliddy hell, Mick, whit huv ye bought um? The full shoap?'

'Ach, ye know, a PlayStation, Scalextric, aw that stuff. It's no aw hus but, there's somehun there fir you.'

'Where?'

'These wans.' He pulled out two presents. 'But ye cannae open um till th' morra, right?'

She put her hands on his waist and nuzzled his neck, trying to get round him.

'Aw, Mick, jist wan, eh? The wee'est wan? Please?'

'Oh awright, er . . . here, this wan . . . Happy Christmas.' He kissed her.

'Thanks. Dae ye want yir present the noo?'

'That depends oan whit it is,' he said with a glint in his eye.

'Ha, ha, very funny. Away in an see yir son.' She looked at the present and shook it.

Mick walked into Jamie's room and knelt at the side of the bed. He looked at him for a second, smiled and kissed him on the cheek. 'Happy Christmas, Wee Man.'

Jamie half opened his eyes. 'Da?'

'Hiya, pal.' He stroked his hair. 'You go back tae sleep. Yir da'll be here in the mornin.'

'Ye promise?' Jamie asked, his eyes closing.

'Aye, ah promise. Ah'll no be leavin ye again, son.'

'Da? See that dug doon th' stair? Jacko.'

'Aye.'

'He widnae let me huv a shot ay hus bike.'

'Would he no, son?' Mick stifled a laugh. 'Niver mind . . . shhh, go tae sleep.' He watched for a moment as Jamie drifted off to sleep. Mick stood up, smiling to himself. 'A dug on a bike? Kids, man, yis dinnae hof talk some shite.'

Nobody understood why Irene stayed with him – even her own family. At times she never knew herself. He was a bastard, a horrible, horrible bastard and she hated him.

He was never like that when she started going out with him, or when they first got married. But she didn't know what lay ahead then: the drink – what it could do to you, get you in its grip. Lately she was beginning to find out. She was becoming like him and she knew it. She'd have half-bottles of vodka planked about the house, places where she knew he'd never look. She needed a couple of stiff voddies before he came home from the pub so she could deal with his crap. If you can't beat them join them, she thought. He never noticed. How could he when he was three sheets to the wind? She could be staggering round the kitchen, steaming, trying to get his dinner ready and burning it in the process but he was never any the wiser.

Last night was the final straw. She'd said it a million times before, but she meant it this time. She thought she'd been dreaming: suffocating; someone was attacking her. She was at the stage where you wake up and let out a warbled cry that comes from deep within. The sound that you hear frightens the life out of you – sounds like someone else's voice, but you realise it's you and it was just a dream, as real as it seemed. Tonight was real. Tonight she woke up choking on food, with a hand round her throat, pushing her into the pillow.

'Ya fuckin rat! Tryin tae poison me noo, are ye? Well *you* fuckin eat it – go oan, ya cunt, eat it!' he screamed.

She could smell the drink, the BO, the stench of his breath – like cowshit. She tried to get up, get her own breath, but he was sitting on top of her, holding her down. The food was slipping down her throat and she was gagging. Every intake of air pulled the food further down her throat. She had to do something. God knows where she got the strength, but she punched him as hard as she could in the face. It was more surprise than anything that caused him to fall backwards. A blow like that coming out of the semi-darkness could have that effect on you.

He reeled along the bottom of the bed and fell off it with a heavy thump. She saw her chance: she had to get out of the house. She knew what was coming next if he got up. She could hear him moving. She jumped out of bed and spat the food on the floor, coughing it up. She looked down at it: sausages. She knew where from too – the fridge. They'd been there for five days. That's when food had last passed his lips. It was always the same when he was on a bender: wouldn't eat, but wouldn't let her throw anything out either. He'd eat when he was hungry, he told her. Four days later he feels peckish and wonders why the sausages are blue-moulded. Alkie logic: someone's trying to poison him.

'Ya fuckin wee rat ye! Surprise merchant, eh?' His head popped up from the bottom of the bed and his eyes narrowed as they focused on her. She shot out of the room, closing the door behind her and dragging the clothes basket in front of the door. She skidded down the stair carpet on slippery heels, landing on her arse a couple of times. She swung round the banister and made for the front door. As she opened it the icy blast hit her. She looked down – she was only wearing her nightie.

'Cunt!' came the roar from upstairs. Then the banging as he tried to get the bedroom door open with his feet still behind it.

She grabbed her coat and fled into the cold night air, leaving the front door open. She ran up the road, feeling the soles of her feet sticking to the ice: it felt like someone was pulling sticky packing tape off them, but they were already too numb to feel any pain.

'IRENE!' he bellowed from the house. 'IRENE, YA FUCKER! GET BACK HERE!'

She ducked down behind a car. She was a good twenty yards away from him. She wrapped her coat round her and breathed her hot breath into it so it wouldn't give her away if he looked up the street. She shuffled on her knees, in the ice, peering round the front of the car. He was walking down the path. He stood at the gate and looked about for her. She looked about too: the street was deserted. It must have been two in the morning and not a soul in sight. Just as well; the neighbours would be getting a real show tonight. Not that it would be the first time . . . she reminded herself that this was definitely the last.

'Irene, come on, git in here – it's freezin.' The shouting had stopped. The tone of his voice suggested that she saw sense and stopped messing about. She huddled the coat round her and watched him wander up the path then stop and look about. He was bending down. What the hell was he doing? She watched as he leaned into one of his rose bushes, snapped off a dead twig and threw it away. The mad bastard. She's out here freezing her tits off and he's pruning the fucking roses! She pictured herself telling Audrey that one over the cup of tea she hoped to get when the coast was clear.

Audrey had heard it all over the years and hadn't once refused her a bed. Irene knew she'd be more than welcome over Christmas. She remembered she had no money. No problem, she'd reverse-call Audrey from the phone box outside the Paki's. Tom would come round and pick her up. He'd have the heater on full and a couple of daft jokes to try and cheer her up. He never asked questions, Tom. A big quiet man. They were a lovely couple. How did Audrey get to be that happy? Luck of the draw?

'WELL, FUCK YE THEN; FREEZE, YA RAT. SEE IF AH CARE!' he shouted up the street, then looked down it in case she was down there instead and he'd been shouting in the wrong direction.

She watched him stagger back up the path and slam the front door. It didn't close properly and slowly creaked open again. She instinctively went to get up to go over and close it: they could get robbed during the night. Fuck it, she thought. Fuck him, his house, his roses, his shitty life. She'd had enough.

She looked about the street: Christmas Eve – again. It had no special meaning these days. It used to be great when the kids were young, but now Evelyn was married she hardly came round any more. You couldn't blame her. Shug was hardly in either: did his own thing these days – young guys were like that. The season of goodwill? she thought. It was a time of dread. She hated it.

She looked across at her house. She'd been meaning to change the curtains and blinds for Christmas, but with one thing and another she hadn't got round to doing it. Her neighbours always envied her blinds – asked her where she got them. She always kidded on she paid top dollar for them, but really she got Audrey to make them. She'd buy the material herself and get Audrey to copy a design from a magazine. She was clever like that, Audrey, and she hardly charged Irene a penny. A good friend. The blinds meant nothing now; they could rot along with that horrible bastard in his fucking pigsty he called 'hame'. She knew the house always looked a picture of tranquillity from the outside. It was just a front for the neighbours. Nice windows, but inside it was the house of madness. Well, she was leaving it before she went as insane as him.

She pulled herself up and tried to walk. She heard the ice snapping beneath her feet, then looked down and saw the blood and skin on the pavement. She went to lift the sole of her foot up and look at it but decided against it: she could imagine. She just hoped she could get to Audrey's before her blood heated up and she started to feel the pain.

She heard a car and looked up: a taxi was dropping off its hire at the bottom of the street. She watched in hope as it drove towards her. Audrey could pay it and she'd pay her back when she got her social through. Irene stuck out her hand, praying the taxi driver didn't have another hire to go to. It pulled up and the door opened.

'Where ye goin, hen?'

'Fourteen Elmbank Crescent.'

'Oh, aye, ah know it. Meter an a hof tonight, you know.'

'Hmm?' She shivered.

'Meter an a hof, cos ay Christmas an a.'

'Oh, aye . . . aye, ah know. It's awright.'

She got in and wrapped the coat around her. She sensed him looking at her bare legs, her feet. He reached out and turned the heater on full blast.

'Cold wan th' night, eh?' he said as he pulled away. The car drove along, crackling on the ice.

'Aye, freezin.' She shuddered and looked out of the window. Her nose started running as the heat began to hit her. She felt the tears streaming down her face. She wasn't sad, she was happy. Maybe it was the relief. She didn't know what she was – she didn't care any more. She wiped her eyes and looked at a house at the top of the street as the taxi slowed to turn the corner. 'Happy Christmas' was stencilled on the window in fake snow. She was determined this year would be. She more than deserved it.

Day Eight: Christmas Day

It had been a nice night. Things looked like they were back to normal.

Sex had often been the cause of arguments between them, mainly instigated by Mick. He usually complained he didn't get it as often as he used to. Evelyn's argument was she never used to: have to go to work, keep a house, cook meals and raise a son like in the 'good old days' Mick was always on about.

Last night was different. Three times, thought Mick. Fuckin marathon.

It was good to be married. There was something righteous about making love with the missus. Comfortable. Safe. You didn't have to pretend. Of course being married had its problems, so does everything, but at least he didn't have to play the 'Game' . . . out there in the clubs; all that shite.

AIDS: fuck that.

He looked down at her, her head resting on his chest.

She looked up at him. 'Ah'v bin dreamin aboot this.'

'Oh aye, so ah'm that good, am ah?'

'No, no that.' She nudged him. '*Us*, bein back thegether like this.'

'Ah know, so huv ah.'

She leaned over the edge of the bed and picked up the shredded baby-doll nightie. 'Pity aboot mah prezzie though, eh? It didnae last five minutes oan. Yir supposed tae tek it aff wi yir hons, gently – no tear it aff wi yir teeth.'

'Aye, sorry aboot that – goat a wee bit carried away. It wus worth every penny though, eh?'

They laughed.

'Oh, that reminds me.' He got out of bed.

'Where ye goin?'

'Tae git yir other prezzie.'

'Oh, bring yours in as well, it's under the tree. An' don't mek any noise, ah don't want um wekin up jist yet.'

He went into the living-room and came back moments later with two presents. He jumped into bed and handed Evelyn a small gift-wrapped box. He shook his own present, wrapped in red and silver paper with a tag that said: *To Mick. Happy Christmas, Love Evelyn and Jamie*. He listened as the aftershave glugged about inside it, pretending not to know what the hell it was.

'Is this wan mine?' he asked her theatrically.

She smiled back at him sarcastically. He did the same routine every year.

'The one shaped like a boatil ay aftershave?' he said, his mouth opening in mock surprise, 'Ah wunner whit it is?' He opened it, his jaw dropping wide open as though he'd just won the lottery.

'It *is* a boatil ay aftershave, smartarse,' she said, carefully picking open the expensive-looking paper wrapped around her present. 'Ah couldnae think whit tae git ye. Ah couldnae git ye claithes, cos ah'v hardly seen ye, an ah know ye like tae buy yir aen . . .'

He splashed some of the aftershave on. 'Hey, ah like it.' He leaned towards her. 'It's crackin – smell.'

'Are ye sure? Ah kin tek it back an git somehun else that ye like if ye don't like that wan.' She threw the wrapping paper on the bed, and looked puzzled at the small, black velvet-covered box. She slowly opened it.

'Ah luv it.' He kissed her cheek. 'Thanks.'

'Omigod.' Her mouth dropped open as she took the gold locket and chain from its box. 'Whit's this? Mick? How much did this cost? It's too much!'

He took it from her and carefully opened the catch. He put it around her neck and fastened it, gently kissing the back of her neck. 'An before ye ask – aye, it's paid fir, wi mah overtime. Go ahead, open it up.'

'Is thur a photie in it?'

'Open it an see.'

She kneeled on the edge of the bed, looking in the mirrored wardrobe as she opened the locket. Inside was a happy family photo of her, Mick and Jamie. She grinned at him and gave him a big bear hug. 'It's beautiful. The best present ah'v ever hud.'

'It's tae remind ye' – he corrected himself – 'it's tae remind *us*, aboot whit's important.' He took the locket and looked at the picture. 'Ye remember that day when we took the Wee Man tae Blackpool laist year? That wis a briwyint day that wis, we were really happy . . . then, a couple ay days later, it aw turned tae shite.'

'Mick, don't, please. It'll no happen again . . . mah brar'll niver come between us again, ah mean it this time.'

He shrugged, then smiled as he looked at the photo. 'Ah know. Dae us a favour, when ye look at that photie, ah want ye tae remember . . . that's aw that's important. You, me, an the Wee Man . . . Fuck everywan else!'

What a romantic.

'Mick, yiv goat such a lovely way wi words.' She heard a rattle coming from the bedroom door. She looked up. The door handle was being slowly turned. She shoved Mick under the covers.

Jamie came in, smiling. He ran and dived on to the bed, landing on Mick, who sat bolt upright with the shock.

'*Aaahh!* Ya wee . . .'

'Da!' shouted Jamie, genuinely surprised to see him.

'Da!' Mick imitated him. 'Aye it's yir da. Who did ye think it wis, Santa?'

He wrestled Jamie on the bed, tickling him. Jamie squealed with delight.

It was the usual Donnelly Christmas. In the morning they'd phoned round all the relatives, and Jamie thanked everyone for his presents. Mick had tried calling Archie's number to check that the old boy was all right and there had been no further attacks, but he just kept getting a 'disconnected' tone. When he reported it the operator said there was a fault on the line and it had been reported to the engineers, so Mick made a mental note to go and visit him in a day or two. The remainder of the morning he'd spent reading and rereading the instructions for the video game, and trying to tune it into a spare channel on the TV. By the time he got it Jamie had lost interest. Within an hour Mick was hooked and couldn't put it down. Jamie went into a huff because he couldn't get a shot. Evelyn sorted it out by coming in from the kitchen, taking the game controller off Mick, handing it to Jamie and giving Mick a plastic basin full of potatoes to peel instead.

Later on, Jamie helped to set the table while Mick sat with a can of beer, watching football. Evelyn came in again, picked up the remote and changed over the channel to the Christmas film.

After dinner, the three of them curled up on the couch watching a Christmas repeat of *Only Fools and Horses*. Evelyn put on her new *Father Ted* video and Mick nodded off and snored for an hour. After his traditional kip and a few more drinks, he put on a CD and pulled Evelyn up to dance. Jamie sat with a cheesy grin watching them: they were back together again. He couldn't stop laughing when Evelyn found an old 70s CD, and dragged him up and taught him how to do the Bump.

* * *

Shug wiped the cold rain from his face and pulled up his collar. He looked up at the flat. He could see Mick dancing about, giving Jamie a piggyback. He turned and booted the door of a parked car before walking away up the street.

Day Fourteen: New Year's Eve

Seven thirty p.m. Evelyn and Mick were in the bedroom getting ready to go out. He had the charcoal grey suit on that he'd bought from Top Man a couple of years ago when one of the boys in work got married. It had only seen the light of day three times in as many years. Evelyn had her back turned to him as he zipped up her black sequined dress and gave her arse a squeeze.

'Don't touch whit ye can't afford.' She smiled, turning round to face him.

'Oh, like that is it?' he said, grabbing her waist and pulling her close. The front doorbell rang. He sighed as if to say 'Typical.'

She laughed and walked out of the bedroom.

Evelyn opened the front door to Siobhan who stood smiling in the close. Her long leather coat hung open, revealing a white silky three-quarter-length dress with a mandarin collar – fat too good for babysitting, thought Evelyn. She hoped she wasn't up to anything, then remembered that she'd never had any trouble with Siobhan in the past. A good level-headed girl. Not like her friend Jaqui.

'Hiya, hen, you look nice,' said Evelyn. 'Moan in.'

'Hiya,' she replied warily. 'Er . . . is it awright if Jaqui babysits wi me?'

Jaqui popped her head round the door, smoking and chewing as usual, wearing a short leopard-print dress under her brown leather coat. She gave Evelyn a cheeky wave. Evelyn's suspicions were raised even higher.

'That depends,' said Evelyn, as she eyed Jaqui with disdain. 'Will she spew all ower mah kitchen units like she did laist time?'

'She promised me she'll no.' She turned to Jaqui. 'Dint ye?'

What was it with people? thought Jaqui. They always liked to remind you of the last time you made an arse out of yourself. She stubbed out her fag on the wall. 'Aye, ah'v nae drink wi me – hoanest, check!' She held her arms up.

Evelyn couldn't help smirking. 'That didnae stoap ye drinkin aw mine, ya wee witch.' She motioned Jaqui to the wall. Jaqui sighed. She knew the routine by now and assumed the position, facing the wall with her feet apart and her arms outstretched. Evelyn frisked her. Satisfied Jaqui was clean, Evelyn gestured with her thumb. 'In.'

They followed Evelyn inside the flat. Jaqui turned to Siobhan and whispered, 'Fuck sakes, man, y'd git less hassle tryin tae git intae Victorias.'

'Noo, are ye sure ye don't mind?' Evelyn asked the girls. 'We'll no be that late.'

'Naah,' said Siobhan. 'We're no missin anyhun th' night . . . we'd jist be ower at mah hoose fir the bells.'

'Aye, listenin tae yir da whingein aboot how shite the telly is,' mused Jaqui, looking about the room.

Evelyn put her coat on. Mick came in fixing his tie. He smiled at Siobhan. 'Hi, pal.'

'Hiya.'

Jaqui sifted through his CDs.

'Awright, spewy,' he said.

She gave him a sarcastic smile and burst her bubble gum.

'Right,' said Evelyn. 'The wee feller's asleep. There's loads ay food in the fridge, so help yirsels. Oh, ah got yis a boatil ay wine. Wan boatil, Jaqui, that's yir loat, right?'

'Aye.'

Siobhan nudged her.

'Thanks,' said Jaqui.

Evelyn scanned the room as though she'd misplaced something, 'Right, we're aff. Is that everyhun? Ah'm sure ah'v forgot somethin, ye know.'

Mick picked up her handbag and held it out to her. She took it off him as he put his jacket on and ushered her to the door. 'Moan, we'll niver git oot at this rate.'

'See yis!' said Evelyn.

'Have a nice time,' said Jaqui.

'Aye,' said Siobhan, 'enjoy yirsels.'

'Aye, yous too.' Mick looked at Jaqui. 'An, hey you, don't be bringin any men in here, right?'

'Ah don't know any men . . . No any real men anyhow.' She licked her lips at him suggestively.

Whit a wind-up merchant, thought Mick. He shook his head as if to say, 'I give up' and walked out of the front door behind Evelyn.

Jaqui turned to Siobhan, puzzled. 'How is it she aywis frisks me an no you?'

'Cos she trusts me,' said Siobhan, pulling a bottle of vodka from her coat pocket and handing it to Jaqui. 'Here, ah'm gonnae check oan Jamie.'

Irene sat in the smoke-filled room and looked about. It was the janitor's room of an old chapel. Chapel, she thought. If only Hugh could see her now he'd have a flakey. So, what was new? If the milkman put the milk on the wrong side of the step Hugh would have a flakey and go out on the drink: any excuse. But she didn't want to think about him, she was here for herself.

Audrey had spoken about Al-Anon a few times, what it had done for her, for Tom, and how they'd managed to piece their life back together.

Irene remembered when she and Audrey used to work at the baker's. They were only in their twenties. Audrey started seeing Tom and less of Irene, then they moved away to Coatbridge where Tom's family came from. That was the last she'd seen of her until a few years back.

She'd been shopping in the town and browsing around Marks and Spencer's, looking at the lovely clothes and wondering how she was going to be able to afford a new skirt. She picked up one and checked the price: twenty pounds. She could feed her family for a month on that – she'd had enough practice over the years. She felt the fabric: lovely. You only got what you paid for. Who was she kidding? She couldn't afford that. Maybe if she hinted hard enough Evelyn would buy her it for her birthday. Aye, she was a good girl, Evelyn, but she wasn't exactly flush herself.

Irene turned and walked to the door: What Every's was having a sale and she'd be able to pick up almost the same skirt for a fiver, the only difference being you'd be able to spit peas through it. If she was lucky it would wash okay – do her a turn.

Then she saw her: well dressed, nicely turned-out, in her fifties, but something strangely familiar about her. This woman looked like she'd money, nice jewellery and a few bob in the bank, but Irene could tell one of her own class a mile off. It was like a second sense.

The woman turned. They made eye contact and instantly smiled. They knew each other, that was for sure. The woman's brow furrowed and she looked away, puzzled. Irene made for the door; she didn't want to be standing staring at a woman in Marks: she might be a lesbian.

'Irene?' came the woman's voice. Irene turned and the penny dropped. She'd got older, but she still had that toothy smile like a female Ken Dodd.

'Audrey?' They both laughed and walked over to one another. They looked each other up and down and smiled. Irene realised she, herself, was dressed like a tramp and felt self-conscious, but it soon left her when Audrey gave her a big hug and a kiss on the cheek.

'How'v ye bin? Yir lookin great!' Audrey said.

'Ach, listen to you,' said Irene, standing back to take in Audrey's new look. 'Ye look like ye've won the pools!'

They went for coffee and talked about old times. Audrey had married Tom, but he loved a drink. If the truth be known he loved it more than her. He'd become devious with it: betting, not paying bills and drinking the money instead. Lying to her that he'd paid the telly – swearing on the wean's life. She used to check the payment book and saw the pages had been ripped out and the amount filled in as usual, but wondered why there was no ink stamp on the stub.

'There's a new woman doon there,' said Tom. 'Ah asked her aboot that but she sais they don't stamp it any mair; you can go doon yirsel if ye like, pull her up aboot it, but ye won't git anywhere.'

That was good enough for Audrey until Granada came banging on the door to get their telly back. Tom got worse and worse until they got turfed out of their home. Tom's mother's home. The poor woman had kept a roof over his head when he was a child – paid the rent on time all those years. She'd only been dead a year and Tom had managed to lose everything she'd worked for. That was when Audrey realised if he could do that to his own mother he could do it to her. She left him and moved in with her sister back in Drumchapel.

Audrey's name had been down on the council's

housing list for years, so after a few refusals she finally got the place she was in now.

Tom saw the error of his ways and started going to Gamblers Anonymous, then quickly realised the root of his problem was really the drink. The compulsion. He came grovelling to Audrey, cap in hand, begging for another chance. Audrey kept him at arm's length for a few months until she'd satisfied herself he was genuinely making the effort, then she started going along to open meetings with him to try and understand his illness. That was the word that struck her more than anything. The *illness*. The 'family' illness. Up until now she thought Tom was just a selfish bastard, but after a few meetings she realised that it was something they all suffered from – they were *all* affected by it: her and her two daughters.

Irene listened intently, relating this to what was happening in her own life. Up until now Irene had just thought that Glasgow men liked to drink – that it was tradition or something. Now she knew it was just another excuse conjured up by alcoholics.

Irene looked about the janitor's room. Pictures drawn by children were stuck on the walls. She wondered what these wee kids had to put up with in their lives and if it was anything like what her own kids had had to suffer at the hands of that bastard. There she was again, letting him into her head. But that was the reason she was in the room – the reason they were all in the room – because of someone else's drinking and the effect it had on them.

She pulled out a cigarette, lit it and listened intently to a man in his seventies describe how he had to clean up his wife after finding her slumped in a neighbour's close in a pool of her own vomit and piss. The woman was seventy-six. A great-grandmother: the mother of a primary school teacher and a midwife. Alcohol was like drugs, it didn't distinguish between class: it could affect anybody. It was affecting this poor man all right.

She watched him swallow deeply and lift his glasses to wipe away a tear. He was close to the edge: his back against the wall. The poor old bugger. He wanted to leave his wife, but couldn't. How would she manage without him? He was having trouble managing himself; he wasn't getting any younger, and having an alcoholic in the house was like having a couple of two-year-olds running round the kitchen when you had the frying pan on: you had to watch them like a hawk.

So this was how the partners of alcoholics spent their Hogmanay? None of them looked like they were too bothered about missing out on the celebrations. Like Irene, getting their head straight was more important to them than any party.

They all had one thing in common: they hated Christmas and New Year. 'New Year?' A small fat woman commented, 'There's nuthin new aboot it – it's the same pish every year wi hum stoatin roon the hoose. That film *The Lost Weekend* disnae huv a look-in – it's mair like the loast month wi hum.'

That raised a few smiles. It was important to laugh.

'Ye huv tae laugh or y'll go mad,' a few of them said. It was true. She'd felt herself on the verge of insanity a million times and it was a long time since she'd had anything to laugh about.

Before they came in, Audrey took her into the janitor's kitchen where a tall woman with a mop of grey hair was shuffling about in a cardigan and slippers, making tea. Everyone who came in for a tea or coffee lit up when they saw her, gave her a hug, a kiss, said how well she was looking. Irene thought she looked a mess – imagine coming out with your slippers on, on a night like this? Audrey introduced them. 'Lilly, this is mah pal, Irene – it's hur furst time.'

Lilly put down the huge teapot she was holding and wiped her hand on her cardigan. 'Pleased tae meet ye. Is it yir furst time at this meetin or yir furst time in Al-Anon?'

'Furst time at Al-Anon,' said Irene.

Lilly smiled at her warmly and leaned closer to dispense some advice. 'Tek whit ye want an leave the rest, hen . . . an keep comin back.'

Irene looked at Audrey, puzzled.

Audrey smiled and nodded back at her. 'This is the wellest wumin ah know in Al-Anon; y'd dea well tae listen tae hur – she knows what she's talkin aboot.'

As they walked into the room a thin, hard-looking woman indicated the empty seats that were either side of her. Audrey quickly grabbed Irene by the arm. 'Here's a couple ay seats over here.' The woman gave Audrey a look that could poison a reservoir. Audrey nudged Irene as they sat down. 'Y've met the wellest wumin in Al-Anon,' she said, then indicated the woman they'd just avoided, sitting with an empty space all around her. 'Ye don't want anything tae dae wi the sickest.'

'Who's that?' asked Irene.

'That's Torn-Faced Betty. Keep away fae hur if ye know what's good fir ye – she's as sick as a parrot!'

Irene was about to ask what she meant when the meeting started. The talking died down and Lilly shuffled up to the top table, carrying her personalised cup; 'Supermum' was printed on the side, with a cartoon of a woman clasping her hands above her head like a champion. Obviously the love Lilly felt from her friends in this room tonight was something she also had in her home life. Irene immediately felt jealous.

'It'll be a good meetin th' night,' said Audrey. 'Lilly's chairin.'

Irene sat throughout the meeting, listening intently to all their stories. Sometimes she was shocked, sometimes she thought these people had it easy compared to what she was living with. Other times she felt herself moved to tears. Occasionally she laughed along with the rest of them, as someone told how they dealt with the madness of alcoholism: took a step back from it, didn't react to the alcoholic, and little by little were now starting to get their own life back in order.

Irene looked about. On the whole these people looked happy. If it worked for them it could work for her. What did she have to lose? She felt safe being in a room with people who understood, lived a similar lifestyle, but were actually doing something about it. The old man, who was earlier close to tears, was now laughing and nodding in agreement as a wee bloated-looking woman in a chemotherapy wig told how her husband, just nights earlier, had been shouting and singing 'The Sash' in the street. She wouldn't have minded so much but he was a Catholic.

When her husband saw he wasn't getting a reaction from the neighbours he came into the house and stripped off in the living-room. He went back into the street, completely naked and started singing 'Fly me to the Moon', bending over and skelping his arse on the 'moon' bit. This had the right effect as the neighbours came out to see what the noise was. Then he decided that if they really wanted something to stare at he would bloody well give them something. He climbed on to his car and did a belly dance on the roof.

'So,' the woman laughed, reaching a couple of fingers under the back of her wig and scratching her head. The wig slid forward, almost covering her eyes. She automatically tilted it back into place and continued her story – 'I thought, Buck ye! If that's what ye want tae dae then that's up tae you. Ah jist went back inside an watched hum through the windae. There he wis on top ay hus motor, dancin away quite the thing, wi aw the neighbours laughin at hum, an he's thinking this is great – whit a comedian – entertainin the neighbours wi his wee dance and his big red erse. Bit whit he didnae know wis they were aw laughin at hus wee wullie disappearing wi the cold.'

Irene held her sides and looked at Audrey: tears of laughter streamed down her face. She shook her head, unable to speak.

'Bit dae ye want tae know whit the best laugh wis,' said the woman. 'He gets up the next mornin like nuthin's happened an looks oot the windae. Next thing is he's gien it laldy aboot someone dentin the roof ay his motor, an how these bastard kids run ower the roofs ay cars fir a laugh. Then, when he calms doon, he only gits washed an dressed fir the chapel, din't he? So he's shoutin me tae hurry up an he's potterin aboot oot the front, talking tae Ella fae ower the road aboot his dented motor. Ah'm lookin through the windae an ah kin see she's dyin tae laugh; she wis at the front ay the crowd last night, pointin at his wee tadger an howlin laughin. Then later on, tae mek matters worse, he's smilin an shakin hons wi aw the neighbours at the chapel!'

The crowd continued to howl with laughter. The woman composed herself and tried to be serious but she was smirking away and shaking her head. 'Ah mean, naebody would believe ye, wid they?' she said, raising her hands upwards. 'Whit ye huv tae live wi . . . See when ah'm getting mah chemo, and the nurse puts the needle in she aywis says tae me, "Think ay somethin nice, hen." Ah jist think ay hum and thank God it's no me!' She dissolved into laughter, momentarily shaking her head at her giggling friend in the seat across from her, who sat tearful with laughing, wiping her eyes.

Irene looked about the room: this was the best New Year ever. She was going back to Audrey's for the bells with Tom and their two daughters – maybe a wee drink. 'So whit if Tom's five years sober,' Audrey said earlier. 'He disnae stoap me fae huvin a drink . . . sais it disnae bother hum. That's good sobriety fir ye.'

Drink wasn't important any more, thought Irene. Just look at all these 'hopeless cases'; people who, if you heard how they had to live, would make you say, 'Poor bastard, Ah'm glad it's no me.' Well it *was* her and she was having the best time she'd had in years – and she was stone-cold sober.

When the laughter died, a woman talked about New Year, what it meant to her. It meant a fresh start. Not crucifying herself for the things she'd done in the past, the people she'd hurt or the mistakes she'd made. She spoke about how she'd started to 'make amends': apologise to people for hurting them, trying in some way to undo the wrong. Some of the people she'd apologised to said it was all in the past and accepted her apology, some still bore a grudge, but that was their problem now, she'd been the one to make the first move.

Irene's stomach churned as the amends that sprang to mind mounted up in her head. Top of the list was her daughter – her beautiful girl. God, what had she done, allowing it to go on? It was the fear, the terror of what

Hugh would do to her if she tried to stop him. Irene had blanked it out of her mind, told herself it wasn't happening . . . but every time she heard wee Evelyn whimper in her room she could only grit her teeth and pray he wasn't hurting her too much. This was a madness she'd lived with for years. It was true: nobody knows what goes on behind closed doors. But in that madhouse they all lived in his behaviour had become par for the course – something that 'just happened'. That's how devious Hugh was: controlling them all, making them gradually accept that what was once unacceptable was now the norm. She knew it never happened in anyone else's house in the close. Everyone else's kids were happy, well balanced. Not hers though, they were terrified.

Evelyn had never spoken to Irene about it. Every time a programme about child abuse came on the telly she left the room or the telly was switched over. It never happened in their house. God knows what that evil bastard had told his little girl to get her to keep quiet for all these years. Yet here she was, happily married to a good man. They had a beautiful wee boy. Both of them worked, they had a nice flat, but whatever happened to Evelyn in the past, she must have locked it away in a wee room at the back of her mind, just like Irene had done. They'd both locked the ugliness of Evelyn's childhood in there, never to be let out. Coming to Al-Anon tonight had made her want to look for the key. Maybe it wasn't time to open the door and deal with it yet, but she would hate to die and not have said she was sorry to Evelyn for letting it go on.

'You all right?' Audrey squeezed Irene's hand and looked at her face, concerned.

Irene realised the tears were running down her cheeks. She wiped her eyes, smiled and nodded at Audrey. 'Aye, ah'm fine.'

This was the start of a new beginning. She wanted her wee girl back. She would phone her tonight at the bells and tell her she loved her. It was time to make amends.

Evelyn huddled up to Mick as they stepped out into the cold night air. 'We should huv phoned fir a taxi . . . it's freezin.'

'It's no bad. Anyway ah telt ye, y'll never git wan – it's Hogmanay, man, they're aw busy. Yir better aff walkin it. We'll probably git wan at the top ay the road.'

'Dae ye want tae nip in tae the Halfway fir a quick drink?' she asked hopefully. 'It's only early yet, an ye kin try an phone fir wan?'

'Ye cannae be that cauld, yir jist oot!'

'Ah um. Ah cannae feel mah feet.'

Shug stared at them as they crossed the road to the Halfway. He lit up a fag and stepped back into the doorway of a neighbouring close.

Siobhan and Jaqui were having a little party to themselves – a dance music CD was playing and they had started on the vodka.

Jaqui was on the phone to her boyfriend, while Siobhan flicked through the channels on the TV. The usual Hogmanay – her da was right, the telly *was* shite: Ricky Fulton again. Did he no die last year? She looked through the videos for something decent to watch.

'How no?' said Jaqui on the phone. 'How no? . . . Jist fir an oor? . . . How no?' She tutted then cracked her bubble gum down the phone.

'Well, fuck ye then. Away an *shag* Stevie. Happy New Year, ya basta!' She slammed the phone down.

Siobhan cracked up laughing.

Jaqui took a slurp of her vodka and coke. 'Fuckin poof. Ah'm finished wi um.' She stuck out her top teeth, imitating her boyfriend. 'Ah'm goin oot wi Stevie, ah telt um laist week ah wid.'

Siobhan held her sides, and laughed even harder.

Jaqui couldn't help but join in. She threw a cushion over at her. 'Ah know where there's a good video,' she said. 'Ah fun it laist time . . . in Mick's wardrobe. A porno!'

'Whit were you dien in hus wardrobe?'

'Lookin fir porno videos.'

Siobhan burst out laughing again. Jaqui got up and wobbled unsteadily to the door. The drink was taking effect. She hoped she wouldn't feel sick; she hated it when that happened. She held on to the handle and crossed her legs. She'd have a good nosey through Mick's wardrobe once she'd been to the bog.

'There's this lassie, right,' she said, 'she's goat these

massive tits; ah swear tae god, man, thir no real – wait till ye see these things.' She laughed as she recalled the video. 'An this guy, right. He's a pizza guy, right. This guy comes in . . .'

She opened the door in mid-sentence. Shug stood in the doorway, behind her.

It was then that Siobhan's insides

Jaqui was none the wiser. She continued, 'He goes, "Ahv brought yir pizz—" '

Siobhan screamed. Jaqui turned round, saw Shug and screamed as well. She backed away from the door.

'Seen it!' said Shug. 'He sais ah'v brought yir pizza. Then he shags her stupid. Ah don't mind watchin it again though. Away in an git it.'

Jaqui picked up the vodka bottle. Siobhan grabbed the remote for the hi-fi and turned the music off.

'Aw don't turn it aff,' said Shug. 'Ah wis jist gettin intae it.'

'WHO THE FUCK ARE YE? WHIT YE DIEN IN HERE?' shouted Jaqui threateningly.

Shug calmly walked into the room. 'No need tae shout. Y'll wake up the wean.' He sat down on the couch. 'De yae no know who ah um? Ah'm Shug, Evelyn's brar. It's awright, ah let masel in.' He waved his key at them. Jaqui put the bottle down on the table. Shug picked it up and unscrewed the cap.

'She's no in,' said Siobhan nervously.

'Ah know that.' He poured himself a drink and looked her up and down. 'Yir Siobhan, int ye?'

Siobhan glanced at him. She remembered meeting him last year, when Evelyn brought him home. But there was something familiar about his voice. She couldn't work out where she'd heard it from. 'Aye, ah um,' she said, her voice quavering.

He laughed at her nervousness. 'Yir awright, Siobhan, nae need tae shit yirsel . . . again.'

Then she knew *exactly* where from.

The air expelled from her body.

'So whit dae ye want?' asked Jaqui, barely able to hide the anger in her voice.

'Ah'v come tae see the Wee Man.' He stared at her aggressively. 'AWRIGHT?'

'Well ye cannae see um; he's asleep!' Jaqui slowly edged towards the door.

'Ah kin see um if ah like. Ah'm hus uncle. Sit doon, yir awright.'

Siobhan knew she had to get out but her legs wouldn't move. She managed to stand up, not wanting to be left alone with him. She slowly started to follow Jaqui.

Shug jumped up, blocking their path to the door. 'SIT DOON, AH SAIS!'

Petrified, the girls sat down on the couch. Shug calmly topped up their drinks with the vodka.

'That's better. Here, huv a drink, it's New Year. Whit aboot this video then?'

Siobhan and Jaqui looked at each other, scared. They turned to face the TV, trying to ignore him.

'Your Honour, my client has always turned up for his court appearances, and has never once skipped bail.'

Whit a fuckin stoatir, thought George, worth every penny, that brief.

George had expected to go down; spend Hogmanay in Bar-L. After his past record for assault he was only one step away from being seriously fucked, and he knew it. The last thing he expected was bail. He'd made a cunt of his relationship with Karen – big-style. Giving women a slap was one thing, but throwing stools across the bar at them? Suppose asking her for a wank would be out of the question?

His temper always got the better of him. A big, stupit, jealous basta, that's what he was. He'd have to screw the nut.

Life was full of surprises lately. What was the judge thinking? Season of goodwill? Mebbe he had a drink in him? Possibly – red-nosed auld cunt – probably hated women as well: 'Go oan yirsel, Georgie boay. Gie em a skelp fae me too!'

George smiled and looked across at the bar. They'd managed to fix the gantry up good-style. Aye, and that was the other surprise – Nancy not barring him: the £300, a bunch of flowers and the head-bowed, remorse routine, turned up full, had guaranteed him of that.

But then again, Nancy always did have a soft spot for him: he kept the shite out of the pub, that's why. Besides, she was no stranger to jealousy herself, and having Karen around the place hadn't been doing her self-esteem any good. Mebbe he'd done Nancy a favour.

He looked across to the bar; Nancy was serving Mick and his missus. Good; he wanted a word with him about that brother-in-law of his.

Mick looked about the pub. It was heaving. 'This place is mobbed th' night.'

'Ah know,' said Nancy. 'It'd be awright if it wis like this every weekend, eh?'

'Whit?' said Mick. 'Y'd never git served.'

'Yir erse! Ah always serve you furst.'

'Aye, that's true,' Mick smiled. 'Ye cannae complain aboot the service; ye kin complain like fuck aboot the beer though.' He looked at his pint for signs of cloudiness.

'Whit!' said Nancy.

He laughed. 'A joke, it wis a joke!'

'It'd better be, son,' she warned.

Big George shouted from across the room: 'MICK! MERE A MINUTE!'

Mick turned to Evelyn. 'Ah, fuck. Ah'v bin dreadin this; ah'm away ower tae see Big George fir a minute.'

'Don't worry aboot it,' she said. 'That business wi Shug hud nuthin tae dae wi you. Just don't be aw night, we're goin soon.'

She watched as he walked over to Big George. George,

all smiles, put his arm around him. Mick stood shaking hands with him and his friends.

'So, where ye aff tae th'night?' asked Nancy.

'Away intae the toon tae meet pals ay oors; tae tell ye the truth ah cannae be bothered wi it. The minute mah pal gits a few drinks in hur she sterts moothin aff at hur man. It's no a night oot when she sterts that carry oan and she'll no shut up till he snaps.'

'Well if they stert their pish, git yirsels back here instead; we'll be open aw night probably, an y've no far tae stagger hame.'

'Aye, that's true . . .' She looked over at Mick and Big George sharing a joke. 'Listen, Nancy, ah wanted tae apologise fir whit happened in here wi oor Shug. Ah'v no really had a chance tae speak tae ye since it happened an . . .'

Nancy held her hand up, stopping Evelyn in mid-sentence. 'Listen, hen, you an yir man are welcome in here any time. There's no need fir you tae apologise fir anyhun, it wisnae you who caused the hassle. But if ye happen tae see that brar ay yours, y'd better tell um tae keep oot the road ay George an hus mates fir a couple ay years at least. After whit happened tae Karen, he'd be better aff leavin the country. Cos when George gets a hold ay um, Shug's a deid man.'

Evelyn took a drink of her Hooch. 'Ah'll no see um. Ah hope he hus left the country.'

'Anyway,' said Nancy, 'forget aw that, it's a New Year. Whit did Mick git ye fir yir Christmas?'

'Underwear, as usual . . .'

'Dirty wee bugger.'

'An this . . .' She felt her neck. 'Aw, basta.'

'Whit? Huv ye loast it?'

'No, it's in the hoose.' She shouted over to Mick, 'MICK!'

'WHIT?'

'MERE A MINUTE!'

He pushed through the crowd. 'Whit is it?'

'Ah forgot mah loacket. Dae us a favour . . . away ower an get it fir us; it's in mah jewellery boax. Ah want tae show it tae Nancy.'

'Show hur it th' morra.' He went to push back through the bodies to George and his mates.

'It disnae matter, hen, ah'll see it the next time yir in,' said Nancy.

Evelyn pulled Mick back. 'Aw . . . please? Ah wanted tae wear it th' night.'

Women, he thought, can't live wi em, can't bury em under the patio either. 'Awright.' He gave her a tenner. 'Here, get them in, ah'll no be long.'

Shug sat on one of the two-seater couches with a half-asleep Jamie on his knee, flicking through the channels on the TV, using one remote, while skipping through the tracks on the CD with the other. Unseen to the girls he'd managed to unplug the phone. No need for distractions, he thought. The girls sat on the couch facing him. They glanced at each other, then the floor; both of them too terrified to speak.

'That's the good thing aboot dein whizz,' he explained. 'Ah kin watch aw the stations on the telly at the same time, an ah kin listen tae music an aw. AH UM IN CONTROL! Eh, Wee Man? Whit's the matter? Tired? Did ye miss yir Uncle Shug? Eh? Wee Man, wek up!'

Jaqui had had enough. 'Leave um!' she said, the vodka starting to give her courage. 'He's tired.'

Shug ruffled Jamie's hair. 'Ah'v no seen um fir ages, he kin sleep th' morra!'

Siobhan turned towards the TV as she heard the newscaster say, '. . . last week's vicious attack on pensioner Archie Prentice . . .' Archie's picture flashed up. She grabbed the remote off Shug.

He looked at her, surprised by her bravery. A sneer came over his face: 'Haw you!' He'd have to teach her some manners.

'It's Archie!' said Jaqui. 'Turn it up!' Siobhan found the volume on the remote and turned it up, just managing to catch the end of the news report.

'. . . Police are appealing for any witnesses to come forward. And now to sport . . .'

Jaqui looked at Siobhan incredulously. 'Whit's happened tae um?'

If your picture was on the news it only meant two things: you were famous or you were dead . . . and Archie wasn't famous.

'Is he deid?' said Siobhan. 'Aw God, ah hope no. Ah'll phone mah mammie, see if she saw the news.'

'Y'll phone naebody,' slurred Shug. 'Is that that lollipop man cunt?'

'Aye, an he's no a cunt – right?' threatened Jaqui.

How did *he* know him? thought Siobhan.

'That's that fuckin child molester,' sneered Shug. 'Is he still alive? The basta!'

Jaqui was trying to be calm, get some answers, but she was shaking inside. 'Whit are you talkin aboot? Whit dae *you* know aboot it?'

Shug sniffed: Big Man. 'Aye, ah sorted um oot, dint ah. He wis touchin up the weans an 'a. The Wee Man an aw . . .' He ruffled Jamie's hair again. Jamie woke up and looked about, bleary-eyed. 'He'll no touch weans up again, ah made sure ay that,' said Shug. 'End ay story.'

Siobhan couldn't get her head round this. What was happening? She started to cry. Jamie struggled free from Shug and ran over to the girls.

Jaqui was incensed. 'Whit dae ye mean, "touchin up the weans"? He's no a molester, he's a lollipop man, fir fuck sakes. He's looked after me an hur' – she pointed to Siobhan – 'better than oor aen das huv, ya stupid-lookin basta! Whit did ye dae tae um?'

'Well, fir a stert aff, ah rearranged hus bollocks wi a Stanley.' He folded his arms and laughed as though he expected them to share in the huge joke.

The girls looked at him with hate in their eyes.

He tried a different approach to make them understand. He leaned forward and held his palms out. 'Look, ah only did whit anyone wid dae, right? Ye cannae let these sick bastas away wi it. Sometimes ye huvtae tek the law intae yir aen hons, right? Fuckin polis are a waste ay time, man. They'll no dae anyhun.'

Siobhan stared at Shug. She felt like her brain was overloading. This wasn't happening. She could see his mouth moving like he was on the telly. ***Blah blah blah*** . . . He was getting further away. Her head was swimming. Any minute now she was about to pass out.

Jaqui wasn't listening either: she'd heard all she needed to convince her he was a psycho. Without any warning she leaped up from the couch and, with all her strength and rage, kicked Shug in the face, knocking both him and the couch backwards. 'GET OOT, QUICK!' she shouted to Siobhan and Jamie.

They ran for the door, but Shug, shuffling on his knees, got there before them. He put his arm across the door, barring the way. Jaqui grabbed the vodka bottle off the table.

'OOT THE WAY!' She dragged Siobhan and Jamie aside and smashed the bottle over Shug's head.

Shug fell to the floor, clutching his head. He tried to get up but swayed unsteadily on his knees. Siobhan wrenched the door open, knocking him over on to his side. He lay there moaning, trying to get his bearings. Siobhan and Jamie ran into the hall and made it to the front door. As Jaqui went to step over Shug he came to his senses, looked up and refocused his eyes on her, grabbing her ankle and holding on tight. She kicked at his hand but he pulled himself back up on his feet and punched her in the chest. She flew backwards across the room, landing with a sickening crash among the bottles and glasses on the coffee table.

In the hallway Siobhan struggled to open the front door, wondering why she couldn't turn the lock. She'd opened this door a hundred times, what was wrong now? She looked through the glass panel and realised someone was on the other side trying to get in. She stopped turning it, allowing Mick to get his key in. She breathed a sigh of relief as he pushed the door open.

'WHIT THE FUCK IS GOIN ON?' he shouted.

'It's Evelyn's brar!' shouted Siobhan. 'He's goat Jaqui.'

'YA WEE COW!' Shug shouted from the living-room, followed by a scream from Jaqui and the sound of broken glass.

Mick shoved Siobhan and Jamie into the close, out of harm's way. 'Tek Jamie ootside!' he said.

She picked up Jamie and made her way down the close stairs, hoping Evelyn's mad brother wouldn't follow them.

Mick barged into the living-room in time to see Shug punch Jaqui in the face. Jaqui, too angry to feel the pain, rode the punch like a prize-fighter and retaliated by trying to claw out Shug's eyes. 'BASTA!' She screamed.

Shug, half blinded, pulled himself away and turned round to see Mick coming towards him. Mick had waited for this for a long time. He put all his weight behind a punch that hit Shug square in the face. Shug reeled backwards and Mick moved in, grabbing him by the collar and throwing him into the hall, banging Shug's head on the corner of the front door. Shug struggled to get his bearings and blindly tried to swing punches back, but he was too slow. Mick gave him two, rapid, right in the face, sending him staggering backwards into the close.

Mick came out of the front door and Shug automatically took a step back to distance himself. He lost his balance and fell down the close stairs.

Mick followed him down the stairs and hauled him on to his feet. He pushed him along the close, out of the door and flung him into the street. Shug landed on a parked car, making the alarm go off. Mick grabbed Shug by the hair, held him over the car with one hand and rained punches on his jaw with the other. Shug threw a couple of rabbit punches back, making contact with Mick's head, which only made Mick angrier and punch Shug even harder. Shug wriggled and kicked until he finally managed to break free and stagger off down the street.

Mick walked over to Siobhan who was still hiding in the doorway of next door's close and angrily took Jamie from her.

'How did he git in?' he asked.

'He hud a key,' said Siobhan defensively. What did he think – they'd let him in?

'Come on,' said Mick, walking back into the close.

He'd check if Jaqui was okay first, then see about getting the locks changed. Great timin, he thought. Whit loack-smith is gonnae come oot oan Hogmanay?

St George's Square was a mass of heaving bodies. Bells were ringing, the crowd was drinking and Shug was steaming. He stood, swigging from a bottle of Buckie and looking about: happy bastards – everywhere. Blokes were coming up to him, shaking his hand. Women were avoiding him: sixth sense?

Through his drunken haze he could see couples kissing. He wanted some of the same. He turned round and grabbed an unsuspecting girl from the group of people he was standing next to and tried to kiss the face off her. 'Happy New Year, darlin.'

She was disgusted but forced a laugh, trying not to offend as she pulled away from him. 'Aye, Happy New Year tae you too,' she said and walked off to join her pals.

He spied a small student-type with a perfect arse. She looked a wee bit like Scobie's bird. Maybe it was. He decided to try his luck again. 'Haw!' He made a grab for her. 'Happy New Year!'

She pushed him away. 'FUCK AFF!'

'Fuck sakes! Ah'm jist tryin tae wish ye a Happy New Year!'

'Aye, Happy New Year. Jist keep yir hons aff, right!'

'Aw git tae fuck, COW!'

Her lanky boyfriend stood towering over a group of

his mates. He turned round when he heard the shouting and saw what was going on. He lurched over and pulled her away from Shug. 'Haw, pal? Whit's wrang, eh?'

'Aw fuck, man, nuthin. Ah wis jist tryin tae wish the wee yin there a Happy New Year an 'a, no? An she teks a flakey oan me. Ah don't mean hur any herm – jist tryin tae be sociable.' He smiled at her patronisingly. 'Sorry, hen!'

The boyfriend could see Shug was pished: no point in starting a fight. Looked like he'd already had one. 'Aye, yir awright, mate, nae problem.'

Shug offered his wine. 'Here, pal, hae a drink oot mah boatil. Happy New Year.'

The boyfriend was a bit reluctant: bad manners to refuse though. 'Aye, awright. Happy New Year, bud . . . here.' He handed Shug a half-bottle of whisky.

They both stood, eyeing each other. Drinking from each other's bottles.

The pipe of peace.

The boyfriend smiled at Shug and offered him his wine back. Shug smiled in return then snorted back a load of catarrh. He looked into the boyfriend's eyes as he spat it into the whisky bottle. The boyfriend watched, gobsmacked, as the catarrh slid down the inside of the bottle and floated on the surface of the whisky. Shug handed him the bottle and took back his wine.

'YA DIRTY BASTA!' The boyfriend squared up to Shug. His mates all gathered round.

Shug smashed the neck of his wine bottle against a bin

and held it up in front of the boyfriend's face. He looked about for an escape route through the crowd. The boyfriend took a step forward. Shug waved the bottle again and the boyfriend and his mates backed off.

'Fuckin loony,' the boyfriend said.

Shug seized his chance: he turned on his heels and disappeared into the crowd.

Mick got out of bed and looked at the clock: 05.22. Another year – what a load of bollocks. He went to the bog and had a slash.

What a fuckin night that had been. If he ever saw that stupid cunt again he'd fuckin *do* him.

Hopefully he'd be banged up in a day or two, now that Evelyn had called the police on him; Mick couldn't believe it when Siobhan told them he'd attacked Archie. Evelyn knew he had a grudge against him but didn't think in a million years that he'd do anything about it. Mick walked to the kitchen and poured himself a glass of water.

What was wrong with that bastard? Chemical imbalance? He must be pure evil, picking a fight with a wee lassie like that. They'd ended up running out of ice, trying to get Jaqui's swollen lip down, and he had to go over to the Halfway to tap some more off Nancy. He'd completely forgotten about Evelyn. She'd been trying to phone the flat to find out what the hell was keeping him but somebody had unplugged the phone. While they waited for a taxi for Siobhan and Jaqui, Mick phoned the hospital to find out how Archie was, but they'd only tell them that Mr Prentice was critical but stable. The locksmith was a non-starter. The ones who actually answered their phones just laughed at him or wished him a Happy New Year. He'd have to go to the ironmonger's tomorrow and pick up a Yale lock himself, that would do.

Mick put the glass back in the dish-rack and turned off the kitchen light. He smiled to himself as he pictured the man Jaqui would end up marrying. Poor bastard. If the guy answered her back she'd kick the shit out of him. It was then that he noticed the door to Jamie's room was open.

Day Fifteen: New Year's Day

Big Hugh stood at the front door in his dressing-gown, holding the purple tin in his hand. 'Ah widnae tell yous cunts even if ah knew.' He scratched his sparse dome and contemplated the piece of flaky scalp underneath his dirty fingernail.

A middle-aged policeman, with a Mexican looking moustache eyed him with disdain: what a way to spend the New Year – taking shit from this fat, baldy, asthmatic cunt, with a big purple face to match the tin in his hand, and a nose that made Karl Malden look like Leonardo DiCaprio. 'Look, if we could jist come in fir a minute.' He raised an eyebrow at his stony-faced colleague who'd been staring at Hugh since they arrived, willing him to say something, anything that would incriminate himself.

'Away an raffle – ah'm no huvin the polis first-footin me. Whit kind ay luck would that bring me, eh?'

'Hugh McNab – yir boay – he stays here, right?'

'You tell *me*. Yir the one wi the computer.'

'Look, Mr McNab. Yir daughter's reported her son, Jamie, missing. We've reason tae believe he may have bin abducted by yir son, Hugh. Did he come hame laist night?'

'No,' answered Hugh, as though they were keeping him from an important engagement. He swigged from the can and stared them down.

The Mexican's stony-faced colleague cut in, trying the *Cracker* approach. 'Ye didn't seem at all surprised, jist now . . . when we told ye yir grandson had bin abducted?'

'Nuthin tae dae wi me; mah daughter niver brings hum roon tae see us. It's bin that long since ah'v seen hum ah couldnae even tell ye whit he looked like.'

The Mexican was starting to get pissed off. He held up a school picture of Jamie. 'He looks like this.'

Big Hugh glanced at it and nodded, uninterested. 'Oh, aye. That's a good photie.'

'Is *Mrs* McNab in?' he asked, putting away the photo.

'She's stayin wi friends ower Christmas an New Year.' Big Hugh grinned and waved the can at him.

'Oh, oot ma fuckin road!' he said, pushing past Hugh. He walked into the house.

Stony-face followed him into the hall, shaking his head. 'Ye try an be nice tae people an look whit happens.'

'Aye, on yis go – come in, why don't yis?' Hugh followed them into the house.

Shug and Jamie had spent the afternoon at the pictures and McDonald's. This was the business, thought Shug. He could get quite used to this. Jamie hadn't even asked for his ma or da once all afternoon.

They arrived back at Big Hugh's, pulling up in a taxi.

Shug scanned the street as he paid the driver. He didn't want his stupid sister or that dickheid Donnelly turning up, ranting and raving. He looked about again and opened the taxi door, happy they were nowhere to be seen. They probably didn't even give a fuck about the Wee Man.

Hugh came through from the kitchen, clutching the purple tin like it was a permanent appendage. Shug took Jamie's coat and hat off him.

'Polis were here,' said Hugh.

'Whit happened?' asked Shug.

'Fuck all. Hud a look about then took aff. Ah don't think they'll be back.' Hugh smiled at Jamie and coughed a rattling phlegm-ridden belter that only the forty-a-day man can. 'Mere, wee feller.' He held out his arms as he sat down. 'Moan an sit oan yir granda's knee.'

Jamie turned to Shug with a look that said it all: who was this strange man, and what was he doing in Grannie's house?

Evelyn sat and stared at the floor of the interview room. Mick gazed at the walls, trying to figure out what was going on. He looked over at her; he could see she was doing the same as him: running it over and over in her head.

Jamie wouldn't just get up and leave the house in the middle of the night. But the things that had been happening lately – the arguing, Mick walking out without saying goodbye to him, and Shug beating up Jaqui, were enough to make a wee boy act out of character. Mick cursed himself for telling the Wee Man about Archie lying half-dead in hospital. Evelyn cursed herself too: she knew she should have taken that key off Shug.

The policewoman reappeared, carrying two teas. The Mexican and Stony-face, who'd just returned from Big Hugh's, came in behind her. 'Mrs Donnelly?'

Evelyn jumped up; excited; frightened. 'Huv ye found hum – wis he there?'

The Mexican shook his head. He sat down and took out his notebook. 'Your father says he hasn't seen hum fir years.'

Mick looked over at Evelyn. 'Whit – *Shug*?'

'No, yir son,' said Stony-face.

'Ah widnae say years, mebbe aboot six – eight months. He drinks; ah don't like Jamie goin there when mah ma's no in. Ah don't trust hum. Wis ma ma in?'

'He said she wis stayin wi friends,' said Stony-face.

Evelyn looked crestfallen. 'Friends? She's no allowed tae huv any. It's the match. It hus tae be the match.'

Mick stood up and looked as though he was going to punch the wall. 'Fuckin alkies, ah'm sick ay the bastas: selfish fuckin stupit glaykit cunts – all of em!' He turned to the policemen. 'Dis he no realise how serious this is?'

Stony-face shrugged as if to say, 'Probably not.' He dealt with cunts like Big Hugh every day. 'How de ye mean "the match", Mrs Donnelly?' he asked.

'Rangers–Celtic, th' morra. He was talkin aboot tekin Jamie the match, bit ah wisnae fir huvin it.'

'Can ye no jist barge in the hoose, see if he's there? Ah'll come wi ye – *ah'll* dae it if ye want?' said Mick.

'It's no as simple as that, Mr Donnelly,' said the Mexican. 'We cannae jist keep walking in an oot ay his hoose whenever we feel like it. That's harassment.'

'Oh, an we don't want tae upset hum noo, dae we!' said Mick.

'Mick, sit doon,' said Evelyn.

'Sit doon? Fuck sakes!' He paced about the room, waving his arms. 'Mah boay's gone missin, bin teken by yir loony brar, who's jist fuckin nearly kilt an auld man an a wee lassie. We've aw given these cunts statements.' He pointed to the police. 'They know he's no safe! So whit are we aw waitin fir? An you want me tae sit doon, huv a cup ay tea?' He swept the cups off the table.

Evelyn started to sob. The Mexican cut in. 'Mr Donnelly, I realise this is hard fir ye. We will git him, bit it's like a game – it's difficult . . .'

'It's no that difficult,' said Mick. He pulled the door open and stormed out.

Shug lay in bed stroking Jamie's hair. The Wee Man was fast asleep. Shug still hadn't heard anything from his ma. He hoped she was all right. Hugh had told Shug she was away visiting his Auntie Jean, but Shug knew better. That old bastard had been giving her a hard time again, probably a black eye too, that's why she was staying away. His family was completely fucked, the whole lot of them: mental with a capital M.

He'd managed to pack some of Jamie's things when he took him out of bed last night. Not a lot of stuff, but just enough to tide him over till they got where they were going. Where to, that was the question? London, maybe? He'd enough money from the Tamazepam deal and what he'd squirrelled away from knocking a few motors for Harry over the past months. They'd get by until he sorted himself out with some work. He knew Jamie would probably cry for his ma and da but Shug was good at pacifying him. He knew the right things to say. In time Jamie would forget all about them. They didn't deserve him, the complete fuck-ups that they were.

Shug and Jamie could disappear in London, no problem. Wouldn't draw any attention to themselves either: a father and son making a new start, that's all they'd be. But first on the agenda was the gemme. After all, he'd promised the wee feller. After that they could get a taxi to Central Station and catch the train to London.

The door handle rattled slowly. Big Hugh was trying to get in. Fuck him, the dirty old cunt; he'd kill him before he'd let him in here.

'Whit is it?' Shug asked.

'It's me, son, ah wis jist checkin tae see if the wee feller wis asleep yet.'

'Aye, he is.'

'Gonnae let us in?'

'Away tae yir bed, Da, he's awright.'

'Whit's the door loacked fir?'

'Force ay habit. Ah'm away tae sleep – night.'

There was a pause as Big Hugh contemplated his options. 'Aye, gidnight then.'

Shug listened as Hugh shuffled off up the landing and shut his bedroom door. Shug knew he had to stay awake, keep a watch over the Wee Man. There was no way he was taking a chance with him. He sat up in bed and reached for his fags. He'd stay awake for days if he had to; anything for the Wee Man, anything at all. If it came down to it and someone said Shug had to eat a piece of dog shit or cut off his balls to save the Wee Man's life: no problem – pass the knife.

He lit up a fag and listened as Hugh mumbled away to himself in the next room. Probably annoyed that he couldn't get near Jamie, thought Shug. He reached under the mattress, pulled out a kitchen knife and placed it on the bedside table. Just let him try and come in here tonight. He'd cut his fucking hands off.

He put his hand into the pocket of his jeans and took out a wrap of speed. He opened it and poured the lot on to his tongue, wincing as he swallowed it. He'd stay awake all night and get the Wee Man out of the house first thing. They could get breakfast at McDonald's then go to the transport museum or something until it was time for the kick-off.

The sooner he got Jamie away from this place the better.

* * *

Korea: the Battle of the Hook. Snipers taking pot shots at his napper. Eighteen years old, running down a road with mortar bombs exploding either side of him. That was the closest Archie had came to death. Merchant Navy, that had its moments and all. Aye, he'd led a charmed life, right enough. Nothing had prepared him for this, though.

He could hear his heart beating and the noise of the monitor in his right ear. **Beep**__/__**Beep**____ /__**Beep**______/__ He was sure it was starting to get slower. Someone was sitting on the edge of the bed.

'Jean?' he mumbled. 'Whit are you dein here?'

'Hiya, darlin. Ah'v missed ye.' She smiled warmly at him and stood up. 'Come on,' she said as she slowly walked across the grass.

Grass? He looked about – he was in the park again. He pulled back the covers and turned to sit on the edge of the bed. All his pain was gone. He slid off the bed and stood on the soft warm grass. This was a good dream. He'd dreamed of Jean a lot over the past couple of years, but this was the best ever. He looked across the park to see where she'd gone. She was sitting on the park bench, waving at him.

He walked over and sat down next to her, watching the pigeon feed from her hand. He looked up at the sky – not a cloud. It was warm and sunny today. Bright, as though the sun was reflecting off a big aluminium plate at the end of the park.

Jean turned and smiled at him. He'd missed that beautiful smile – it could light up a room. Maybe it was her smile that was lighting up the park? It was like she'd never been away. He just knew they wouldn't be apart again; it had been too long.

She slowly stood up. The pigeon flew away. Jean turned and smiled at him and held out her hand. Archie stood up and took hold of it. She led him off towards the light.

__Beep__/_______Beep__________/__
_________Beeeeeeeeeeeeeeeeeeee-
ee_________________________________

Hugh woke up, feeling like he'd slept with his head in a vice. He sat up in bed and reached for his fags, He lit one, staring at the fag burns on the stained duvet, trying to figure out what he had to do today. It was New Year's Day . . . or was that yesterday? Was there enough drink to see him through? Then he remembered Shug and the Wee Man were staying. He'd better get up and make them something to eat. There was some bacon in the fridge, maybe a couple of eggs. He'd been to Asda and bought a few messages the other day. He had to – that bitch would rather he starved. Fucking gallivanting off with her pals. He'd have words with her when she eventually decided to show her face.

He pulled himself up, sat on the edge of the bed and looked across at a half-full glass of whisky on the bedside table. No sense in wasting that, he thought, reaching over for the glass. His hand shook as he picked it up. He immediately put it back down again before the lot spilled. He leaned over so his mouth was closer to the glass, and shakily raised it to his lips, inhaling some spilled ash off the bedside unit. The whisky burned his throat as it went down. He felt it curl around his empty stomach and burn inside him like acid. He must have an ulcer, surely to fuck? Whisky never used to burn his guts like that before?

He opened the door and walked barefoot along the sparse landing carpet. The door to Shug's room was open. He peered inside and saw it was empty. He went downstairs, expecting them to be sitting watching TV but the living-room was empty too. His eyes focused on the empty whisky bottle next to his seat and the ashtray that overflowed on to the floor. An overturned bowl of soup sat glued to the rug in front of the fire and the TV hissed away loudly in the corner. The screen was like a small snowstorm with an aggravating noise that made him wince. He located the remote control down the side of the couch. He switched off the TV, went through to the kitchen and looked in the fridge. There was an egg and a can of lager. He looked in the bread bin and saw there was only one slice of bread left. That bastard comes back here, eats all the grub and then fucks off without even a note? Just like his mother, a selfish cunt. And where was the Wee Man, come to think of it?

He supposed they'd be back soon enough. He opened the can of lager and took a long satisfying swig: icy cold, numbing the back of his throat – just what you need in the morning when you've a mouth like one of Gandhi's flip-flops. He glanced at the blackened pot that sat in the sink, covered in thick, greasy water with pieces of scrambled egg floating on its surface. It suddenly hit him: that was the last of the drink. No food in the house either. No money in his pocket, and the next giro over a week away. Probably two weeks with these workshy bastards at the social off on their Christmas holidays. They didn't give a fuck about him, oh no. Just so long as they were happy over Christmas, fuck everyone else.

Then inspiration struck:

A provi cheque!

He went into the living-room and opened the small drawer of the drinks cabinet, searching through the various policies and telephone books for Irene's address book. He pulled it out and looked through it for Ann Wishart's number. Ann was an agent for Provident and was used to getting called upon at this time of the year. People had families to think of, unexpected guests to feed. She'd understand. He dialled the number and cleared his throat.

'Hullo?' said Ann.

'Ann, how's it goin?'

'Who's this?'

'Hughey McNab, darlin.' He tugged the cord for the venetian blinds and squinted as the sunlight hit him.

'Oh, Shug . . .' came her less than happy reply. 'How are ye?'

'Aw the better fir hearin yir beautiful voice. Huv ye no left that man ay yirs yet?' he joked.

She tried to play along, wishing he'd piss off. She knew what a drunken bastard he was. 'No yet, Shuggie . . . bit you'll be the furst tae know when ah dae, eh?'

Big Hugh laughed: he could still pull them. Big charming bastard that he was. He got to the point.

'Listen, darlin, the reason ah'm callin: we've hud some family turn up unexpectedly, an ye know whit it's like; we've awready stocked up an aw that, bit it wis jist me an Irene plannin a quiet time at hame this year, ye know? Anyway, we're a wee bit short at the minute and wondered if ye could see us awright fir a wee provi cheque?'

'How much?' asked Ann cautiously.

'Jist twenty quid, that's aw.'

There was silence on the other end of the phone for a few seconds. Hugh held his breath and prayed she'd say all right.

'Is Irene okay aboot this? You know ah usually deal wi hur?'

'Aye, aye,' he said. 'She's jist away tae the Paki's fir some milk; said tae gie you a call and ask ye.'

'How dis she want tae pay it back?'

He hadn't considered that. 'Er, same as she always dis?'

'Two pound a week?'

'Aye, that's it.'

'Well if yir sure it's okay wi Irene?'

'Aye, nae bother. Ah'll be up in an oor then, is that awright?'

'Aye, aye, ah'll see ye then. Cheerio.'

'Bye, hen.' He put the phone down. 'Ya fuckin dansa!'

He put the kettle on to boil some water for a shave and hurried upstairs to find something to wear. He'd make an effort: get dressed, have a quick wash and a shave and comb his hair. He'd nip round to Ann's, pick up the twenty quid provi, be down the Paki's within half an hour and get fifteen quids' worth of bevvy for the cheque off Mohammed – the money-grabbing wee cunt that he was. Still, Hugh was only losing a fiver – small price to pay for a full day's swallay.

After the police had got nowhere with Hugh, Mick decided to pay him a visit himself. He banged on the front door and hammered on the windows. He knew he was in there, the old bastard, but he wouldn't come to the door. Mick went to the phone box and phoned but nobody answered. He went back and shouted through the letterbox, calling him a blue-nosed cunt and telling him what he thought of the Queen, but Hugh still never took the bait.

Mick went back to his ma's and sat in the kitchen with

his head in his hands. She couldn't understand why the police weren't doing anything. Neither could he. 'We're doing all we can,' is what they told him. If that consisted of sitting on their arses then they were doing a splendid job. His da thought Mick should be at home with Evelyn, but as far as Mick was concerned it was over. If anything happened to Jamie, he'd never forgive her; wouldn't be able to look at her without remembering what a stupid bitch she'd been by letting Shug keep that key.

The only thing he could do was sit it out and wait for the match. Shug was a dense bastard. The one place he'd take Jamie and not expect anyone to know where they were was Ibrox. Kick-off was an hour away. In one hour he'd hopefully have his son back.

Irene sat back on Audrey's comfy couch, looking down at Audrey's two teenage daughters curled up in front of the TV. Shona had got a videotape of *Legends of the Fall* for Christmas, and she and her sister Kirsty had been winding Irene up about fancying Brad Pitt with his long hair.

Normality, thought Irene. It was a long time since she'd seen anything like it. Here were two girls with an alcoholic da – well balanced and laughing and joking in his company. Irene watched the way they acted around him – they had nothing to fear. On New Year's Eve they both gave him a hug and a kiss and wished him a Happy New Year. It struck Irene how genuine the girls were.

They could hug and kiss their da like that without pulling away, repulsed. She tried to imagine Evelyn doing that to Big Hugh but couldn't for the life of her. She supposed it must be because these girls weren't living with the drink and knew it would be a different story if they were. She glanced over at the phone and thought about giving Evelyn that call. With all the celebrations last night it had completely slipped her mind.

Tom came in, putting on his jacket. 'Ah'm away the pub tae git *steamin*,' he said. Nobody batted an eyelid.

Audrey watched Brad Pitt on the TV. His long hair blew in the breeze as he rode a horse through a field of corn. 'Aye, well try no tae git too drunk, eh? If yir no back in time fir yir dinner ah'll gie it the dog.'

'Aye, see ye later, eh?' He gave her a peck on the cheek.

'Enjoy yirsel.' She reached for a box of Black Magic on the coffee table and started unwrapping the Cellophane.

'Bye, Irene,' said Tom, amused by the expression on her face.

'Bye.' She managed a confused smile.

He zipped up his jacket, ruffled Shona's hair and walked out of the door.

'Bye, Da,' said Kirsty.

'See ye later, pal!' Tom shouted from the hall before closing the front door behind him.

Audrey offered the Black Magic to Irene. Irene shook

her head. 'He's no away fir a drink is he?' she asked, concerned.

Audrey laughed at Irene's naivety.

Kirsty turned round to Irene. 'Irene, you are so easy to wind up.'

'He aywis says that when he's away tae the pub,' said Shona, 'same pishy patter aw the time.'

Irene looked at Audrey, concerned. 'But he says he wis goin the pub?'

'Aye,' said Irene, 'tae watch the Rangers/Celtic match on Sky. He meets a few of hus auld pals there. Ah'v warned hum no tae be gittin intae rounds wi them any mair though; they aw drink pints – he only drinks fresh orange an lemonade.'

'Aye,' said Shona, turning round, 'they were aw tekin the pish, weren't they, Ma?'

'Jist you watch the film, madam,' said Irene. Shona turned back to the TV.

Audrey saw Irene's surprised expression. 'Ye didnae think . . .?'

'Ah didnae know whit tae think when he said that.'

'He'll go an shout an scream at the telly wi the rest ay them doon there, bit the difference is he'll come back the same way he went oot: sober. That's whit ah'v goat tae be grateful fir today.' She popped a chocolate in her mouth and turned back to the film. She nudged Irene and indicated the TV. 'Here's where he teks hus shirt aff.' She grinned. 'Bet ye widnae say no, eh, Irene – ah know ah widnae.' She threw her head back and laughed out loud, exposing her chocolate-covered teeth. Irene laughed too, relieved.

'Mu-um, that's disgustin,' said Kirsty, turning round.

'Yir a pure embarrassment,' said Shona.

Irene watched the screen as Brad Pitt pulled the thick linen shirt off over his head. Her mind was elsewhere. She tried to imagine Hugh going to the pub to watch the Old Firm match, sitting drinking fresh orange and lemonade with his cronies. In another life, maybe. Not this one. She hated the Old Firm match – the memories it held. She looked up at the calendar on the wall and shuddered as she remembered what date it was.

2 January 1971

Irene stood at the sink doing the dishes. She turned on the radio to find out the score of the Old Firm clash. The score would determine what mood Hugh would come home in: happy if Rangers won, depressed if they lost. Either way he'd be pished.

No sooner had she flicked the switch on the radio than the music stopped and the announcement came on.

'And the latest news we have of the Ibrox disaster is a confirmed fifty-eight people have died.'

Irene dropped a plate: it smashed at her feet.

'Reports of more deaths are coming in by the minute. The disaster happened today when the steel barriers gave way to a surging crowd on Stairway 13 at the Rangers end of Ibrox Stadium.'

Irene heard a scream. She looked out of the window and saw Agnes Burns running down the street, wearing just a towel. This couldn't be happening – Hugh was at the match.

She ran out into the close and looked around: neighbours were wandering about with tears streaming down their faces. She ran down the stairs and out of the close, looking in the street for signs of him. He was nowhere to be seen. Her heart pounded as though it would burst out of her chest. He was dead, she knew it. Every time Rangers played at home, as regular as clockwork, he'd gone to the match. She hoped, by some strange twist of fate, that he hadn't gone this week.

She remembered how happy he was the other day when he came in with his ticket. This was no ordinary match – it was the New Year Old Firm match: tickets only, and after weeks of trying he'd finally managed to get one.

She ran off down the street in the direction of the Two Bells, hoping somebody in there had seen him at the match and would be able to tell her if he was okay or not.

Her bottom lip curled downwards as she struggled to fight the tears. She knew it was hopeless. Hugh would be dead. This was how death occurred – when you least expected it. They'd only been married two months. You read in the Sunday papers about these poor women this kind of thing happened to. She never imagined she'd be one of them. 'Poor lassie, only merrit a couple ay months an hur man was wan ay they bloks killed at Ibrox.'

Hugh had gone out of the door this morning with a bad dose of the shakes after a night on the drink. She'd been nagging him about what a state for a man in his twenties to get into. He said he'd only enough money for a wee curer and he'd be back for something to eat before the gemme. He never came home. That was Hugh all over: a liar to the end.

She burst open the door of the Two Bells and looked about. It was full of men, most of them crying and watching the TV for news of the disaster. Hugh was nowhere to be seen.

She pushed through the crowd of men, searching, asking anybody, 'Huv ye seen mah man? Hus Big Hugh McNab bin in?' Guys she'd never seen before shook their heads, unconcerned. They were too busy with the report on the telly.

It was hopeless. She burst into tears but nobody batted an eyelid. It was just another person greeting – on a day when Glasgow was full of them. She turned for the door, praying that he was all right and by the time she got home he'd be sitting there waiting for her.

'Irene!' came the man's voice. She turned round to see where it was coming from.

Wee Iain Bruce the barman came up to the edge of the bar. 'Ye lookin fir Hugh?'

'Aye,' she blurted out, hopeful, unable to stem the tears.

'He's ower there in the corner,' he said.

Irene was unable to take it in. 'Mah Hugh? Big Shuggie McNab?'

'Aye,' said Iain, 'he's lyin pished but . . . ah hope y've come tae tek hum hame.'

Irene elbowed her way through the crowd to the back of the room and there he was, slumped over the table. She ran over and hugged him. He lifted his head up. She saw his eyes were red. He'd been crying. 'Irene, they're deid . . . the boays are deid.' He cried. She hugged him tight. She'd never been so glad to see him – the stupid drunken bastard that he was.

She got him to his feet and took him home. He lay in his bed for two days. All she got out of him was: 'It should huv bin me, Irene, it should huv bin me.'

When he finally surfaced he told her what had happened: he'd gone for his curer in the morning with enough money for a half and a beer. He'd got the taste for it and the feeling was starting to come back in his body again, but Iain had refused him credit: once bitten twice shy. A couple of Rangers supporters were looking to buy a ticket for their pal, and Hugh, weighing up the pros and cons of the situation: (a) he needed a drink; (b) he had a ticket in his pocket; (c)these boys had money; and (d) he'd been to plenty of Old Firm games before and didn't think he was going to miss much, came to the conclusion that selling the ticket would make everyone happy – especially him. This unwittingly saved his arse: he usually stood right in front of Stairway 13. The man had the luck of the devil. He also had his temper.

In the weeks that followed he became more moody and irritable, snapping for the slightest thing. If Irene thought he could be an evil bastard before, then he'd become ten times worse now.

When things had calmed down he took her out. She was happy to see him back to normal; they were starting to act like a couple again. They went to the Barrowlands for a drink and a dance and all seemed to be going well. Hugh had a drink in him but he was happy, smiling and joking for the first time in weeks and that's what really counted.

She watched as he got up to go to the bar. Couples were dancing everywhere. She laughed as a guy carrying a tray of drinks skidded on his arse on a wet patch on the dance floor. His arms jutted upwards to cushion the effect his fall had on the tray, while his arse took the full force. Gingerly, he pulled the tray down in front of his eyes and his face lit up – not a drop spilled. Irene howled with laughter. A crowd of people at a nearby table stood and applauded him. The guy stood up and took a bow.

Irene looked across to the bar. Hugh stood finishing his pint, then stopped and turned to face a young guy standing next to him who was drinking with his two mates. She knew that look, even from this distance. Something was wrong. Hugh calmly tapped the guy on the shoulder and tilted his head for him to lean forward so Hugh could say something in his ear. The guy leaned forward and Hugh took a step backwards. There was a sound she'd never forget to this day as Hugh calmly pushed the pint glass into the guy's face. It broke around about his mouth in a second, sending long shards of glass into his cheeks and throat. Irene felt sick to the pit of her stomach. One of the guy's mates grabbed a beer towel and quickly wrapped it round the bloke's neck. The other looked like he was going to square up to Hugh, then quickly changed his mind as the bloke with the beer towel dragged their bleeding friend to the exit.

Hugh turned from the bar, marched over and grabbed her hand, pulling her out of her seat. 'Moan, we're goin,' he said. She wasn't arguing. He never spoke all the way home in the taxi, just sat and fumed.

When he calmed down he told her what he'd overheard. 'Ah wis stonnin at the bar mindin mah aen business, when ah hears these bloks talkin aboot the Ibrox disaster, right? So, ah'm stonnin there, earywiggin, waitin tae git served when ah hears this cunt sayin tae hus mate; "There wisnae enough ay they orange bastards killed fir my likin. Sixty-six? Should huv bin six hunnert an six!" An he's fucking laughin wi his pal! So I turns an looks at hum and ah gies hum a mad grin. The cunt fuckin grins back at me like ah'm a pape – in on the fuckin joke or somehun – so ah sais tae hum, "Haw, mate, mere," an he fuckin leans in, so I goes, "See every time ye huv a shave y'll remember the second of January, ya cunt!" An ah sticks mah glass in his fuckin coupon. Cunt'll no forget that in a hurry.'

He looked at her as though he were waiting to be congratulated. She stared at him unbelievingly. What was going on? What was all the heartbreak over the past few weeks about if people were going to carry on like this, as though nothing had ever happened? Nothing would ever change – how could it? As far as Hugh was concerned the cease-fire was over; he'd made sure of that. She shook her head. Hugh noticed and tried to explain.

'Irene, ye don't come oot wi comments like that at the dancin withoot expectin some cunt tae chib ye. The cunt wis oot ay order an that's that!'

She looked at him, gobsmacked. He could see he wasn't getting anywhere.

'Ye jist don't git it, dae ye?' he said.

'No ah don't.' She shook her head.

He looked at her like she was an alien. 'Ah, fuck you,' he said, 'ah'm away oot!' He got up, grabbed his jacket and stormed out. Little did she know but it would be his battle-cry from that day on.

Mick dialled the number. Someone picked up the phone at the other end.

'Radio cars?'

He put ten pence in the call box and looked across the bar to see George coming back to their table with another whisky for him. He'd told George he didn't want to get pished, but George reckoned Mick needed a wee dram in him to settle his nerves.

'Hi, ah need three taxis . . . goin fae the Halfway in Drumchapel tae Finlays in the Gallowgate. How long will it be?' asked Mick.

'Aboot ten minutes. Whit's the name please?'

'Donnelly.'

'Be there as soon as we can.'

'Thanks.' Mick put down the phone and went over to join George.

'How long?' asked George.

Mick knocked back his whisky. 'Ten minutes.'

'Right, boays, drink up, we're in business. Did ye phone Ronnie?'

'Aye, ah phoned hum this mornin.'

George looked as if to say, 'Well?'

Mick nodded. 'Aye, he'll dae it.'

'Don't worry, Mick. We'll git yir boay.' George gave the nod to the boys. They finished their pints, placed their glasses on the bar and filed out of the pub: a small infantry, decked out in blue and white.

Day Sixteen: The Old Firm Match, Ibrox, 2 January

Have you seen the Glasgow Rangers?
Have you seen the boys in blue?
They are loved where ere they go boys,
for they are loyal and they are true.
They have played away in Monaco,
far away in the USA,
but the greatest game in history
is the game on New Years Day!

Jamie pulled the jaggy scarf away from his neck and looked about the ground. He'd never seen this many people before in his life – only on the telly. Everybody in Glasgow must be here, he thought. Who's driving the buses, serving in the shops? Maybe everybody went back to their work after the football?

'Uncle Shug, are we goin back tae mah hoose fir wir tea?'

'Aye, aye – tea, yir jist here.'

'Dis mah mammie know?'

Shug looked about at the crowd. 'Aye, ah phoned hur – she says its awright – stoap worryin.'

A roar went up as the Rangers team filed out on to the pitch. Jamie looked across at the crowd as a huge cloud of steam belched up into the rafters. A man further up the aisle was bent over, being sick on his shoes. He turned round and saw Jamie looking at him. Jamie smiled. The man wiped his mouth, smiled back and gave Jamie the thumbs-up.

Shug grabbed Jamie under the arms and picked him up so he could get a better view of the players running down the pitch towards them.

'See hum, Wee Man? First player tae be transferred fir a million quid between two Scottish clubs. Imagine how many sweets ye could buy wi a million quid, eh?'

'Aye.'

'An hum – four an a half million! There's yir goalie. An see that loat ower there . . .' He pointed to the Celtic end.

'Aye.'

'That's the enemy.'

A guy sitting next to him, wearing a Rangers bonnet, shared Shug's sentiments. He grinned. Shug clocked it: an audience.

'Whit does the Pope smoke, Wee Man?' prompted Shug.

'Dope.'

The guy laughed: *Out of the mouths of babes.*

'Well, you tell that loat then,' said Shug, pointing to the Celtic end.

'THE POPE SMOKES DOPE!' shouted Jamie.

A bunch of blokes sitting behind Shug laughed at the gallus wee feller.

Jamie turned and laughed back at them. He looked up at the flag they were waving with a big red hand in the middle of it.

'Gies a song, Wee Man,' said one of the men holding on to the flag.

Jamie started singing: 'Hullo, hullo, we are the Billy Boys!'

The men behind them joined in, raising their flag high and scaring the life out of him with their booming voices:

HULLO, HULLO, WE ARE THE BILLY
BOYS, HULLO, HULLO, Y'LL KNOW US
BY OOR NOISE,
WE'RE UP TO OOR KNEES IN FENIAN
BLOOD, SURRENDER OR YOU'LL DIE,
FOR WE ARE THE BRIGTON DERRY
BOYS!

'Jist here, mate.' Big George pointed to the house with the closed curtains. The taxi pulled up. George got out, walked up the path and knocked on the door. He'd sent Mick ahead in the first taxi. No point in telling him about this wee detour. George's mates went to get out of the taxi but George shook his head at them.

The front door opened.

Fuckye!

Hugh's main concern, as he hit the deck, was the whisky spilling from his glass, not the fact that someone had just stuck the nut on him.

He looked up. Big George waded into the hall and grabbed him by what little hair he had left. 'Where is he, ya auld cunt, ye?'

'Whit? Whit?'

'Y've goat two mair chances. Ah want tae know where Jamie is – an ah want tae know noo!'

Hugh felt his head: his hair had been pulled out by the roots. 'Ah don't know.' He ran his hand over his face and looked at the blood on his hand. Split eyebrow – bastard.

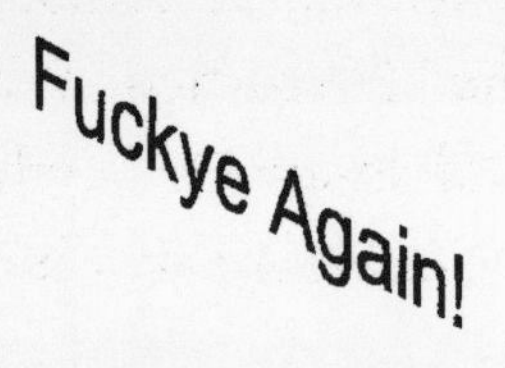

George stuck the boot in to his kidneys.

'AAAAHHHHGGG.'

'Last chance!'

Hugh gave up. He wasn't fit for this shite any more: terrorising folk was a young man's game now. 'THE GEMME, THEY'RE AT THE GEMME!'

George looked down at the pathetic old bastard. His da always talked about Big Shuggie McNab as if he were some kind of superman – used to rule the roost around here, get respect. How the fuck could anyone respect a jakey old cunt like that?

The only man George respected was his da. Years ago, when his da worked for the parks and gardens, some bastard burst into the hut and attacked him with a blade. Hasn't worked since. Walks with a stick. Never complains, just gets on with it. They never did find out who did it. If George ever found them he'd . . .

He closed the front door behind him.

Mick walked into Finlays with the squad of boys, dressed in blue and white. He went over to the bar. Ronnie's mates acknowledged him with a nod of the head, as though there had been a death in the family.

'Awright, Mick,' said Ronnie.

'Thanks fir yir help, Ronnie.' He shook his hand.

'Nae bother; moan, wir wastin time.' He turned to the boys wearing the Celtic colours, and laughed. 'Right, you loat, aff wi they colours and git some ay this blue shite oan.'

The Rangers boys took off shirts, scarves and hats and started handing them over.

Big George came in, smiling. 'Haw, Ronnie, here's a skerf fir ye!'

Ronnie came over and shook George's hand. 'Happy New Year. Who'd'v thought we'd'v seen the day, eh?' He took the scarf off George and tied it round his neck. 'Mah granda'd be spinnin in his grave if he saw this. It's jist fir today, mind – business as usual tomorrow.'

'Aye, only to be expected,' said George, handing over a dozen tickets for the Rangers end.

Wee Eck, one of Big George's mates, didn't want to miss a golden opportunity. He took out a disposable camera and lined everyone up against the bar.

FLASH.

In the dimly lit police room that overlooked the ground a couple of senior officers milled about at the back, leaning on a table, drinking tea and talking about football. Evelyn perched on the edge of her seat, next to a white-moustached guy in his fifties who gave her the impression she was sitting next to a Des Lynam look-alike, not the match commander who was busy watching the Rangers crowd through the CCTV.

Evelyn pointed to the corner of the screen. 'Can ye try ower there?'

The commander moved the joystick and the camera zoomed into the crowd. Evelyn scrutinised the screen. Nothing.

Mick sat looking out of the window as the bus pulled into Ibrox. It had come true, if only for a day: Rangers and Celtic supporters travelling to the match together – on a Celtic supporters bus – laughing and joking as well. Pity it had to have happened under these circumstances. He looked up the aisle of the bus. The boys were studying the snapshot of Shug before passing it on.

He hoped to fuck Jamie was all right.

Ronnie got off the bus and heard the familiar sound coming from the Celtic end of the ground:

Hail! Hail! The Celts are here.
What the hell do we care,
what the hell do we care?
Hail! Hail! The Celts are here,
and what the hell do we care now?
For it's a grand old team to play for
and it's a grand old team to see,
and if you know the history
then it's enough to make your heart
go . . .
We don't care what the animals say,
what the hell do we care?
For we only know that there's gonna
be a show
and the Glasgow Celtic will be there!

This was too weird. Ronnie followed close behind George, Mick and the boys as they approached the gate to the Rangers end. He felt his insides churn as he handed in his ticket and walked through the turnstile. He could hear the Rangers supporters winding up Celtic.

Hail, hail, the Pope's in jail!
What the fuck do we care, what the fuck do we care?
Hail, Hail, the Pope's in jail,
what the fuck do we care now?

'Ye awright?' Mick asked Ronnie.

'Aye.'

'Ah'm no,' said Mick. As they climbed the stairs they could hear the whole of the Celtic supporters singing at the other end of the park above the noise of the Rangers crowd.

I'm sick and tired of slavery since the
day that I was born,
and I'm off to join the IRA and I'm
off tomorrow morn.
We're off to Dublin in the green –
FUCK THE QUEEN!
Where the helmets glisten in the sun
– FUCK HER SON!
Where the bayonets SLASH the
Orange SASH to the echo of the
Thompson Gun!

'Let's git intae these Fenian bastards!' shouted Jamie.

Shug laughed and looked down at him proudly, like Spike the dog from *Tom and Jerry*. 'That's mah boay.'

Rangers were attacking the Celtic defence.

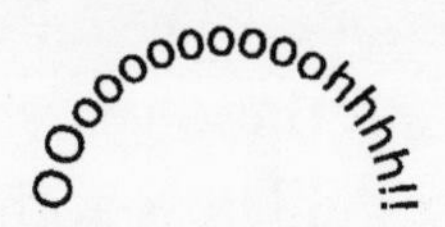

The crowd let out a gasp of disappointment as Rangers nearly scored. Shug started a chant.

HULLO, HULLO, WE ARE THE BILLY
BOYS, HULLO, HULLO, Y'LL KNOW US
BY OOR NOISE,
WE'RE UP TO OOR KNEES IN FENIAN
BLOOD, SURRENDER OR YOU'LL DIE,
FOR WE ARE THE BRIGTON DERRY
BOYS!

The crowd around about him started joining in. Twenty yards behind him George, Mick, Ronnie and the boys made their way to their seats, taking in the enormity of the crowd and the deafening sound of the Rangers end.

HULLO, HULLO, WE ARE THE BILLY
BOYS, HULLO, HULLO, Y'LL KNOW US
BY OOR NOISE,
WE'RE UP TO OOR KNEES IN FENIAN
BLOOD, SURRENDER OR YOU'LL DIE,
FOR WE ARE THE BRIGTON DERRY
BOYS!

The train slowed down as it approached Bridge Street underground. The doors opened and Chic stepped on to the platform, looking up at the writing above the stairs. **Deeks ya dick**. It was still there after all these years.

It was meant for Derek McLean, Chic's old boss at the furniture removal place he'd once worked at. Derek, or Deeks, as he liked to be known among the boys *was* a dick who had it in for Chic from day one and was instrumental in getting him the sack. Deeks travelled into town every day, leaving his car at Bridge Street car park while taking the underground. Chic had simply left him a little message to remind the sleekit bastard, every day, who he was.

Chic smiled to himself as he trudged up the stairs. He knew it was childish, but he'd done it. Five years ago. It must have had the effect of Chinese water torture on poor old Derek by now.

He walked through the single turnstile and felt an umbrella dig in his back. He turned round. A guy in a suit stood behind him searching in a briefcase. Chic gave him a look that said, 'Dae ye fuckin mind?' But the guy was oblivious and continued his search, holding up the queue in the process.

'*Beg Eshoo*, sur?' A *Big Issue* seller waved a copy of the magazine at Chic as he came through the turnstile.

'Naw thanks, mate.' Chic pulled out a car key with a key fob attached.

'Any spare change?'

Chic pretended he hadn't heard as he walked past the ticket office and out of the entrance.

'Soarry fir askin, sur,' the seller said to Chic, then

turned to the guy hunting in his briefcase, hoping he was looking for his wallet. '*Beg Eshoo*, sur?'

Chic stepped outside and looked among the rows of cars as though he'd forgotten where he'd put his. 'Black Orion 1.6i Ghia, H reg.' He looked about and pressed the key fob. The indicator lights on a black Orion flashed at him from over by the Habib Bank.

'Nice wan, Harry,' he said under his breath as the Park and Ride punters raced past him to get to their cars.

Harry had been up to his usual tricks, fitting an alarm to the car of an unsuspecting punter. Chic had paid a couple of visits to the guy's address but the car was nowhere to be seen. Harry suggested Bridge Street car park because the bloke had told Harry he was going to the Old Firm match and couldn't be bothered with all the hassle of trying to park near Ibrox; Bridge Street was an easier option for him. Easier for me, thought Chic as he walked through the rows of cars.

Then he saw it: a black Calibra, full body kit, alloys, with a mobile sitting in a holder and a laptop bag on the back seat. He felt a surge of excitement as he thought of the possibilities. He'd get at least four hundred for the laptop – keep that money-grabbing wee bitch off his back for a while. Not to mention what he'd get for the phone. He looked again: looked like one of those new slim Nokias. Then there was the car. If he could get that over to Stranraer without Harry knowing he'd be quids in. 'Ya fuckin dancer.'

Fuck the Orion – it could wait. He looked about the

car park as people started driving up to the exit barrier. He reached into the pocket of his combat trousers, pulled out a screwdriver and sidled up to the driver's door. He put it into the barrel. A quick couple of bangs with the palm of his hand and the barrel fell inside the door. He reached in and pressed the bar.

Clunk. It opened. No alarm.

He jumped into the passenger seat, took the mobile out of its holder and pocketed it. He turned round and hauled the laptop bag on to the passenger seat. It felt heavy. There was definitely a laptop inside. He felt another surge of excitement running through his stomach and down to his groin. He was sure he was getting a hard-on. This game was better than sex, especially when you had daft bastards leaving stuff like this lying about. What the fuck were they thinking: that they'd come back to their car and find it all just as they'd left it? Stupid cunts like that had more money than sense: they deserved all they got. He slammed the driver's door shut, grinning to himself as he pictured a fat wee businessman standing in the empty space, looking about, scratching his head.

ZZZZZZZTTT. The doors locked.

'Wait a minute?' Chic tried the door handle but it wouldn't budge. Fucking central locking – all tied into the ignition. He pulled out his screwdriver again and wedged it under the plastic steering column, levering it downward to burst the panel off. He'd soon have this baby hot-wired and ready to roll . . .

Whooo Whooo Whooo Whooo. What the fuck? *Now* the alarm starts to go off! Never mind, a couple of seconds more and he'd soon have the fucker sorted . . . He looked up to see if anyone was about. What was that cunt doing? The *Big Issue* seller was walking towards him, talking into what looked like a radio. Chic looked across the road. Police were dodging through the traffic, running towards the car park.

'Basta!' He pulled at the door handle again. Nothing. He looked at the *Big Issue* seller standing in front of the car, grinning at him and shaking his head. 'The cunt's polis!' Maybe if he'd given him some change he would have left him alone?

He felt the panic rising and tried the passenger door but it was closed tight. He picked up the laptop bag and swung it at the window but all it did was bounce back. He looked out of the driver's window again: the police were pushing past people at the bus stop, making their way over to the car. Chic looked up at the grinning *Big Issue* seller as he pulled out his ID and flashed it smugly at him through the windscreen.

It was a honeytrap. How could he have been so stupid? He'd seen it on TV a million times – on the same programme that showed him how to block phone boxes for fuck sakes. He glared at the *Big Issue* seller and gripped the steering wheel in anger, contemplating banging his head off it. But he knew it would only make this grinning cunt's day.

'Fuck, fuck, fuck, fuck, fuck, ***FUUUUUUUCKKKKKK!!!!!***'

* * *

'There! Over there!' Evelyn pointed at the screen. The match commander moved the joystick. The camera zoomed in on Jamie and Shug. Evelyn breathed a sigh of relief. 'He's awright.'

'Is that yir son?' asked the commander.

Evelyn nodded and smiled, relieved.

The commander picked up a chart of the Rangers end and got on the radio: 'B272 from police room.'

Evelyn reached into her bag, took a cigarette out of the packet and shakily lit it up.

A voice from B Division came on the radio: 'Go ahead.'

'Proceed to the fifth row from the front. Intercept the bloke, wearing a black anorak, black jeans – goat a wee boay beside him. That's yir man. Proceed to police room.'

'Received.'

'B486 from police room.'

A policewoman came on the radio: 'Go ahead.'

'Wait fir B272 to intercept the guy in the fifth row. Return to the police room with the wee boay sittin next tae um – tell him his mammie's waitin fir hum.' He looked at Evelyn. She breathed a sigh of relief, exhaling the cigarette smoke across the room. She shook her head at him as if to say, 'If you'd any idea what I've been through . . .' He smiled at her, knowingly.

'All received,' said the policewoman through the radio.

* * *

Ronnie and his pal sat, watching the Celtic crowd singing 'The Fields of Athenry'. They turned and looked at each other, wishing they were over at the other end where they belonged. Ronnie's pal started humming along. Ronnie nudged him and shook his head: they were too young to die.

Big George turned round and looked up the aisle. Something was going on. A policeman had just finished speaking into his radio and was walking down towards them. Fuck, that's all he needed. He followed the policeman's field of vision across to a policewoman; she was down near the pitch, heading their way too. George looked down at the rows of heads in front of him. One of the heads turned round and said something to the head behind him. Wee Eck looked up at Big George's face for clues. Then George recognised Shug. 'It's hum!' said George. 'The basta! . . . Moan!' George and Eck made their way along the aisle, pushing through the seated crowd until they got behind the unsuspecting Shug. They crouched on their hunkers behind him. George tapped Shug on the shoulder. Shug turned round. 'Awright, Shug man . . . remember me?' grinned George.

'Naw, mate. Who are ye?' Shug gulped.

'Don't tell us that yiv forgoat me awready? Ah'v brought ye a wee message from ma ex-burd . . . Karen.' He pulled out a thin Kitchen Devil.

'FUCK!' Shug dived out of his seat and made a run for it, down the aisle towards the pitch, knocking the policewoman over in the process. George's mates started running towards the barrier. Mick started running from the left. Rawhide – round em up. ***Yee ha!***

Who's that team?
For ever and ever, we'll follow the Gers,
The Glasgow Rangers, the Teddy Bears,
For we will be mastered, BY WHOM? by no Fenian Bastard,
we'll keep the Blue Flag flying high!

Blue-nosed dicks, thought Ronnie as he came bounding over from the right. George steamed straight ahead, throwing objecting bodies out of the way, trying to get to Shug. Shug dodged the police and made it to the barrier. He climbed up and went to jump on to the pitch. Big George came slamming into the barrier, managing to get a hand to Shug's scarf as he jumped. Shug landed on the pitch, half throttled as the scarf tightened round his neck.

For it's here I am an Orangeman, just come across the sea,
For singing and for dancing, I hope that I'll please thee,
I can sing and dance with any man, as I did in days of yore.
And it's on the twelfth I long to wear the Sash my Father wore!

George tried to reel Shug in like a fish but Shug wriggled free of the scarf and ran off down the sideline, tearing towards the Celtic end. Two stewards from Rockstead Security tried to stop him, but he body-swerved them both and carried on running.

The policewoman picked up the bewildered Jamie and set off towards the police room with him. Mick came running up to her, breathless. 'It's awright, ah'm hus da,' he panted.

'Da!' exclaimed Jamie, surprised to see him at the match. Mick picked him up, holding him tight as he followed the policewoman. He gave the crowd a final look: he never did like the Old Firm game – ninety minutes of pure hate. If they knew what he was he'd be dead.

Rangers attacked the Celtic goalmouth and put the ball in the back of the net. The Rangers supporters went wild. Mick looked at Jamie's face; he was scared by what was going on. He wasn't the only one. Mick clutched Jamie closer to him and bounded up the aisle, trying to get away from the noise.

IT IS OLD BUT IT IS BEAUTIFUL, IT'S
RED IT'S WHITE AND IT'S BLUE,
IT'S WORN ON THE SLOPES OF IBROX
PARK, AND A PLACE CALLED
PARKHEAD TOO,
MY FATHER WORE IT AS A YOUTH IN
THE BYE GONE DAYS OF YORE,

AND IT'S ON DISPLAY EVERY
SATURDAY EVERY TIME THE RANGERS
SCORE!

Shug pelted along the sideline, looking like the mad greyhound on the cover of Blur's *Parklife*.

Celtic supporters, annoyed at the Rangers goal, roared 'OFFSIDE' and threw scarves on to the pitch. Shug continued to run. Without losing momentum he did a forward break fall with the skill of a black belt and picked up a Celtic scarf. He landed back on his feet, tied the scarf round his neck and ran towards the Celtic supporters.

The ref disallowed Rangers' goal: the Celtic supporters went wild. Shug stood on the pitch in front of them. 'OOH, AAH, UP THE RAH, SAY OOH AH, UP THE RAH!'

He dived over the barrier to be welcomed like a long-lost brother.

JINGLE BELLS, JINGLE BELLS,
JINGLE ALL THE WAY;
OH WHAT FUN IT IS TO FUCK
THE HUNS ON NEW YEAR'S
DAY, HEY!
JINGLE BELLS, JINGLE BELLS . . .

The match commander zoomed in: Shug had his arms around Celtic supporters' shoulders and was jumping up and down, singing. The commander smiled: now he had him.

Mick carried Jamie into the police room. He put Jamie down and watched him run over to Evelyn. She threw her cigarette into the ashtray and picked him up, almost squeezing the life out of him. Mick looked across at her and smiled.

'Oh, son.' Tears ran down her face. She hugged him tight and swung him from side to side.

Mick walked over and stood in front of her. He looked at her, stony-faced. 'Ah think y've goat some explainin tae dae, don't you?' he said.

She studied his expression. Was he serious? How the hell did he know what had happened in the past? Had he been in touch with her ma, beat it out of her da? What? Whatever it was, the cat was now definitely out of the bag. She felt cold, sick to the pit of her stomach. There was no going back now. She had to explain. She stared at the floor, thinking of a way to tell him.

'Look, ah wis jist a wee lassie; he made me think it wis aw mah fault – that the social would come an tek me away if ah telt anyone.' She glanced up at him.

He looked amused, puzzled by what she was saying. 'Whit ye oan aboot?' he asked.

She stared at him for a second. Had she heard him right? 'Er, whit are *you* oan aboot?' she said.

He indicated the lipstick-covered cigarette ends and the one that still burned in the ashtray. 'Ye promised me y'd gie them up in the New Year.'

Fuck. He was on about the fags. 'Oh,' she said, realising he was none the wiser, 'aye, ah will . . . ah will noo.'

He looked at her, suspicious. Something was going on that he didn't know about. What was this business about the social? 'Whit wis aw yir fault?' he asked.

She took a deep breath. 'Mick, ah'll tell ye when we get home, ah promise.'

'Aye, like ye promised aboot the fags?'

She took her cigarettes and lighter out of her bag and tossed them into the wastepaper basket by the door. 'Ah mean it this time,' she said. 'Nae mair secrets.'

He put his arms around her and hugged her. 'Ah hope so.'

A policeman popped his head round the door. 'Kin y's stick aroon fir a few minutes – jist a couple of wee questions an we'll arrange a car tae tek ye hame, eh?'

'Sounds good tae me,' said Mick.

The commander picked up the chart for the Celtic end and scanned it to see where B Division had placed their officers. He looked back up at the screen: he'd gone.

He couldn't have disappeared? He'd only taken his eyes off the screen for a second. The commander slowly pulled back the joystick and leaned forward in his chair. 'Now wait a minute . . . he was there a minute ago.'

As the camera pulled back and the frame opened up, it became more and more difficult to see where he was. Shug was lost in a sea of green and white.

* * *

Wee Eck sat at the bar in Finlays, looking through his photos. He pulled one from the pile and laughed. Francie stood, checking off an order. Wee Eck called him over. 'Haw, Francie, here a photie fir ye.'

Francie looked at it and smiled. 'Aye, mind that?' He went to hand it back.

'Keep it – ah kin git another.'

'Cheers.' Francie pinned it up behind the bar.

Wee Eck looked up at the photo and took a swig of his Beck's. The camera never lies: Big George shaking Ronnie by the hand. All around them, a team of boys, decked out in blue and white, standing in front of the bar.

But that was days ago. Wee Eck suddenly realised that he shouldn't really be in here, now that it was back to 'business as usual'. He finished his drink and slowly edged his way out of the front door.

The bus pulled out of Buchanan Street bus station, heading towards the M8. Shug folded his jumper, put it up against the window and leaned his head against it. He thought it best if he stayed away from Glasgow for a while. In four hours he'd be in Liverpool. He'd phoned Scobie and got the name of the bar Malkie was working at. He could just imagine Malkie's face when he showed up. He could hardly wait.

He thought about Jamie, what life would be like without him. He felt choked. He'd stay away for six months, a year at the most – wait till things died down, then he could pay the Wee Man a visit. He wished he'd been able to say goodbye to him, explain where he'd be. He hated to think of Jamie getting upset. What kind of uncle just takes off without an explanation? They were the best of pals after all, but there was nothing else he could have done in the circumstances but disappear.

He had it all figured out: he'd get a job with Malkie for starters, then put the feelers out and ring a few cars. He could punt a bit of smack and make some decent money, then come back for the Wee Man. He'd take him away from those bastards he called family before they did him any more damage. But he'd do it properly next time. He could explain it all to Jamie when he saw him again. Jamie would be a wee bit older then. He'd understand.